the Darren Effect

Also by Libby Creelman
Walking in Paradise

the
Darren Effect

a novel by
LIBBY CREELMAN

Edited by Bethany Gibson.
Cover photograph copyright © tiburonstudios, istock.com.
Cover and interior design by Julie Scriver.
Printed in Canada on 100% PCW paper.
10 9 8 7 6 5 4 3 2 1

Library and Archives Canada Cataloguing in Publication

Creelman, Elizabeth, 1957-
    The Darren effect / Libby Creelman.

ISBN 978-0-86492-506-0

    I. Title.
PS8555.R434D37 2008   C813'.6   C2007-906578-3

Goose Lane Editions acknowledges the financial support of the Canada Council for the Arts, the Government of Canada through the Book Publishing Industry Development Program (BPIDP), and the New Brunswick Department of Wellness, Culture and Sport for its publishing activities.

Goose Lane Editions
Suite 330, 500 Beaverbrook Court
Fredericton, New Brunswick
CANADA E3B 5X4
www.gooselane.com

For my children, Andrew and Clara

When Benny Martin died, his wife was there, but her feelings towards him had been impossible to read for some time. There were nurses too. He sensed they were helpful, caring, nearly intimate, but he found this complicated and wished they would disappear.

Benny's son Cooper was home asleep, dreaming a dream that would return throughout his adolescence: the two of them had caught a long iridescent fish that could both fly and swim, but resisted being reeled in to shore. It flew above the misty surface of the river, leaving in its trail colourful watery loops.

Heather Welbourne had awoken suddenly in her dark house and left her bed. Dazed, she misjudged the location of the doorway and nearly collided with the wall, but lifted a hand to protect herself at the last moment. For many years, Benny had struggled with his desire for this woman.

Darren Foley, a man Benny had never met, was in his basement tending to an injured Atlantic puffin, which would outlive Benny by an hour and nine minutes.

PART ONE

Chapter One

She went to see him in the hospital only once. As it happened the hospital staff were happy to give away information about him. It was different later when he was in the palliative care unit. But now they told her without hesitation — without even looking up from the station — that he had a private room on the fifth floor. She found it easily. She passed up and down the corridor, making sure he was alone.

She had imagined this all a number of times: entering his hospital room. He would recognize her without making eye contact, as though using a sixth sense, then turn to a statuesque nurse standing nearby in a crisp white uniform and say, Would you mind asking that woman to leave? But expecting this from him was silly. He might be angry with her, but he would not be ungracious. She would tell him it had been all her fault. It would pour out of her: she was a monster, a madwoman. She would ask his forgiveness, and at last they would talk about his prognosis. There would be a discussion of treatments, drugs, hope. What's new with you? he would ask, and she would shrug and look away, and say, Nothing's new. Except I'm here now and I love you. But first she would have to win him over, she would have to get him to forgive her for locking him out in the rain.

It was a Thursday morning nearing eleven thirty at the end of September. In the corridor, a trolley of lunch trays seemed to have been aimlessly placed and forgotten. The odour reminded Heather of eating as a girl at a friend's house, where the food was always alien and a bit sickening. The nurses wore baggy salmon-coloured uniforms and did not look her way once. As she entered his room, she felt she might be floating. Her shoes made only a whisper of noise across the floor, and she moved slowly, as though the air in the room were trying to hold her back.

He was propped up in the hospital bed, looking out the window. He didn't seem to realize anyone had entered, or if he did, he didn't care. But as she approached him, he turned. He looked startled and then delighted. He looked at her and smiled as though he'd like to drink her in, as though all the fuss in the car had been some great lark, a game, something that only served to charge whatever was going on between them now.

But what was going on between them now? She felt wobbly. It was the anticipation and then the fact that he didn't appear angry with her. All these weeks. She had thought he would be angry. Shouldn't she know him better than that?

"Well. Hello," he said. "Here you are."

She could barely smile. She felt excruciatingly shy.

"I didn't expect a visit from you."

He was still smiling. Smiling as though he liked her very much. There was an obvious lack of force behind his speech and she knew she was an idiot for not having come sooner.

"I thought I might stop by. I know you didn't want me to."

"It's good to see you. You don't know how good it is to see you."

"I'm so sorry." She was about to cry but couldn't do that. Someone might walk in at any moment. "I was terrible."

"Don't be so foolish."

"How are you?"

"Sick. I'm pretty sick."

He turned and glanced out the window again. There was nothing out there. Although it was a clear, bright September day, from inside the hospital the sky looked white. You couldn't be sure it was even sky.

"I'll be going home in a few days."

"Really?"

"What I've learned. People like me. We're in and out."

"I better not stay. Isabella might be in."

"Just left. You probably passed her."

Heather shook her head. She would have noticed that: passing Isabella Martin in the corridor. She felt a familiar, fleeting bitterness.

"Don't leave yet. You just got here. What's new?"

"Nothing."

"Oh, come on." He laughed and reached for her. "Come closer. I've missed you so much."

He looked the same but different, which was what she had expected. The bed was made and he was resting above the blankets in new jeans and a yellow polo shirt that made him look washed out. He hadn't shaved yet that day, but his hair seemed to have been recently trimmed. His teeth had darkened. That was easy to see because he was smiling so widely at her. The last time she had seen him there had been the suggestion of fragility, but today was something else entirely. It caused her to ache all over.

He squeezed her hand and closed his eyes. Suddenly his face tightened.

"Are you okay?" She drew closer to him. "What is it, Benny?"

He opened his eyes and smiled at her. "It's just so good to see you."

Here she was. Here he was. Where she had been longing to be for weeks. Yet she found she couldn't get a single thought to stay put in her head. Suddenly she needed to leave.

But then it was too late, the world was narrowing to include only a handful of white stars.

"Is there someplace I could sit?" she whispered. The only chair was on the other side of his bed. She wasn't sure she would make it.

He moved his legs to make room for her on the bed. As soon as she sat, he reached for her and pulled her head to his chest. He groaned softly. Her sick feeling immediately passed and the terrible coolness was followed by peaceful warmth. She never wanted to leave. It was remarkable that despite everything that had happened to him, the smell of him remained the same. In the past she had often smelled him for days after a weekend together. Despite showers and a change of clothes, and the time and distance, his smell would linger. He would seem to have left something permanent in her olfactory memory.

"I hear it's Indian summer out there."

She nodded. "It's hot." His legs looked like poles.

"How come you're not in shorts?" He shook her weakly. "Or a dress? Uh? Where's that one we bought? What do you call that pattern? That floral thing?"

"Paisley." She felt a twinge of impatience. He *always* asked that. He seemed to be determined to forget the word. "I called your house," she told him.

He sighed. "I know, Heather."

"I shouldn't have."

He let out a long breath. The calling was not important. Not at this point and because she had nothing to do with his house and home anyway. Only a fool would entertain hope now — for a genuine public life with this man but also, she saw, for his recovery. She sensed a new frontier between them. She wanted to stroke his hair, run her hand across his chest and into the hard dip at its centre, but it wasn't her territory. She couldn't move. She would hate herself for this later. She felt she had become desensitized to the world around her. She felt a terrifying, soft floating.

"I'm going to miss you so much," he said.

She couldn't find the right words. She pressed her face into his chest, but all she felt was the fabric of his yellow shirt. She lifted her face and pressed it against his.

He had a way of saying goodbye, on the phone, in the car, on the sidewalk, that day at the hospital, that was soft and unmanly. His way of uttering those two syllables had always surprised her. It seemed to signal an exceptionally sad parting, even though there had never been a reason to be this sad before.

She had thought, so this is goodbye, before. But this, *this* was goodbye.

Outside the hospital she stood bewildered, unable to make a decision and move in any one direction. There was her office, but it was Saturday. She could go home, but she would only think of his visits, slipping in the back door, often unexpectedly, never knocking. Everything around her — people irritated by her blocking them on the sidewalk, the shimmering cars, the sky, all that baking concrete, even the parking meters — was coming at her in waves, beating at her face and hands and urging her to an action she couldn't fully imagine. She had left him sitting on the edge of his bed, dejected, alone, brave, pale, watching her as she backed out into the horrible smelling corridor. If she were a different woman she would muscle in on Isabella Martin. She would insist on some right to participate. To spend hours in that hospital room. Hold his hand, kiss his brow. To care for him, too.

But was that something *he* wished for?

How was she going to get through the next few weeks and months, the rest of this insane, unseasonably hot day? The weather reminding her of meeting him in Spruce Cove six years ago.

That day had been record-breaking in its heat. Early June and hot, even in the morning. She'd been the first awake and strolled down to the beach alone. She was wearing long pants and a turtleneck, and told herself repeatedly to return to the cabin she was sharing with her sister to change into something cooler. But the ocean drew her away from the cluster of cabins that lay in the field behind the parking lot and beach. She was admiring the blue-grey humps of hills that armed the bay, so far away they had looked soft as paint, and beyond them, the white clouds that blurred the meeting of sky and sea. Everything — the water, sky, hills — seemed to speak of heat.

The dog had appeared out of nowhere, barrelling across the sand with a speed that paralyzed her. A dripping wet black Labrador retriever. Its name was Inky, she would later learn, in the prime of its short dog's life. It stopped two feet from her and flopped back ungracefully on its haunches. Its curiously housed penis, she saw, was grainy with sand; its expression, fierce and brutish. Lowering its nose to the sand, it released a saliva-encased tennis ball at her feet, then looked up at her, its ears soft tents rising, and nudged the ball closer until it touched her toe.

Then it began to bark. It rose — barking — front legs splayed as though it might pounce — barking, looking her straight in the eye. Heather wondered if it were rabid. She tried turning away from it, to snub it, to savour the view again. But the barking would wake everyone in the cabins, certainly everyone in the campers at the edge of the parking lot. She remembered hating that dog. Imagine, hating Inky — a creature perpetually cheerful, agreeable, loyal.

Now, as she crossed the hospital parking lot, she smiled, thinking how terrorized she had been. The smile felt good on her face, then sparked a terrible moment of clarity — she was no longer on that beach but outside this hospital, minute by minute increasing the distance between herself and a man whose dying seemed incomprehensible.

She had walked away from the dog and beach — not quite tiptoeing. When she looked back, she saw it hadn't moved, not even followed her with its eyes. But it was still barking and it was the barking she wanted to escape. She stepped off the sand and across the small lot where several cars had parked in no discernible pattern. She made her way to a minivan and moved behind it, blocking her view of the sea and the dog, and realized the level of her distress. I'm such a coward, she thought, closing her eyes and leaning against the warm metal of the van, but just let that demented dog run off and persecute someone else. This was what she had been thinking when she opened her eyes and found him standing just feet away, watching her.

She assumed he was a tourist. Ontario, possibly the New England states. But when he spoke, she knew he was from St. John's.

"What are you doing?" he asked.

Not, she would later tease him, Can I help you? Are you all right?

"Hiding from a horrible dog." He was short and athletic looking. She noticed his hair was untidy and flying off, though there was no breeze at all. It might not have been combed in days.

He laughed. "You're not referring to Inky?"

She realized the barking had stopped just as the dog came trotting around the side of the van. It was covered in sand and panting.

"Where's your ball?" the man asked the dog in a calm, business-like voice. The dog stopped and looked at the man. It retracted its tongue and with some difficulty closed its mouth around it. Heather watched its head swing left, right, left. Then it did two complete turns and looked again at the man.

"Where's your ball?" he repeated, this time, it seemed, more intimately.

The dog sprinted back down to the water and Heather made a move to go. She could feel the sweat collecting beneath her breasts along the underwire.

"By the time he's finished rolling on top of that ball, he's forgotten it exists," the man explained.

Heather tried to appreciate the remark. She had no interest in dogs.

"Camping?" he asked.

"No, no. We're here for a writers' retreat."

"You're a writer, are you?"

She hesitated. She was warmed by his voice, his confidence and easy curiosity about her.

"Yes, we're staying in the cabins," she said. "For the weekend."

A week later when they met again at the lecture, she was forced to tell him she was not a writer. She was a social worker, tagging along after her younger sister, Mandy, who was the aspiring writer.

He moved towards the van and leaned against it, letting her know it was his. He was looking at her, thinking something about her, and although she would have liked to have known what, her instinct was to offer him nothing more, and to ask him nothing about himself.

She had said goodbye abruptly and walked away from the man with his van and dog and returned to her cabin. At first she thought nothing more of him. There was an afternoon poetry workshop out in the field, under the few trees and in the face of some welcome, unpredictable sea breezes. Before the readings could begin there was competition over the shadiest spots to sit, then argument about someone's suggestion they delay supper in order to avoid the hot kitchen, but eventually they all sat back, fanning themselves with their manuscripts.

Heather stared at each face without listening. It wasn't until she lay flat on the grass and looked up at the sky and tried to focus on the one misshapen cloud that she realized her distraction was formidable, uplifting and irresistible. She spent the remainder of the weekend returning every hour or so to the beach, but the man, dog and minivan had vanished. She nursed a small fantasy: reliving the meeting, rewriting the conversation. His expression. Her appearance. She emitted confidence, she spoke to the dog and even stroked its bony forehead and soft creased ears. She wasn't sweating and the man asked her what her plans were for the rest of the day.

It was a public lecture held on campus. Had she known anything about him, she would have known he was married and, surely, she would have avoided eye contact, pretended she could either not remember him at all, or not remember where she'd met him. But she did not know anything about him and she went straight up to him. He stood by the table with the books and refreshments and he waited for her, watching her approach — only a few seconds, really — and when they started talking they could have been talking about anything under the sun. When he asked if she'd like to go for a drink after the lecture, she wasn't even relieved. She knew then who he was — not his name or what he did, but what he would come to mean to her — and she knew that he knew.

His name was Benny.

It was a fluke either of them had been there. Later, Benny would call it fate, though only half seriously. It was the last in a series of public lectures for the year — that night on outport architecture. Benny had felt obliged to attend. Heather was there to meet Mandy and Mandy's partner Bill, a university professor, but they didn't arrive. Heather suspected they had quarrelled, but she never asked.

Heather made it as far as her car and got in. Her keys were in her hands. It was a busy day at the hospital, but even on a slow day, parking here was impossible. In her rear-view mirror she watched with detachment as cars went up and down the lot, hunting for a space. Many, seeing her sitting there, stopped and waited. Make up your mind, they seemed to suggest. She felt her heels digging in. Detachment gave way to an unwillingness to behave. She might sit there until nightfall, if she wanted. She might still be there when the lot began to empty and the heat of the day began to lift and a dark Volvo pulled in beside her. Isabella Martin would disembark, distraught but refreshed, in slacks and a white cardigan. Benny's son Cooper would tumble out the other side.

What would Heather do? Would she get out of her car? Would she make an appeal, apologize, beg?

Heather imagined Benny's wife walking through her as

through a ghost — undetected, unseen — and on into the hospital to her husband. The Volvo would rock slightly, and in the back seat Inky would sit up. He would glance about with his ears perked until he found and recognized her, and their eyes would lock.

"What is it?" Benny had asked, just before she left the hospital room.

"Nothing," she had said.

Heather sat with her hands on the steering wheel of the silent car and considered rolling down a window. The heat was extraordinary and the only thing in the physical world making an impression on her. She started the car. Hearing the engine come to life nudged her like an unseen hand and she burst into tears.

Chapter Two

The Indian summer did not last. Heather's impression of October was of darkness and cold. Eventually she learned from a teary client they were having a record-breaking streak of bad weather: thirty-two consecutive days of precipitation. Heather had nodded. Really? She had not known.

Now it was November, coming up to a long weekend.

She pulled her chair up close to her desk — she preferred this when clients entered her office these days — but it was a tight squeeze with her coat cradled in her arms. At a time like this she required something to hold on to.

He had a right to be angry with her, if he wanted to be. That was the worst of it. She had been cold and unsympathetic. She couldn't stop thinking this, even after seeing him in the hospital and knowing it was the furthest thing from his mind.

She shivered. She seemed to be chilled all the time. And bone-tired. She had turned the thermostat on bust the day before, just before going home, but now it was eight in the morning and the air in the building was parched and stifling.

Was she really so bad? So cold, cruel and heartless? Most people did and said things they regretted once in a while. Heather was sure of it. Her mother, for instance. Her sister Mandy. Even Benny, goddamnit.

She pushed herself away from her desk and went out into the hall where it was even warmer, past the empty reception cubicle and into the washroom where the poster of the bruised, dejected-looking girl beneath the caption "Love Doesn't Have to Hurt" caused her, as always, to look quickly elsewhere.

She looked in the mirror.

Her face was red and blotchy. Her nose was swollen and her eyes looked foreign and dark. It was time to pull herself together. You couldn't change the past. She splashed cold water on her face, dried off, took a deep breath. She applied face cream, which helped. It gave her skin the springy feeling of regeneration and hope. And as she began to feel better, she began to resent the cause of her sadness. She was better off without him.

But she *was* without him.

She looked at herself in the mirror again and watched her eyes well up, her chin and then her mouth collapse.

"Stop it!" she whispered to the mirror, ashamed of herself, then splashed on more cold water, dried her face, and applied another coat of face cream. She had ten minutes before her first appointment. She'd be fine. She had a solid capacity for recovery, her mother had always said so. In ten minutes, no one would know she'd been crying. She checked her teeth. Looked around for a comb, gave up and ran her fingers through her hair. She felt a surge of energy.

She returned to her office, picked up the phone and called her mother, waking her.

"Did you discover anything?" Heather asked.

"You really want me poking around?"

"Yes! I asked you to. I want to know anything. *Where is he? He's not at the hospital.*"

"He's not?"

Heather paused and took a moment to consume her exasperation. "No. I already told you that. Because I called. At least he's not where he was. He may have been moved."

"I could ask around. You know this town is small. A person would be a fool to have an affair in this town, Heather."

"It's too late for that advice."

"Don't yell me at me, honey."

Heather was aware of her mother sitting up and reaching for her pack of cigarettes.

"*Mother!* Please."

"Honey —"

It was lit. The first inhalation.

"What?"

"I'm worried about you."

"I'm *fine*. But I'm busy —"

"You're busy? Right now? It's not even nine o'clock."

"No. I'm just busy. I mean, I don't have much time. I just feel so *rushed*."

"I wonder if you should see someone. You seem in such a panic. It's awfully early in the morning to be in such a rush and panic. How many cups of coffee have you had?"

"None. Do this. Just do this."

"On one condition."

"Absolutely no conditions."

"You stop —"

"No."

" — driving by their house."

Heather paused. "How did you know that?"

Exhalation. "It's a small town."

Mandy was driving, which made everyone a little nervous. Bill sat in the front beside her, and Heather in the back, causing her to feel tolerated yet banished, like a child. When Mandy braked at the stop sign at the bottom of the street, Bill pitched forward in his seat like a rag doll, as though he had expected Mandy to sail through the intersection. Heather suspected he and Mandy had just had sex.

Bill straightened, then glanced into the back seat, and Heather gave him a weak smile. She felt remotely embarrassed. She knew she looked wrecked and that Bill would have been told, at the very least, that it was the result of a disastrous love affair. Bringing her along on these outings had become a habit of theirs, but Heather knew it was Mandy's crusade, not Bill's.

Mandy parked directly in front of the Legacy Café and Heather watched Bill glance up to see two women in conversation just outside the entrance. When he turned quickly back to study the dashboard, Heather took a better look at the women. One was staring into the car at Bill, nodding, chatting with her companion, even laughing, but she had clearly fixed her eye on Bill. Heather longed to escape the next few minutes.

Mandy pulled her scarf in at her throat, then gathered up her purse and keys and gloves. Neither Heather nor Bill had moved.

"Hold on a minute, Mandy," Bill said. Heather thought it was a mistake to have said anything. Better to just walk on in.

"How come?"

"That woman."

"Oh, for the love of..."

Mandy leaned across Bill to look up at the café. Other than these two women, there was no one else out on this raw November morning. Remembrance Day. They were all sleeping in, Heather thought, respecting the holiday.

"Which? The blond in the hat? Or the one in the blue jacket?"

"Blue jacket."

"Let's go. She's too old to be a student."

"I wouldn't say she's too old to be a student," Bill said crossly. "Theoretically, nobody's ever too old to be a student."

But Mandy was out of the car. She shut her own door with some force, then opened Heather's and said, "Come on, let's go. It's freezing."

Heather obeyed and Mandy flew up the steps and into the café, not awarding either woman standing there a single glance. Heather and Bill followed. Heather had never seen the woman before.

They took a booth by the windows. Mandy opened Heather's menu and then her own, as though there were some chance she would not order the vegetarian omelette and Earl Grey, and Heather, nothing at all, and said, "Now let's see. What would you like, Heather? What do you feel like? Bill's treat." Then she leaned over the table and whispered harshly, "Who is she, Bill?"

"Honestly, I don't really know."

Heather was aware of Bill glancing at her. She liked Bill, but had never been entirely convinced he and her sister were right for each other. Bill was a good deal older than Mandy. They often bickered, Heather thought, because they didn't really know each other. Normally she helped them through this. Changed the subject, made a joke. Got them back on track. But she couldn't think of anything to say. She looked out the window and felt her eyes welling up.

"Yet we all avoid her?" Mandy demanded.

"Mandy, I don't know who she is."

Heather sensed he was telling the truth. Outside it looked almost cold enough to snow.

"I wish you would order something, Heather."

Heather glanced at her sister, whose face looked too tight and unhappy. Mandy wasn't going to let this go.

"Bill, if I discover — "

"She's nobody. I promise you, love, I don't even know her name."

"Well, it's your last warning."

"What does that mean?"

Before Mandy, Bill had had relationships with women that were casual, upbeat, short-lived. After Mandy, he had, he claimed, embraced monogamy, and Heather believed him. The woman in the blue jacket could be anyone from his past: as much as a weekend girlfriend, as little as a woman he had once exchanged glances with at a party — but someone, unfortunately, whose name and face he no longer remembered.

Mandy turned to Heather and smiled, though her eyes were still glittering in a way that made Heather uneasy. "They were asking about you at the Writers' Cooperative last month. Someone mentioned that epic poem you wrote about a horse named Joy. They miss you. You haven't been to a workshop in years. Why don't you come next week? It'll be good for you."

"You mean I can work through my troubles by writing about them?"

"Or you could come along and keep me company."

"Mandy, I attended a grand total of three writing workshops, the last one at Spruce Cove . . ."

The time she met Benny.

"Bill really liked that poem, didn't you, Bill?"

Bill looked startled, as though he hadn't realized he was still part of the conversation. Heather thought it wasn't fair to put him on the spot like that. After all, he taught in the Anthropology Department, not Literature and Language. And her poem had been dreadful.

"I think the horse was named Happy," Bill said. "Not Joy."

Heather nodded. "It was meant for children. It was dreadful, wasn't it?"

"Well, I can barely remember it."

"Say no more," Heather said, laughing for the first time that day. "It's all over your face, Bill." She realized they were staring at her, relieved by her sudden, though marginal, lightness. For a moment, she felt herself sharing in it.

"I'd like to write a story about desire," Mandy said a second time.

"Could we have missed the turnoff?" Heather asked. "Desire?"

They were en route to the Writers' Cooperative meeting, and Heather was beginning to wonder if they were lost. It was night, and raining.

"Yes, but not just any desire. Desire for a time that no longer exists," Mandy said. "A lost opportunity."

Heather was watching the slick black road. She had to force herself to consider her sister's idea.

"You mean like an opportunity for a relationship? You just missed the turnoff, Mandy. Stop."

"I can't believe you said that, because listen to this." Mandy pulled over and stopped the car. Her look was inspired and familiar. The windshield wipers were on high. Zip, zip, zip. Heather had to stop looking at them. "This happened to me last week, and already I've been thinking, what a great story. Which way?"

"The turnoff's back there. Just go back — slowly — you can't miss it. I'm listening."

"I was driving along Empire Avenue where they're widening the road, right?"

"Turn here, Mandy."

"And I got stuck behind this poky guy in a truck. You know how I'm always barrelling around town." Mandy removed her hands from the wheel and Heather looked on as she pumped her arms up and down as though speedwalking. "There was something so familiar about him. I could see a bit of his face in his rear-view mirror and the way he was looking around, curious about the road construction. Who cares about road construction, Heather? I could feel his interest like it was my own, and suddenly I realized, I know this guy. Maybe I even said it out loud. I will in the story."

"This must be it. The first house past the Irving."

"Plus the shape of his head. I recognized that. He's as mild as May, but he looks like a bulldog. Nothing like Bill."

"So who was he?"

"Darren Folcy. Biologist. Don't you remember I used to live with him?"

"No."

"He was into birds."

"Birds?"

"Yeah. But Heather, it was uncanny. I've been feeling lonely, and I know you're thinking I have Bill."

"No, no, I wasn't thinking that. "

"When I saw Darren it was so weird. What I remembered of him seemed as intimate as though we *had* been intimate. He'd been interested in me, but I had just met Gary."

"I think you can park here. I don't remember Gary."

"Darren and I were strictly domestically intimate. Shared the groceries, the bills, the bathroom. So I find myself tailgating this guy and it's him. I can predict the movement of his head, even though I haven't seen him in years. Even his thoughts."

"Sounds like you have the start to another great story," Heather said, opening her car door.

"It's not enough," Mandy said, not moving.

Heather's right leg was already out and getting rained on. She rested her head on the back of the seat and closed her eyes. "What do you mean?"

"I was thinking about calling him, asking him out for a drink. In the service of my craft."

"I see. This is your story about desire?"

"Or maybe just follow him around town, on the q.t."

"What?" Heather slowly drew her leg back into the vehicle. "Like stalk him?"

"It would be an adventure. I'm fed up with Bill. I think he's got something for that woman."

"What woman?"

"The one we saw last weekend, at the Legacy Café."

"I wouldn't assume there was anything to that, Mandy."

The idea was bizarre, even alarming, and Heather knew she should seriously caution her sister against it. But then, most of the writers in the Cooperative wrote about themselves, and Mandy was only suggesting taking the process one step further. Heather couldn't write about herself. Not surprisingly, she'd only written the one poem, for children, about a horse.

Now that they were here, getting out of the car and attending the workshop was the last thing in the world Heather wanted to do. *Do you feel hopeless, unreasonably sad, ever find yourself thinking there's no reason to go on living?* This was the litany she gave clients. Like a blood test, an X-ray. A lot depended on their answer. Of course, they had to be telling the truth. They had to be honest with themselves.

The workshop had already started. There were a few shushes

and severe looks. She and Mandy slumped down on the floor, their backs to the wall, hidden by the dining room table already set with refreshments. Mandy reached up and slipped two asparagus sandwiches out from under their plastic wrap. She handed one to Heather.

If Heather wrote a story fuelled by the desire for a time that no longer existed, she would need to give her central character a name, and she would never be able to decide on one that fit, other than Benny, which, of course, had been his name.

Someone was reading a poem about an island. Someone else likened it to Walt Whitman.

Or she could begin: A woman and a man meet. She is a clinical social worker, single. He is an architect, married, with one son. Six years later, he becomes sick.

She was in his home only once. It was in that time between winter and spring. He told her over the phone no more than the plain fact: he'd been diagnosed with cancer. She cancelled the rest of her appointments for the day and drove immediately to his house.

He was there alone. His son was in school and his wife — a substitute teacher — had been called in that morning. It was afternoon, but there was still the smell of toast and coffee and something sweet — syrup? — in the kitchen, where they stood a while awkwardly. She could see that everyone had rushed away to their day: a bowl half-filled with milk and soggy cereal, dirty mugs and spoons, a plate with crumbs, the tub of margarine and jar of jam, all still on the kitchen table by the window overlooking the park. And beside the sink: a stack of gunk-covered plates and pots and pans from supper the night before. An opened bottle of white wine stood on the counter, someone's plan to return it to the refrigerator unrealized.

As Heather followed Benny upstairs, she felt a vague desire begin to surface. She paced herself as she ascended the staircase, passing the family photographs hung on the wall: babies with wizened faces, fresh from their births at the hospital; adults in crooked birthday hats; a delighted woman in her wedding dress, holding a champagne glass; a toddler with his hair in his eyes, hanging from the neck of a young Inky; the still-coiled body of a man golfing, his chin up as he scans the sky for the outcome of his shot.

"Is that you Benny?"

Benny was standing at the top of the stairs, watching her. He said, "Those were all taken before I knew you."

It sounded like an apology. She looked up at him, wanting to hear more, but he had turned away.

And then the smoky black and whites: three young men in graduation costume; a string of women in long skirts on a rocky beach, hands over their eyes as though the sun might carry them off; a young woman with silky movie-star beauty, posed naked to her shoulders, the rest of her body artfully dissolved; someone's grandmother in an apron, standing by the Christmas tree, smoking, caught in the act of shaking her head, Don't take my picture, I'm not prepared.

At the top of the stairs Heather can't face Benny. It isn't just his bad news. It's that all this time she has failed to recognize what it is she should have desired: to inhabit the body of the woman who lives in this house. She wants to stand in the centre of this woman's family — the centre of this universe — and be entitled to all her history and expectations.

She wants that family album — both tastefully and ostentatiously displayed along the stairway — to be her own and of her own making. She wants Inky, struggling to rise from the carpet at the foot of the master bed to nuzzle her in the crotch, to have been hers. She wants to have known him as a puppy, rubbed his nose in his accidents, retrieved him from the pound. She wants to have been part of every decision that was ever made about him. And about the cat, curled over a pile of magazines in the window seat, and the iguana, rabbit and gerbils she will never see.

And about his son, Cooper, whom they can hear coming in the house.

Without a word to each other, Heather and Benny return downstairs. In the kitchen, the boy shakes her hand. He has dark hair and a blanket of nutty brown freckles across the bridge of his nose. She sees that the act of employing everything his parents have taught him about manners does not come easily to him. He turns back to the counter and places a cold pancake between two pieces of toast. He is an unusual boy. She had never known this.

She looks at Benny and realizes he loves his son dearly. The boy is eleven, but already it is obvious he will not be tall. A miniature Benny.

Benny jokes, "We suspect he doesn't eat his lunch at school," and the boy is embarrassed.

"So I gave you those papers?" Benny asks her.

Heather stares at him. His question confuses her, but he sees that and says, "The Spruce Cove project? It's important we have the designs completed by the end of the weekend."

He's telling her he wants to get away for the weekend with her as soon as possible. There is a twinkle in his eye. Looking forward to this seems to be enough to sustain him, but Heather knows it won't be enough for her.

Benny turns back to the boy. "She's going now. What do you say?"

The boy hesitates, blinking. "Nice to meet you, Miss," he mumbles.

As Benny escorts her to the front door, Heather glances into the living room. There is a pile of stuffed toys in the centre of the room. She would have thought the boy too old to be playing with these, but then, what does she know about children?

"What the hell is he doing?" Mandy whispered.

Heather was thinking that if a client came to her, talking about gallivanting through the woods in order to spy on a man in order for that client's sister to write a story about desire, she would have to ask, Do you really think this is wise?

"And I'm freezing."

"You're freezing, Mandy, because you're dressed for the catwalk, not the outdoors."

Mandy grinned. "I know." She was wearing a bulky faux fur coat, but it clearly did nothing against the cold. Snow had come early this year — though the experts were saying it would not last — and both had worn inappropriate footwear: Heather, waterproof calfskin boots that were apparently not waterproof and Mandy, oxfords whose fleece trim was already soiled.

"Did you bring your cellphone?"

"Yeah. You?"

"Yeah."

They had followed Darren Foley by car from the Canadian Wildlife Service parking lot nearly a hundred kilometres up the Southern Shore, and then, as their elation wore off, on foot over an old woods road through a forest of freakish trees crusty with ice and draped in some kind of fungus or parasite, giving them both a feeling of having miscalculated in some profound way. Darren had brought snowshoes, causing Mandy to remember him as "that little smartie," but ATVs had already been out and packed down the snow, making their hike easy, if not leisurely. Despite her cold feet, Heather realized with surprise she was enjoying the excursion. She took a big deep breath, closed her eyes and breathed out with a happy hum.

"Closet nature freak, are you?" Mandy asked, shivering.

"Hey, this was your brainstorm."

They looked down at Darren tracing and retracing his steps along the water's edge on the beach below.

"He's wiping his eyes an awful lot," Heather observed.

"Maybe he's crying," Mandy said, squinting. "Water's some blue, isn't it?"

30

"I know, looks almost tropical. So what does he do? Is this actually his job?"

Mandy shrugged. "He was studying clutch size when I knew him."

"Clutch size?"

"Something to do with eggs."

"Is he married?"

"Not sure. Did he finally get married? I can't remember."

They had come over the top of a treed ridge to see Darren stopped below at the cliff's edge. He glanced up and Mandy, who'd been in the lead, fell back onto Heather in a panic, swamping Heather with her vast coat, but Darren did not appear to see them. He removed his snowshoes and stood them in the snow, pushed his way through some shrubs and scrambled down a rocky slope to the beach below. They watched rocks loosen and run ahead of him, hitting the beach with a narrow, mean sound that failed to echo, and then he disappeared from view. Heather suggested they backtrack, so they made their way out onto a point — barren except for a patch of tuckamore under which they crawled. There was just enough space to sit cozily side by side, their knees drawn up to their chests.

"What the hell is he doing?"

Heather was staring out to sea. "Look at the size of those white birds, Mandy. Do you suppose they're seagulls?"

"He's kicking at something with his foot. He looks lonely, doesn't he?"

"Really? I thought he looked happy."

"Then why was he crying?"

"Did we decide he was crying?"

Mandy slipped her fingers out of her leather gloves and tried to warm them with her breath. "Maybe he can cry and be happy at the same time?"

Heather didn't say anything.

Just then, Darren removed his orange cap and rubbed vigorously at his forehead and ears. He shook his head like a wet dog, Heather thought.

31

"Maybe I take myself too seriously?" Mandy suggested. "Maybe this is a retarded idea for a story?"

"I didn't say that."

"Look at him now."

"He's found something."

"He's sitting down."

"What is that?"

They watched him fiddle with something several minutes, then toss it down the beach. It looked like a black rag. Then he lifted a large pair of binoculars Heather hadn't realized were hanging from his neck and appeared to search the horizon. He would know what those birds were.

"Do you still have those binoculars?" Heather asked her sister.

"That cute little pair Bill gave me? Yes. Never used."

"Bring them next time, okay?"

"Next time?"

"It would be nice to pin a name on those birds."

On the beach below, Darren had stopped moving. The sisters sat side by side, leaning into each other for warmth, frozen as much by cold as by indecision and puzzlement. Heather turned to look out to sea, still flooded with light, though the tropical turquoise colour had paled. She thought of Benny for the first time in an hour. For weeks her body had seemed plugged with mud. It was such an effort to do anything, sometimes even to smile at a client or remember to nod or ask appropriate questions. There was a sorrow inside her she couldn't shake off, and a stubborn hope that drove her crazy.

But being out here in the fresh air, as though on the edge of the world, helped in some way. She thought of driving by Benny's house, of phoning that house and hanging up the moment someone answered, even before she could know who had answered. The feeling then was short-lived, but restorative, like taking a deep breath and letting it fill your lungs with oxygen.

Until she visited Benny at home, Heather had known only what she could see from her car as she drove past. The house was in the old part of town and one in a row that backed onto a park. They put their Christmas tree in the northeast corner of the living room, and used only white lights and favoured an abundance of looping garlands. For Halloween they also hung lights — orange pumpkin-shaped ones — that framed all the windows of the first of the three stories. In summer two pots of drooping annuals were suspended outside the front door.

Heather searched the beach. With the coming evening its details had blurred and all she could see of Darren was his orange cap. But she didn't want to leave yet.

While she had been driving by his house for years, the phoning had begun only in the past several months. When she discovered Benny's cellphone number was no longer in service, she began calling him at home. She hung up because she was afraid of what Benny might say to her. That he might scold her. That he might say, Enough is enough. And then she would start crying, pleading, upsetting him.

"How's everything going?" Mandy asked. "With that man?"

"I can't find out anything. I'm just waiting."

"For him to die?"

"Mandy."

"Sorry. I just meant . . ."

They were whispering. "Maybe. I don't know. But wouldn't that be cruel?"

"No."

"Perhaps I'm hoping for a miracle in cancer care. In case a miracle comes along, I'd want him to be alive for it, right? I wouldn't want him to have missed the miracle because I thought it might be better if his suffering ended." Heather closed her eyes and clenched her jaw. "Sometimes I don't know what I'm saying."

"Is he suffering?"

"He would have to be."

"Let's go. I need to stretch my legs. And I have a funny feeling about this."

"Why?"

"Not sure."

"Hold onto that feeling. It will give your story atmosphere."

"I'm sorry I ever dreamt this up."

"Don't be, Mandy." Heather turned and took her sister's hand in her own. "This was wonderful."

Chapter Three

Tracey Quigley was scheduled for eleven but she was late. She didn't drive, was afraid of buses and rarely had money for a cab. Heather knew it was unlikely that either her husband or sister would give her a lift if they didn't feel like it. She suspected Derm and Donna of wielding control over Tracey that was, at best, unfair, but she believed home was the best place for Tracey, at least in the short term.

The day was dark. The lights from a synthetic Christmas tree could be seen blinking out in the dingy hall, though the tree itself was not visible to Heather, who wondered what decorations, if any, surrounded Benny. Would they have such things? If they did, it would be for the family and medical staff as much as for the patient.

That morning her mother had telephoned to report he had been moved to the palliative care unit.

"I wish you would consider a leave of absence," her mother had said again. "I'm concerned about you, honey. I think this is too much for you."

Heather looked at her watch. She hoped Tracey would arrive soon.

At twenty after eleven the door opened and there followed a brief scuffling in the entrance. Heather stayed behind her desk, out of sight. The building was empty. There was no one in the waiting room and her receptionist had taken the morning to do some Christmas shopping. Anyone could walk in off the street.

Then the Quigleys were there, crowding the doorway. Heather stood. Tackling all of them seemed beyond her capacity this morning.

"Tracey is scheduled for today, Derm. Just Tracey."

She could see by Derm's expression that he already knew this. But there was something on his mind. Tracey was Derm's wife, and Donna was her sister, but Tracey's illness had brought Derm and Donna together in such a way that they often behaved as though they were the young woman's parents. Although Heather recognized the stress and responsibility facing Derm and Donna, she did not trust either one of them.

"I can see you for a few minutes at the end of the session, Derm."

"You don't mind if we have a smoke, then?"

"No Smoking" stickers decorated the building, but then so did ashtrays. Heather nodded.

Derm and Donna left the room and Heather rose to close the door. Returning to her desk she reminded Tracey to take a seat. Heather liked Tracey. Her face was plain, intelligent look-ing. Her brown hair was pulled back in a ponytail and her bangs were cut a good inch above her eyebrows, straight as a ruler. Had she passed her in an airport Heather might have optimis-tically imagined her to be a geneticist or violinist. But Tracey was neither. She had not finished high school and had never had a job, not even for a day. She suffered from bouts of intense phobic fear: sweating, breathlessness, heart palpitations, diar-rhea. The attacks lasted as long as two hours and were most debilitating at night. Occasionally — Heather had been told this more than once but never by Tracey — she soiled herself, so paralyzed with fear she was unable to get out of her bed.

"How have you been feeling, Tracey?"

"Same."

Heather felt a perilous inability to concentrate. She wondered whether she and Tracey might discuss her own dilemma instead: how to cope with the idea of Benny in that palliative care unit when she couldn't actually imagine him there. When she couldn't imagine how wasted and sick and unhappy he must be. When she couldn't imagine him dying. Never seeing him again.

Heather realized Tracey was watching her. They had been sitting in silence too long, though how long Heather was not sure. She had forgotten to review Tracey's file and now struggled to recall where they had left off in their last session. Relaxation techniques.

"Did you get a chance to read that article I gave you?" she asked Tracey.

"Yeah, bit. Well, no."

"Were you able to put into practice any of the relaxation techniques we discussed?"

Tracey shrugged.

"Tracey?"

"No."

"Oh, dear."

Tracey's eyes widened. It was an atypical response from Heather and one that Tracey seemed to find intriguing.

"How could those simple exercises do anything?" Tracey prodded.

"I see your point. But studies do show —"

"Plus, I was on a diet." Tracey sat back and began chewing on a nail.

Heather nearly smiled, though it was not funny. Tracey was of average weight, thin if anything. Heather wondered if she'd ever told Benny about the Quigleys. She couldn't be sure. Sometimes she couldn't distinguish between what she *had* told him, face to face, and what she had planned on telling him — or told him when he wasn't there — a rehearsal.

Tracey put her hands in her lap. "I had an interesting dream."

Heather sighed. "Would you like to talk about it?"

"We're driving down the road —"

"You and Derm?"

"And Donna. And I sees these two dogs going at it, right?"

"Yes."

"And like, the male, he was stuck. There on the corner in front of the Red Circle. And everyone was just driving by, not noticing."

Stay with the image, Heather told herself, don't over-interpret.

"They weren't fancy breeds, but the female was right tiny."

"I see." But Heather was unable to stay with the image. She felt her thoughts spinning crazily. Stay, she told herself. *Stay.* "Are you taking your meds, Tracey?"

"They don't work."

"You have to give them time. It's possible they might not eliminate the attacks completely. Dr. Turner explained this. It's called — "

"Symptom breakthrough. I know." Tracey leaned forward. "There was another dog. It was just standing there, not looking at the other two but barking at them. Barking, barking, barking. You could hear it for miles around."

Heather thought of Inky barking at her on the beach at Spruce Cove. Her face grew warm.

There was a knock on the door. Derm poked his head in and looked at Heather with raised eyebrows. He'd only been able to wait fifteen minutes, but Heather found herself nodding.

Derm took a seat beside his wife. "She told you, did she?"

"About the dream?" Heather asked, confused and slightly worried.

"What dream? I'm talking about her trying to leap from a moving vehicle."

"I opened the door, that's all," Tracey told Heather. "He's after exaggerating. He's an exaggeration expert."

"She threatened to leap from a moving vehicle. This is a waste of time. Surely to God Dr. Turner's got some better drugs for her."

Donna, who had appeared in the doorway, indicated her agreement with a rushing swallow of air.

Tracey was back working away on the nail.

"Give it up, girl," Donna said. "You're gonna have them hands chewed to the bone."

Derm was looking at Heather. He was struggling to keep a smile from his face. "It was after we seen some dogs. She tell you?"

Donna produced a fierce, snorting giggle.

"Donna," Heather said, knowing she sounded too impatient. "Could you return to the waiting area?"

Donna gave her a poisoned look, then backed slowly out of the room.

Heather turned back to Derm. "Dogs? Tracey was just telling me about a dream with dogs."

"That was no dream. Christ, that was on our way here. She flipped out on us. That's why we were late."

"I just didn't care for the barking, that's all, Derm."

"She tried to leap from a moving vehicle!"

"We'd stopped at a red light."

"It'd turned green."

"No it never."

Heather put her hands up. "Stop!"

Both Tracey and Derm looked surprised.

"So it wasn't a dream, Tracey?" Heather asked more gently.

Tracey shook her head.

"Did you ever for a moment think it was a dream?"

Tracey's hands had begun to shake and she was not making eye contact with anyone.

"That was no dream," Derm repeated, chuckling.

"Would you shut the fuck up?" Tracey whispered.

Derm's mouth fell open and he turned to Heather. "See what I got to put up with?"

Heather felt unprofessionally repulsed by this man, though it was not the first time. She knew Tracey was starting to withdraw and wished it was within her power to forestall the terrible night the girl likely had ahead of her. Shouldn't it be within her power? Was that not why Tracey was here? Heather was doing

39

more than wasting people's time; her uselessness was hurting them.

Perhaps her mother had a point about a leave of absence. For Tracey's sake, if not her own.

Heather leaned forward over her desk, doing her best to pretend Derm was not present. "Tracey, listen to me. It's very important that you stay on your meds." Heather spoke softly, almost inaudibly, knowing that sometimes this was the best way to reach a person.

Tracey's eyes flickered.

"A waste of time," Derm said. "That's what this is."

"Tracey," Heather repeated. "The meds won't work unless you take them as prescribed. You won't get better."

Tracey looked at Heather. "I know."

Early in their relationship, Heather and Benny had embarked on a number of sightseeing adventures. In a sense, Heather later realized, they had been dating. One day they drove south to look for whales, Benny manoeuvring the car too fast on the twists and rises, yet Heather lulled by the movement of the car. She had a cold and had suggested going another day, but he had arrived that morning with cough drops and decongestants, juice boxes and tissues, a hot water bottle and blanket. She had laughed at him, at his persistence, as he ushered her into the car and propped her up, telling her she only had to sit there so he could glance over every once in a while to look at her.

They were on their way back, as far as Witless Bay, when he pulled over. Out on the water hung the cloudy remains of a whale's blow. A whale-watching boat was heading directly for it.

Dazed, and knowing she should be in bed, Heather nevertheless joined Benny at the edge of the road, not wanting him to know she'd lost all interest.

He had just seen the whale. He said he was disappointed Cooper wasn't there to see it too.

"This would be just the thing to get him off that bloody television. He watches too much of it. Isabella lets him. I told her she's lazy and just wants to avoid an argument."

Heather saw the whale come high up out of the water and crash onto its side. She could hear the blissful cries from the tourists, all crowded onto one side of the boat now idling five metres from the whale.

"You called her lazy?" Heather asked. She thought she might be losing her voice.

"A pushover, that's why kids like her."

"You were teasing her?"

"Perhaps a bit."

"When did you have this conversation?"

Heather tried to imagine Benny and his wife in their house. In the kitchen perhaps. He is bringing plates in from the dining room table and she is stacking the dishwasher. They start to talk about their son.

"A few nights ago. Look. Heather, you missed it, the whale."

She blew her nose. "Where?"

"Right there!" He laughed. "Look where I'm pointing."

"No. Where did you have this conversation?"

"Come on," he said sadly. "Why do you ask me these things?"

She turned to him, surprised. "Just curious."

"Look! You missed it again. I think there's two of them." He glanced at her. She wasn't sure, but she sensed he had to stop himself from stepping away from her. "It was after we had gone to bed. We often discuss Cooper then, because he's asleep. It's a convenient time for us. Don't give me that look."

"When was the last time you and your wife had intercourse?"

"The last time?"

"That you had intercourse."

"A few nights ago."

"A few nights ago?"

"What do you expect, Heather, after ten years of marriage? It happens. Particularly if I've been away."

"Away with me?"

"The sex is mechanical."

Yet he did it. He couldn't stop himself. If he could stop himself, wouldn't he?

"I thought your marriage was a shell."

"Heather, it is. *It is.*"

He was looking at her with astonishment. "You don't want to possess me, do you?" he asked.

Heather shrugged. She felt herself backing down.

"That's not what I want," he said. "To possess you."

She never asked him such a question again. If she had, she knew it was unlikely he would be so honest a second time.

"You don't look so well, Heather. Let's get you home."

The Quigleys were her last appointment before lunch. As soon as they were gone, Heather grabbed her phone and began dialing Benny's home number, then stopped and put the receiver down. It was pointless. He wasn't there.

Outside the day was overcast and dimming. She imagined going into the palliative care unit and explaining. It was never about possessing you, Benny, it was about being able to count on you. To be there at breakfast, or in the middle of the night. To be there if I woke up and discovered there was something I'd forgotten to tell you. So I wouldn't have to make mental notes, I must remember to tell Benny this.

That wasn't about possession.

"It was about expectation," she said aloud.

But Benny was dying. That wasn't what you said to a dying man, whether you loved him or you didn't.

She left her office. The snow was mixed with rain as she crossed LeMarchant Road. She was bareheaded and her hands were cold and she was wearing only a raincoat. She thought of Benny's habit of enveloping her cold hands in his hot ones.

She stopped, dug out her cellphone and standing there on the sidewalk, called the hospital.

"Are you family?" the nurse asked.

A man came out of a stone house and stopped when he saw Heather. He smiled, and in the midst of her distraction, she wondered what kind of a smile it was. Lecherous or sympathetic? What did he see on her face?

"I just need to know how he is," she told the nurse.

"I'm sorry, my love, we're not allowed to give out information except to family."

"I just need to know — "

"I'm sorry, my love."

She wandered up and down the short streets, unable to locate her car. By the time she did her hair was lank and soaked; gazing at it in the rear-view window, she saw that nothing remained of the feeble styling she had given it that morning.

He died two days later, the third of December, just after midnight. Heather's mother heard of it first, but didn't call her daughter with the news until the following evening.

Heather was sitting on the edge of her bed, eating crackers, when she answered the phone. At first everything around her seemed to recede as though sucked away with an enormous outgoing wave. Then the room grew still. She put the crackers on the bedside table; they would sit there for weeks. There had been some things she still needed to tell him. All day he had been gone and she had not known.

"You waited all day to tell me?" Heather said to her mother. "Were you afraid I'd go crazy? Whose side are you on?" She slammed the phone down. She was aware that reason had left the room. She was not sorry to see it go.

Chapter Four

Heather and Mandy arrived at the Canadian Wildlife Service building early one Monday in mid-January and discovered Darren Foley's green government truck by the rear entrance, the tailgate still down. This was a relief to Heather. They'd had mixed success finding and following this man, but today had risen particularly early. In fact it was only just getting light out now. Heather parked at the back of the lot, behind a dumpster, and the two waited in silence. Though it was the time of year for short stormy days, the air was still and almost mild. When Darren emerged from the building a few minutes later lugging his gear, it was Heather who saw him first and grabbed Mandy's arm. The two slunk down in their seats.

An hour later the three of them were in the woods. There was little snow and Heather could see here and there patches of green luminous moss. The sky was cloudless and blue. Moose had trampled the earth and made the paths slick with mud and droppings. Occasionally they heard a remote, muted crash and were aware of an odour reminiscent of horses.

"How's the story coming along?" Heather asked her sister.

"What story?"

There was a junction. A narrower, less used route turned

right and inland. Oddly, this was the path Darren's tracks had taken. Heather stepped onto it.

"Heather. Hold on a minute."

Heather turned to see her sister place a hand against a skinny fir, which bent slightly, its roots lifting a mound of moss. "You know what I think? I think Darren Foley is boring."

"Maybe he's meant to be boring. Maybe that's the point."

"Yeah, and maybe he's a sicko. He walks miles into the woods. Finds a beach, then mutilates what we think are dead birds."

"How is that boring? Besides, I thought you two cohabited? I thought you knew him by the way he looked around at road construction?"

"How well does anyone know anyone?"

"How's it going with Bill?"

Mandy grinned. "Bill? Bill wants to know what you and I are up to all the time."

"Have you told him?"

"No."

"Good."

"I don't know. Bill's instincts are usually pretty good on this stuff. He thinks I should write more sex scenes, for example. Did you hear that?"

"What?"

"Branches breaking?"

"No."

"Oh, now fuck."

"What?"

"I've got crap on me, from that tree."

"It's probably sap. Smell it."

"I am not going to *smell* it."

They looked at each other.

Heather was following a man she'd never met through the woods and enjoying it. What was it she felt? A yearning. Like an addiction. The promise of intoxication.

She remembered getting in her car and circling Benny's

house, something she could no longer do. She dismissed the memory.

"There's been a lot of intersections, Heather. Are you convinced we're still following the man of the hour?"

"Definitely. The beach can't be far."

"We're nowhere near a beach."

"Listen, another half hour and we'll call it quits?"

"All right."

"Mandy?"

"What?"

"Just wondering if you brought your binoculars?"

Mandy flung her backpack onto the ground, splattering it with mud, but Heather knew not to comment on this. She just wanted to keep going.

"In case I see some birds," she explained.

"Is it this way? You can't be serious, this isn't a proper path."

"Those are his boot tracks. Who else could they belong to?"

Mandy passed her the binoculars before going on ahead. "Don't drop them."

Heather put the binoculars around her neck. Darren Foley never went anywhere without his heavy black binoculars hanging from his neck, and he generally walked with one hand placed on them, as though they were an extension of his body. Mandy's binoculars were much smaller and more ladylike, but Heather was anxious to get a good clear look at a bird and identify it. She was aware of flocks darting through the canopy, the only proof they were there a surge of high-pitched calls and whistles.

She longed to stop them somehow and give them names: chickadee, kinglet, warbler, siskin, flycatcher, vireo. Identifying them would be like hunting: having one in her sights, understanding what it was, pulling the trigger. Though she didn't want to kill the birds. She simply wanted to place a name on them.

She headed after Mandy, but slowly, establishing some distance between them. After a while the path grew even muddier and less defined. As she pushed aside the branches of trees and bushes, the smell of fir and dank earth rose up. The tracks were so abundant it was impossible to make out an individual print — man or woman or moose. Heather was aware they were heading south, when they should be heading north, or even east. South would only carry them deeper into the interior of the headland. On second thought it might be best to keep up with Mandy. The path made a bend around a massive rock outcrop and dropped into a basin of small pools and stunted trees. Heather stepped onto a hummock of moss — its surface looked so solid and dry — and sunk to her knees. A clump of dead grass topped with white orbs rose inches from her face. She pulled herself free, one hand protecting Mandy's binoculars.

She stood rigid and listened.

"Mandy?"

The path left the bog and passed again into woods. Heather had to assume Mandy had continued this way. She glanced up and saw the day had clouded over. The sky was small, close and white. For the first time, the woods seemed gloomy and hostile. The path had entered a dense lowland. In the darkest areas, the trunks of trees snaked along the ground for several feet before twisting upwards in unison. Heather noticed a patch of lightness off to one side, where perhaps the forest thinned, but as she stepped towards it, she saw through the tangle of vegetation a pile of rocks and some white boards leaning against each other. Oddly, evidence of human activity made the hair on the back of her neck lift. She felt cold.

She needed to stop her fear before it engulfed her. She stepped back onto the path, or what remained of it. She wished for an outdoor adventure someplace more friendly and civilized, like Spruce Cove.

She and Benny had returned to Spruce Cove regularly, usually in the spring before it got busy. Being seen and recognized together had always been a concern.

Why had she never come right out with it and asked him to leave his marriage? Was it ambivalence? Was it fear? She had asked herself this many times in the past couple of months. There were occasions when she had been unable to look him straight in the face. How had that been, she asked herself, to love a man who spared his family but did not spare you? There had been sporadic, sneaky pain so aggressive it erased everything else, but it had not become steady company until the end.

No sign of Mandy at all.

Fear. There it was again. Heather took out her cellphone and dialed Mandy's cell. She made several attempts, thinking she might have made an error, her hands were shaking that badly, but it rang for a while and then abruptly stopped.

It was on one of their first visits to Spruce Cove together that Benny had strolled down to the water with several tennis balls and his racket, which he used to hit the balls down the beach, over and over again, for Inky to fetch. Finally the dog collapsed onto the sand with his tongue nearly leaping out of his skull, no longer barking, and Heather was grateful.

After that, whenever they brought Inky, Benny would bring the racket and balls.

Heather remembered the pollen and slowed, noticing for the first time the snow flurries. She had forgotten about the pollen. It had been everywhere, coming off the evergreens around their cabin as though from an aerosol can. She could see it in even the weakest of breezes: yellow-green clouds of seeds lifting from the cones. A film of it on the windshield she drew her name in — a cocky, adolescent act. Down at the beach it rode in on the sea and formed a narrow band in the surf. At first they couldn't figure out what it was. They thought pollution, some kind of spill. There was another ribbon of it higher on the beach. Heather rolled it between her fingers.

"I think it's pollen," she said.

He pressed his hand against the small of her back. "You're a genius. I should bring you everywhere."

She sat down on the sand and alternated between watching the pollen weightless on the water and Inky racing after the ball and, for several minutes, had been satisfied — smug — with herself for identifying the pollen. Then something happened. It happened only a few times, all those years, before they knew about the cancer.

He tossed the ball up and struck it with his powerful smooth forehand.

She wanted more than this. She wanted Benny to leave his wife. If not now, then she wanted to hear him say there was at least a chance, someday.

Instead he said, "How's work?" dropping the racket and sitting beside her on the sand. He put an arm around her waist and dragged her towards him, pretending it was a great effort so that she grinned, then he picked up one of her legs and placed it across his own.

"Now then, missus," he said. "Who was on the roster this week?"

It was not appropriate to tell him details of her clients' lives, but Heather was rarely interested in denying Benny anything. What's more, it was difficult to resist the way he listened — his soft attraction to her.

She considered her week, the clients she'd seen. She recalled her last appointment on Friday with a sinking feeling.

"What is it?" Benny asked.

"Rosemarie," she said. "I've been seeing her for months. Yesterday I sent her back to her psychiatrist."

"Why?"

"She needs someone who can write a prescription." She laughed, but it wasn't funny. She looked at Benny. "For a serotonin re-uptake inhibitor."

Three couples — a crowd for this time of year — were coming down to the beach. Seeing them, Inky began to dig frantically in the sand for his ball, then ran off to greet them. Heather thought it was unlikely she'd see Rosemarie again.

"You can't save everyone," Benny told her. He glanced at the people and slowly pulled his leg out from under hers and created a few inches of space between them. Heather didn't think it would make any difference. Anyone looking at them would know.

"What's Rosemarie's problem?" Benny asked. "What's wrong with her?"

There was nothing *wrong* with her. But Heather didn't say this. "She's obsessive-compulsive."

He nodded.

"She has an elaborate counting routine."

"What does she count?"

"Benny."

"Tell me. Come on, I want to know everything."

"It's not *what* she counts."

Rosemarie did everything in threes, Heather explained, because she had three children. Three candy bars, three cups of tea, that sort of thing. If she had two children, she would do things in twos.

"But recently," Heather said, "her behaviour patterns have become more elaborate. Her children are aged two, four and eight. So she selects the second box of cereal from the grocery shelf. Then the fourth bottle of ketchup. Then the eighth carton of eggs. It's complicated and time-consuming."

"Why does she do that?"

"She thinks something horrendous will happen to her children if she doesn't."

"That's crazy."

Benny's expression was astonished and childlike. She wanted to touch him, reassure him, but there were those inches of space between them. Was he thinking of his son? Was he feeling guilty? Not knowing what was going through his head made her nervous.

Inky was barking at the people. He wanted them to throw his ball. One of the women looked over.

"Better call Inky," Heather said.

Benny half rose and shouted for the dog, but immediately turned back to Heather. He was like that: he would not drop something that interested him. He would not allow interruptions. Heather thought it was admirable, but intimidating.

"What can you do for someone like that?" he asked.

"I treated her." Heather tried to sound matter-of-fact, as though there had been some hope. But Heather had never believed she'd be able to help Rosemarie in any permanent way. She didn't tell Benny about her sour smell, her shapeless cords, the sweatshirt with the yellow — possibly curry — stains below the collar.

"She sat in my office and I had her drink *one* glass of juice, eat *one* candy bar. The most important thing was for her to get some sleep. Her routines can delay her bedtime considerably."

"What about her kids?"

His question made her feel tender towards him. "I believe they are quite safe."

"Is there a husband?"

Heather had not met the husband, though she had suggested several times to Rosemarie that he come in.

"He has a heart problem. He can't work."

Inky was still barking. Heather rose to her knees and whistled. It was completely ineffective. "This can happen to people," she said. "It starts out as normal life worry, disappointment, sadness, then mushrooms into debilitating anxiety."

They began making their way back to their cabin. Inky saw them and rushed up and on ahead.

"She had been showing a lot of improvement," Heather said, wishing she could put a happy ending on it for Rosemarie. "But her son fell off the roof on Wednesday. It was a minor accident, not what it sounds, but her relapse was severe."

As they passed his car on their way back to the cabin, he reached over and wiped away her name where she had written it in the pollen on his windshield. He looked over at her, as though to apologize, but it was unnecessary. If he hadn't done it, she would have.

There was more snow in the deeper woods. Heather could see it banked up around the trunks of trees. The path had widened, but Heather was only concerned with finding Mandy. The area was heavily criss-crossed with woods paths. There was no reason to be frightened.

At the top of a small rise where the trees were stunted and yellow, she became aware of scratching sounds. She froze. The sounds were faint, but getting closer. She felt a weakening across her shoulders and down her arms, and an inability to look to either side. Then the sound was on top of her: a harsh chattering rising in volume. She tipped her head back with great effort and saw dozens of birds crowding the top of a spruce tree. They were only metres away.

The relief made her insufferably warm.

Several minutes passed. Slowly she lifted Mandy's binoculars to her eyes. Stout rust-red birds were crawling over the cones, grasping the branches with their feet and bills like parrots on the Discovery Channel. But surely these were not parrots. Parrots inhabited warm regions like South America. Their strangeness scared her. She wanted to dig out her new field guide, but it was buried in her backpack and she felt paralyzed.

Suddenly two of the birds dropped and swung side by side, cartoon-like, from a branch, holding on with their bills. Their legs dangled and their wings lay folded at their sides as though not involved with flight in any way.

There was a voice-clearing behind her. She lowered the binoculars and turned, but she already knew: here was Darren Foley, standing in the path in his orange cap, old canvas knapsack, massive binoculars, the boots with the deep cleats.

Where was Mandy?

"See anything interesting?"

"What?"

"Birds? See any interesting birds?"

"Oh no. Sorry. I mean, I don't know what they are." She pointed to the trees above her. "They remind me of parrots."

He laughed. At her?

"Those are definitely not parrots. Red crossbills. I noticed them on my way through earlier. It's exciting to see them."

"Isn't it? Yes, it is. What are they called again?"

"Red crossbills."

"I'm going to look that up."

"Are you alone?"

"Yes." She slipped off her backpack and began rummaging through it. "No."

"Actually, it's a subspecies we have here on the island, the Newfoundland red crossbill. They were rare on the island for at least a decade, and now they're everywhere. A buddy of mine at Wildlife has been studying them."

"Oh, is that where you work?"

He nodded slowly.

"Red crossbills?" She was flipping through her field guide.

He had the tall person's manner of hanging his head. He did not face her directly, but looked at her sideways out of the corners of his eyes. It made him seem shifty, submissive, forlorn. She hoped he hadn't noticed her drenched legs.

"They're very interesting little birds," he said, watching her flip through her field guide. "Yes, that's them. See the crossed mandibles? Hence the name. The bird sticks his bill into the cone and pries apart the scales. Then his tongue lifts out the seed."

Heather concentrated on the page with the birds, then carefully lifted the binoculars to her eyes. Her hands were shaking. He was right. Red crossbills. Unmistakable. What a delight. She felt the space around her expanding.

She lowered the binoculars and glanced at Darren. She noticed he needed a shave. That was something she and Mandy would not have been able to see on previous occasions. Also, that he smelled of soap and might be condescending.

He laughed again. *Was* it at her? "You know, if you're a beginning birdwatcher, I'd suggest you start with a backyard feeder and see what you can attract there. You could get frustrated coming out here, trying to get a good look."

"Oh, I'm not discouraged." Her voice had gone high and breezy.

He looked puzzled. "Of course not. No reason to be." He glanced up at the trees and she tried to memorize his face. The cold had made his skin slack and raw, though the occasional snowflake landing there melted immediately. Mandy would want every detail. He looked nothing like a bulldog. He looked like the Marlboro Man. Mandy better be grateful for that tidbit.

"I saw some other birds a while ago. Flying over the water. Huge white birds."

"Gannets."

She smiled, grateful for the information, but decided to look the birds up in her field guide later. Her fingers felt too cold now to turn the pages.

"Hear that?" he said. "They're moving on. Sometimes I wish I'd gone into passerines." He glanced sideways at her again and she realized how close they were. She wondered if she'd tried to get close to him for warmth instinctively, like a wild animal. Both took a step back.

"The weather is changing. I'd suggest cluing up for the day."

What were passerines? "Have you seen any other people?" she asked.

"Today?"

She nodded. Of course she meant today! She realized she was freezing from head to toe.

"It's rare to see anyone out on this headland. The odd wood-cutter. Do you know your way out? You're not lost, are you?"

"Of course not. I've been here a thousand times."

As soon as he was out of sight, Heather put the binoculars and field guide away inside her backpack. A story about desire? And that man was involved?

Her shoes were squishy with water and her feet were beginning to cause her some shimmering, icy pain.

Was she insane? Maybe she was, maybe she wasn't, but stalking was illegal. It could amount to a criminal charge. Gradually she became aware of her cellphone ringing in her coat pocket.

It may have been ringing for a while. A cold flash was followed by a hot one.

Her hands were shaking. "Hello?" she whispered.

"Heather?"

"Mandy?"

"Where are you?"

"Mandy, I tried to call — "

"My batteries were dead. Sorry about that. What? I'm borrowing a phone — "

"Where are you?"

"Being rescued. Bill's cousins from Calvert. They have ATVs. Roger and Vince. My feet were freezing. And I was lost. Here, they want to talk to you."

After speaking with Roger — or Vince — Heather closed her phone and began pacing back and forth in front of the boulder split in two, each half topped with a thin layer of soil and moss and looping trunk, just as she had described it to Roger — or Vince — on the phone. He told her to continue east another ten metres, then turn left onto a narrow path terminating at a cabin, where she was to await their arrival. Instead, she paced back and forth, struggling with the temptation to dart off the path and run blindly into the woods, to slip into the spaces between the narrow trees and escape rescue.

It occurred to her that she was exhibiting displacement behaviour. Like a cat who wants both to flee its attacker and stand and fight, but instead sits and begins grooming vigorously. Like so many times seeing Benny after a period of separation and not, at first, wanting to get too close. The desire had always arisen in her to pace crazily through the restaurant, airport, hotel room or coffee shop.

She had grown accustomed to seeing Benny around town. To anticipate running into him when she left the house, particularly on weekends and at certain places: Shoppers Drug Mart, the symphony, the soccer field beside the school where he might be out with Inky and his son, or just crossing Church Avenue with his hands in his pockets and a DVD tucked under an arm, always a little underdressed for the weather. After the first year, she hardly thought about it. It was as though she bore antennae with a mind of their own, fixed yet slightly aloof, so that although they searched for him day and night, they did so without wrecking her in any way when he was not discovered.

The symphony was where she first saw Benny with his wife. She was slightly taller than Benny and strong looking, with dark hair cut helmet-like around her head. Heather had been surprised by her bold, expensive clothing.

She could hear the far-off grinding roar of ATVs.

But later, there was that day at Dominion. By then her antennae were tuned to the wife as well. Heather joined the speedy checkout behind Benny's wife and son, who was five or six at the time and using a bandaged hand — a burn, Heather later learned — to repeatedly slap his mother's leg. Heather had never been so close to Benny's wife and was dismayed to find she was so attractive.

"Spank you, Mommy, spank you, Mommy," Benny's son was singing.

Benny's wife had looked back at Heather with an aloof, almost aggressive glance, as though daring Heather to judge her. While Heather was certain this woman knew nothing about her, the encounter left her unsteady.

Heather stopped pacing and turned left onto the narrow path, though it took her a moment to see the cabin built up against a rock outcrop and hidden by trees and enormous yellow ferns. As she approached the gaping entrance, her feet sunk into another small bog cleverly disguised by moss. She pulled her feet free — they were remarkably insensitive to temperature now — and peered inside the cabin. It was constructed of pressboard, rotted and covered with green algal film. Two mugs hung from the ceiling and on the stove sat a white kettle. Bunks had been built into the back wall and broken pieces of Styrofoam lay scattered across the floor. A number of poles supported a sagging ceiling. Heather stared, confused. It took her a while to realize the poles were not part of the original construction and that on balance the cabin didn't look safe at all.

Two rusted kitchen chairs with plastic orange seats were inside the cabin, a third outside. She took the one outside, though it was leaning dangerously to one side, and felt the water in its ripped seat instantly flood the seat of her pants. She rested her feet on a stack of roofing shingles half sunk into the ground. The only creatures living here now are the squirrels, she thought.

She waited for the ATVs to close the last distance. Then they were there and Heather found her legs wouldn't move.

"Ah, look at you, girl. Where are your shoes to?" Roger or Vince said, coming to her and taking her elbow. But she was unable to rise. He had a kind face. One of his front teeth was gone. Benny had also had a kind face, in the mornings, she recalled.

"Wow, listen to her teeth chatter," Mandy said.

"I feel fine. A little too warm, actually. I wouldn't mind a bit of fresh air."

There was a gentle tug again on her elbow, which was irritating, but Heather ignored it, wanting to be polite.

"I still have your binoculars, Mandy."

"That's okay, you can keep those if you want," Mandy said in a funny voice. "Did you see anything interesting?"

Heather tried to shake her head, but her neck had become astonishingly stiff. She hugged herself and fell forward over her knees.

Another tug. She shook him off.

"Wait. I did see something interesting," Heather said, popping back up. "I saw the Marlboro Man."

"She's pale, Roger."

"Let's get you back, girl."

Chapter Five

"I'd like to write a story about desire," Mandy told Bill.

He paused. She had asked him to massage her shoulders, which were hard as stone. "Is this a new idea?"

"No. I've had it a while."

"What does Heather say?"

"She's still getting over the frostbite."

"True. But what does that involve? It's been weeks." He leaned into her neck and kissed her. "I don't know about that sister of yours."

"Bill!"

He returned his hands to her shoulders.

"What do you mean?" she asked.

"I'm not sure she likes me."

"She's probably jealous of you, Bill."

He smiled at her behind her back. Mandy, Mandy, Mandy. The world revolved around her. He kissed her neck.

"Bill."

Sometimes she looked so tiny, perched naked on the edge of their bed, complaining of neck and shoulder pain, that Bill would think, she really is not for me.

"You should have seen her feet when they finally got her shoes and socks off."

She had told him already. She had been thinking a lot about those feet. And about the lost girl, Suse.

"Heather wouldn't cooperate at all."

At the end of the day, Mandy had a few sentences, several beginnings to a poem, an idea for a screenplay.

"They looked like frozen chicken. Honest to God."

"Poor Heather."

"You were so nice to her, Bill. You know that?"

They were not married, and she was fifteen years younger than he was, yet her airs of wifely expertise were not unconvincing. When she was twenty-one, he had lusted after her an entire term. He wrote her ludicrous, lovesick letters, which he later discovered she had not only saved — he had specifically asked her to destroy them — but had shared with her girlfriends — other students of his.

The result was that he didn't entirely trust her. Before he told her anything, he asked himself, do I want this repeated?

Heather sat in an armchair lodged between her bed and window, her feet propped on a footstool. It was now late February and she was aware that six weeks was an alarming length of time not to have dressed or left her bedroom except for perfunctory visits to the bathroom and kitchen, although there were the two trips to the hospital to have the bandages changed and then removed.

And a couple of visits to her doctor.

And hanging the new bird feeder from a tree in her backyard.

Heather had not called her mother, and she had made Mandy promise not to pass on any information about the frostbite. Heather had been cool to her mother since Benny's death, though now she could not quite understand why. She knew only that it had seemed necessary to erect a wall around herself.

Whenever she was angry at her mother, Heather thought of her first date. Grade eleven, Justin Tucker. He worked part-time stacking shelves in the corner store where she worked the cash. She at the front of the store with the customers, he at the back with the dry goods and dairy products and sour-smelling coolers that lined the back wall. Theirs were different but complementary roles, not just in the store but in the universe. These were the thoughts she had when she was in love with him. They embarrassed her later.

When he rang at her house for their first date, Mandy and her mother had raced to the door, pretending to fight over who would answer it and have the first look. Heather was in her bedroom, fresh from the bath, and until that moment, delighted with herself. But she could hear their giggles and scuffling.

He wore the same blue trousers every day. They were short and disfigured where the hem had been reworked too often. He was standing there at her door, in those same trousers, when Heather came down the hallway. Her mother and sister were in control of themselves by then, but the awkwardness had already set in. At the store he was always confident and inscrutable, but now he stood clumsy, uncertain.

They told her later they weren't making fun of her, or him. Sure, it was only a bit of foolishness. But Heather had gone and stayed with her father, refusing to speak to either her mother or sister for weeks.

It was the type of incident to occur in the years immediately following her parents' divorce, as though the divorce had corrupted the family unit, not only by removing one parent from the household, but by triggering a fundamental transformation in the other. Heather did not want a mother who was approachable and silly. She wanted one who was distant and aloof. There was an essential *parent-ness* that her mother no longer exhibited, that she seemed to have cast away, but without which Heather did not feel as safe in the world. Later, when Heather was at university, she was able to step outside her own experience and see that her mother had been doing her best to cope. For a while, at least, her mother had not wanted daughters, she had wanted friends.

*

Heather wondered in what ways the woods had changed with the warmer, longer days. When she closed her eyes, she saw the red crossbills dangling upside down in the trees.

She had sent Mandy to the library for more field guides and sometimes fell asleep at night with them open — on her chest, her belly, the pillow beside her head — the way other people slept with pets. She began to dream of birds, species of her own imagination who were intimate and benevolent, with human voices.

She read about the red crossbill — a monumental example of specialization. The scissor-like bill allowed the birds the luxury of getting at the seeds before the cones fully ripened and unlocked. As a result, Heather read, red crossbills evolved a flexible reproductive physiology, nesting any time of year, in dry hot August or wet slushy February, in areas where — and as long as — there is adequate food. She imagined the fearless olive-green females sitting on their four eggs: pale blue spotted with light brown and lavender. It starts to snow, and gradually, through the night, the small birds are blanketed. Who decided this was flexible? Heather wondered. Wouldn't *accommodating* be more fitting? To be ready, at any time, for the business of a rushed courtship? Wouldn't it be more satisfactory to have a life like everyone else?

Heather froze. Half a dozen birds had arrived at her feeder. Though she knew what they were, she reached for her field guide and flipped through the pages, just for the pleasure of being certain.

Conspicuous white outer tail feathers. Slate-grey hood, like an executioner's. Juncos.

Heather heard someone enter the house. She put her book down and waited.

Her mother hesitated in the doorway, glancing around the bedroom, avoiding eye contact with Heather. In one hand she held an unlit cigarette. She crossed the room to peer out the window at the feeder and several of the juncos flew off. "I don't remember any bird feeder."

"You're not going to light that in this room, are you?"

"Of course not. I'd never dream of such a thing." When she turned to examine her daughter, the outdoor light fell across her face, revealing foundation the colour of caramel. It nearly matched her hair. "How long have you been in that bathrobe?"

"I thought you were quitting."

"I'm trying all the time. Why didn't you tell me you'd finally taken some time off?"

Heather shrugged.

"It was the Melvin man who informed me he'd been delivering groceries here for weeks, and when I called Mandy, what did she say? Basket case, I think."

Heather laughed, perhaps a little too harshly. "Basket case? That's what she called me? Are you aware of the origins of that expression?"

"No, and if it's unsavoury, I don't want to either."

"It's from World War One. It's how they referred to the quadruple amputees, because they were carried around in baskets."

Her mother fiddled with her cigarette.

"It's understandable if they went out of their minds," Heather continued. "Imagine, being lugged around in a basket? Were there lids for the baskets, I wonder, in case it rained?"

"I suppose you're trying to get rid of me?"

But Heather didn't really want her mother to leave. In fact, she was glad she was finally here.

"Mandy said you injured your feet. Hiking? What's this all about?"

"I'm sorry, Mom. Sorry."

"You never called me. You're so stubborn."

Until her father's death eight years ago, her parents had successfully avoided each other for decades. But Heather knew there would have been unavoidable encounters. It was unreasonable to hope they would never pass one another coming in and out of Dominion, or be invited — unintentionally or otherwise — to a Christmas party, or find themselves bumper to bumper at a traffic light. Heather knew what it was like to discover one day that not only had you committed to memory the make and year and colour of another person's car but his licence plate number as well.

"Heather," her mother said gently, "I bet you'd feel better if you washed your face and hair. And got dressed."

The dictionary will also tell you, Heather knew, that the expression basket case evolved from soldiers to some-*thing* that is no longer functional, like a country unable to pay its debts or feed its people, and to some-*one* unable to cope, like a woman who couldn't dress or go to work.

Basket case? Heather looked down at her feet. Indeed, she had nearly lost them.

Once they had convinced Heather to board the ATV, she and Mandy were taken to Vince's home where a small, anxious crowd had gathered. Most agreed Heather's socks should be removed and her feet submerged in lukewarm water. She was placed in an armchair in the parlour, which was gloomy but warm. Family photographs, framed string art and a portrait of Pope John Paul hung over rosebud wallpaper. Linoleum in the most astonishing shades of red, orange and purple peeked out from beneath a square of carpet. Heather could see into the kitchen where a woman in knitted pink slippers stood talking on the phone, occasionally glancing in at Heather. After that, Vince wrapped a second blanket around her and someone brought her a cup of tea. They already had her socks off and were again discussing placing her feet in the tub of water, when she put her head against the wing of the chair.

When she woke Bill was standing in front of her and her toes hurt. She leaned forward, thinking of standing, then saw her feet: they were red and swollen. The windows rattled violently, and she recalled Darren Foley's comment that the weather was changing.

Bill knelt in front of her. "We're going to take you into the hospital in a minute, Heather. Do you understand? Good. Mandy's already in the car. You understand what I'm saying, don't you? You were mildly hypothermic when they brought you in. You're fine now, but you might need some medical attention. Heather?"

"What's that on my feet, Bill?"

"Blisters. Not to worry." He smiled unconvincingly.

The pink slippers stopped by. She said something to Bill, and Heather looked up to see her swatting him with the back of her hand. The woman was hugely buxom and had tight red curls and a generous face. Bill rubbed his arm in an exaggerated manner. Something crashed in a nearby room and a short sausage-shaped dog trotted up to them and sniffed the untouched tub of water near Heather's feet. Then he turned his rump to them, his ears folded back, and growled. The woman with the pink slippers kicked him and said, "Go on. Get out."

The dog bolted from the room. A door opened and cold air swept into the room and the dog began barking, but he was outside now and the sound came to them as though wrapped in a thick sweater.

"Won't talk to you," the woman said. "But he's a nuisance for barking."

Bill said to Heather, "My second cousin, Helen."

"Pardon me?" Helen said, swatting Bill again. "Second cousin once removed."

They were flirting. Heather gazed up at the woman, liking her anyway.

On the way back to St. John's, Heather sat in the back bundled in blankets, her feet, which were becoming fiercely painful, resting on the seat. It grew so warm that Mandy, in the front, stripped off layer by layer, but never complained.

"Where's your car, Heather?" Bill asked.

"Cape Broyle," said Mandy.

"We'll get it in the morning then. Mandy and I."

"I'm sleeping in," Mandy said.

"You can sleep in."

It was snowing heavily now. It covered the windshield within seconds of the wipers clearing it. Bill was driving slowly. "Not the time of year I would have chosen for a hike up the Southern Shore."

Both women ignored him.

"Listen," Mandy said. "I saw something weird out there. Like a white cross."

"In the woods?"

"Yes."

"I saw that too" Heather said, only now realizing what it had been.

"So that's where you were," Bill said. "Way out there. Christ, the two of you. That was Suse's Meadow."

"Suse who?" Heather asked.

"That's right. At the edge of a meadow," Mandy said. "I nearly walked right by it because of the fog. Creepy. That's when I called you, Bill."

Heather wished her sister would be quiet. It was maddening. "Bill," she said. "Suse who?"

"Suse. She went cow hunting one day and was never seen again."

"How old was she?"

"When was this?"

"They looked for her but all they found was her sunbonnet, out on a bog. My guess is she was about thirteen, fourteen."

Heather tried to lean forward. "Suse *who*? Did she have a last name?"

"She was a servant girl. Her family was from Brigus South. Years later they found her bones. Suse Hayes."

"Oh. My. God."

"Who found them?"

"Some fellas out hunting. They thought at first it was a lost sheep. But the hair was still on her head."

"Oh. My. God. Are you enjoying this, Bill?"

"They brought the bones back in a biscuit box. It was later they put the cross out in the woods where she'd been found."

"Cow hunting?"

"Her bones all fit in a biscuit box?"

"That's the story I heard."

"I don't believe that," Heather said. "I don't believe she just got *lost*."

"Neither do I," Mandy said.

"Why not? You two got lost."

"What do you think, Mandy?"

"My first thought was rape and murder," Mandy said quietly.

"Me too," Heather said, feeling close to tears. "My first thought."

"I wonder if this is some fundamental difference between men and women," Bill said. "I thought it was an interesting story."

"An *interesting* story!"

"Well, from a folklore perspective."

"A girl gets lost in the woods," Mandy said, gulping. "She either freezes and starves to death over several days, though no one can find her, or — more likely — she is tortured and killed, and you say it's an interesting story?"

"Freezing to death takes less than several days. You two don't realize how lucky you are."

But both Mandy and Heather were crying. Heather couldn't believe how horribly sad it was. She put her hand on her sister's shoulder, and Mandy took it in her own. They cried more.

"Jesus," Bill said.

At emergency they also told Heather she was lucky. The frostbite was not severe; they did not expect gangrene to be a concern.

"You're a lucky gal," said the intern, not from Newfoundland.

She hadn't eaten all day, the temperature had dropped ten degrees in two hours, and she had been wandering in stockinged feet through the wet, snowy woods for no one knew how long, but she was lucky. When they said *lucky,* she imagined a wide blue sky that never closed above a bog and on the bog, a tattered sunbonnet.

"There's some terrific hiking in this province, isn't there?" the intern said. His hair was flattened at the back of his head; it was clear he'd been recently asleep. "I'm ordering antibiotics. That's routine. I like to tell hikers to be prepared. Appropriate clothing, especially footwear —" Heather wondered if he knew she'd lost hers — "and always carry plenty of food and water, a map and compass if you've got one. Now, is there anything you need to tell me?"

Heather shifted on the bed. "Like what?"

"Like any medical conditions?"

"Why?"

"It's a routine question."

"None that I can think of."

A nurse came in carrying a tray, and the intern jumped back. "The nurse is going to clean and dry your feet, then wrap them in sterile bandages to prevent infection. Frostbite is like any injury." Gradually, the intern was moving closer to her again. "It's due to the formation of ice crystals in the tissue but also to decreased blood flow. Imagine the blood in your extremities thickening and turning sludge-like. When your body gets cold, it gets smart."

"Can I get in here?" the nurse asked, and the intern jumped back a second time. She glanced at Heather and rolled her eyes. The intern was still talking, but Heather found it difficult to look at him. Instead, she watched the nurse, who was working silently on Heather's feet. She wore a small embroidered pin resembling a pumpkin pie.

"As soon as your body temperature drops, those tiny blood vessels in your skin and extremities narrow. This keeps blood flowing to vital organs like your heart and brain. Of course, that comes at a price, as we see here."

Heather tried to smile at him. He couldn't have been more than twenty-five. His bright enthusiasm was commendable, but give him ten, fifteen years and it would be like pulling teeth to get this kind of information from him. He wasn't wearing a ring, but it was likely he was engaged. Years of family life lay in wait: the house, the renovations, the cars. The neighbourhood, the pets, the schooling. The first serious illness.

"Now if those blisters had been filled with bloody fluid —"

A second nurse appeared in the doorway. "Doctor," she said flatly, and the young man spun around and jogged out of the room.

The first nurse took a deep breath and patted one of Heather's bandaged feet as though it were a bundled infant all fed, washed and tucked in for its nap. "That's grand," she said. "Let's pray for a speedy recovery. You don't want to be coming back here."

"What do you call those birds?" Heather's mother asked, looking at the feeder. "Lovely, aren't they?"

"Juncos."

"I didn't know you were a hiker. Did you join a club?"

"No."

"Are those your crutches? What's the verdict on your feet?"

"Mom."

"Oh, no. You're not crippled, are you?" her mother joked.

"Mom, listen —"

"Actually, I have a little speech." Her mother laughed self-consciously and moved closer to the bed, gesturing with the unlit cigarette. "Let me just say one thing and then I'll go outside and smoke this. I did understand, honey. And I *do* understand. I wasn't taking sides. If I took sides, it would be your side."

"I know, Mom."

"I just didn't want you to feel endless sorrow. You always knew how I felt about that man. Sitting on the fence, the way he did."

"I'm pregnant, Mom."

Her mother straightened. She studied Heather's bathrobe more carefully.

"You're showing, too."

Heather nodded.

"Well."

They stared at each other a while, Heather trying to look apologetic, though she didn't really know how she felt. The window of opportunity for terminating the pregnancy had passed, though she had never made a conscious decision to keep the baby. In fact, she didn't think she did want the baby.

"So what *is* the verdict on your feet?" her mother asked at last.

"That I'm lucky."

Her mother laughed and took a seat on the bed. She let her shoes drop from her feet. They thudded — one, two — on the hardwood floor. Heather relaxed.

"I'll have to think about this."

"I thought so."

"I'll have to get used to the idea."

"Yes."

"It's his?"

"That's a fair guess."

"Who else knows?"

"Only you, Mom." The conversation was predictable and soothing. "And my doctor."

"Mandy?"

"Well. I had to tell Mandy."

"How are you feeling?"

"A little tired. But pretty good. A breeze so far."

Her mother didn't smile. "Everything is as it should be? On schedule?"

"Yes."

"I wonder if you have a pack of cards anywhere in this place?"

They played rummy 500 or crib and outside winter gave way to spring. At least once a visit, her mother told her to stand so she could see how far along she was getting. Other than that, Heather did her best to avoid any discussion of her condition.

One day Heather told her mother the story of Suse Hayes.

"They say she went cow hunting, Mom. Does that make sense to you?"

Her mother had just dealt and was moving her cards around in her hands. "What? Cow hunting? Why not?"

"Cows don't run wild."

"They did at one time. Occasionally one wouldn't come home, I guess, so they had to go find it. What is it with you and Mandy and cows? She's asking me the same questions. Is this a movie you two saw?"

"I just told you. Mandy and I saw a memorial cross in the woods."

Her mother put her cards down on her lap. "Can I just say one thing?"

"If you criticize, you leave. That's the rule."

"Yes, the rule, I know." She raised her cards again. "One of the rules. Your discard."

Heather laughed. "I don't have that many rules."

"Don't smoke. Don't criticize — though who distinguishes criticism from comment, I don't know. Don't ask any personal questions."

"That's not true."

"It is."

"Then how do you know so much about my life?"

It had been years since Heather had seen her mother in slacks, though she could remember her wearing them every day, and in summer, a pair of white shorts. Now she wore one of two polyester skirts, which she claimed fit her so comfortably she could not bear to put anything else on. Her blouses were continually coming out and gathering folds at her waist, the one part of her body that had gained weight. Each day she sat pencil-straight on the edge of Heather's bed, and Heather marvelled at the endurance of her back.

Her mother said, "I suppose it helps to be a shrink."

"I'm not a shrink."

"Do you know what I read recently? I read a very interesting article about something called disenfranchised grief."

"Don't you think I know about that?"

"I'm just trying to help. You don't have to snap at me."

"Labelling doesn't help. It doesn't make any difference. I'm angry you would even bring that up."

"What would you say then to a patient in your position?"

"*Clients*. They aren't referred to as patients."

"What would you say?"

"I'd say, I can see you are experiencing a lot of pain and it is real."

"You're being deliberately cold."

"I'd pass over a box of tissues."

Heather's backyard was turning green. The sky was bright blue, but all morning round cold-looking clouds had been passing quickly overhead — a sign it wasn't as warm outside as it looked. Many people were interested in clinical psychology because they were curious about themselves; it was a means of self-discovery. Heather had not thought this was the case for her. She'd thought, at one time at least, that she simply wanted to help people.

Disenfranchised grief was for those unable to publicly acknowledge their loss — homosexuals, the families of AIDS victims, women who miscarry and, yes, women in love with other women's husbands. Heather found it difficult to compartmentalize her feelings, or her relationship with Benny, in that textbook manner. The study of grief — the models, stages, expressions, process — it all seemed pointless in the face of grief's blind impersonal energy.

Her mother closed her hands around her cards. Occasionally, like today, she went without the considerable makeup. Heather found the more familiar racoon look impossible now to recall. Her mother appeared defenceless, just-born.

"Go ahead, open the window and have a cigarette if you want."

"Absolutely not. You're pregnant."

Heather shrugged and her mother stared at her.

"I'll step outside."

As she watched her mother slip stiffly from the bed and back into her shoes, Heather considered the task of waiting for Benny to die from afar. But the truth was, she had longed for it to end.

She heard the back door open and close and her mother exit the house.

Waiting with tremendous dread and almost unconsciously, but she had been waiting all the same.

The day Heather visited Benny at his house, they had stood together at the foot of his bed. They did not touch each other, did not even graze an elbow or hip. After greeting Heather, Inky settled at their feet. Why were they in this room — the master bedroom? By then, she was aware of feeling fragile. There had been the walk up the stairs, all those family photographs.

He was telling her about something. A new chapter in his life? The management of his illness? A need for self-preservation? The challenges ahead?

He sounded jittery and elated.

When she reached out to touch him, he stepped back. He had become slightly unrecognizable.

He asked, "Do you think a person can change overnight?"

He was being patient. His patience was giving him power, feeding him.

"I'm trying to explain something very important to you, sweetheart, and you seem distracted."

Was he saying his illness had already changed him so much he didn't love her anymore?

For six years she had allowed their relationship to be what it was: alternating periods of longing and joy. She wondered if he'd told his wife this news. Of course. First his wife, then Heather. It would be a reasonable progression of events.

There was a peculiar look about him. He seemed calm, almost tranquil, while she was racing to keep up with everything. Shouldn't there be a team of experts in the room with them — people to whom she could make some medical inquiries? What about expectations? Hope?

"Heather, you don't need me."

Was he trying to let her go?

"Of course I need you."

"Tell me why you need me."

"Because . . . " She wanted to say: because of your face, your eyes, your hands, your hair. But how would that sound?

"Tell me. Heather, tell me."

"Because I think about you constantly."

It was the right thing to say. It was as though he had been holding her over an embankment, a precipice, a crashing falls, and was considering releasing her. Was it only a sense of responsibility that stopped him, an inability to hurt this woman who loved him and thought about him constantly? By the time they heard his son coming in, he had changed again — retreated. He wouldn't let her go, not yet.

"When will I see you again?" he asked, just before they went downstairs.

Chapter Six

A few weeks after Benny told her he was sick, they went to Spruce Cove for the weekend. It would be their last trip.

It was a sunny spring day. A house for sale caught Benny's eye just minutes from the cabins and he suggested they stop to snoop around. The house was deserted — a sign with phone number was posted in a front window. They wandered into the backyard past a shed and sagging clothesline, then followed a narrow path through old snow to a view of the coast.

The pack ice was in. It covered the water as far as they could see, a blanket of white under a sky so brilliant and blue it bore down on the landscape as though it might ignite it. Heather was unable to reconcile it with her expectation of ocean. Just where she thought she would see water, she saw a white sparkling desert. Steeples had formed where the ice rode up on itself, pressing against small grey-green islands where gulls stood silhouetted. It was an environment that seemed to exist without reason. Heather stared at it a long time before she noticed the surface undulating slightly, as though a giant animal stirred beneath it.

"A gazebo would be nice out here," Benny said. "For the summer."

"You'd only need a blanket, a book and sunblock. A gazebo would ruin your view from the house."

He took her hand and said, "You're right." She tried to feel happy.

But that evening they seemed to have little to say.

"Where is it?" she asked eventually.

"I'm told it started in my stomach."

"Started? What are you talking about?"

He shook his head. She could see how difficult it was for him to speak about it, but she couldn't stop herself. "Can't you elaborate at all?" she asked gently.

For several minutes he was silent. "I was meant to have tests two years ago. I never went."

"What tests? You never told me. What tests, Benny?"

"I can't talk about it right now. I just want to be here with you, sweetheart, okay?"

The following day there was a driving rain from dawn to dusk and they spent most of their time in bed, yet there was a distance between them. Heather began to feel weightless, almost unable to register his hands on her body when they did touch. He was talkative, but only about certain things. He grew cross if she tried to discuss his illness or the future. She realized he had been speaking for several minutes, something about the cold utilitarian quality of these cabins, yet she had heard little of it. Although the desire to touch him, smell him, watch him, seemed overwhelming, she felt banished and void, and eventually so disengaged from herself she would not have been surprised to discover she could no longer form words.

In the evening he volunteered to make supper. She sensed he found the growing silence between them unsettling. He needed to move about, to act. He dressed and she followed him into the kitchen and watched him crack eggs into a bowl and then begin whisking them. He added salt and pepper and just before dumping the eggs into a pan, poured in too much milk. She wanted to say something but didn't, though she knew that when the eggs were done she would struggle to finish them. How childish of her, still squeamish about scrambled eggs.

He scooped the eggs onto two plates, each with toast and slice of orange, and glanced at her. She had done nothing to help him. She had sat there, half dressed, and watched him — when his back was turned, she watched his back and shoulders; when he faced her, she watched his arms and hands; and when she sensed he was about to glance at her, she looked at the table. The eggs were as she had anticipated: grey watery milk was leaking out from them and pooling on her plate. As she nudged her toast to dry safety, she wondered if she should tell the story of staying with her aunt and uncle one of those weekends her parents were working strenuously against divorce.

But it wasn't really much of a story; why in the world had she preserved its memory? She and Mandy had awoken in the morning and come down to the kitchen, and there was their uncle, wanting to know what they wanted for breakfast. Heather suggested scrambled eggs and her uncle, who was childless, was delighted. A request he could manage. It was the end of June. Heather had just finished grade six and Mandy, kindergarten — for the second time — but they could both see he had been worried about breakfast. Where had their aunt been? His scrambled eggs must have been one part egg, one part milk, Heather thought now. Mandy was excused from eating them because she was generally excused from things. But her uncle would not allow Heather such grace. She was twelve years old. She better eat up. Hadn't she said she liked scrambled eggs? Hadn't she expressly ordered them? But Heather couldn't eat them. She sat beside her uncle at the table in the dark little kitchen, while her hungry stomach growled and a homesickness she never believed possible climbed into her.

Heather and Benny went to bed early, the rain turning to drizzle, neither one wanting to go out in it. Worrying, unable to sleep, she was up several times. In the early hours she was there at the kitchen window to see the clouds move off and the moon emerge. She had wrapped herself in a thin blanket that dragged behind her across the spruce floorboards. The electric heaters were on, filling the small room with a biting, strangling warmth. Outside the moonlight fell brazenly on cars, picnic tables, cabin roofs. The light was also making its way indoors, so that Heather could easily read the warnings about water usage and the disposal of garbage taped by management to a cupboard door. Curtains were tied back on either side of the window, their ruffled borders edged with moonlight in a beautifully decisive way that depressed her.

She had not eaten the eggs, but her uncle had found a means of punishing her later that day. Friends of his had a new swimming pool, and they were all invited for the afternoon. But first, there was the issue of bathing suits. Mandy could wear her underwear, no complaints, but Heather was too old for that, even her aunt agreed. Heather knew this family; she knew there was a fifteen-year-old daughter who would be wearing a stylish suit. Heather herself had a new two-piece, but it was at home. Home. Home was empty this weekend, and locked, but it was not far, a seven-minute drive, and everyone knew where the key was hidden. But her uncle went up into the attic and came down with a bathing suit that had been Heather's aunt's. It was perfectly reasonable for her to wear it. Why didn't she try it on? It came all the way from California and looked to be exactly her size. Why bother everyone with a stop at a locked house when there was a perfectly acceptable swimsuit here in this house? What was the matter with Heather that she couldn't even try it on?

Heather turned from the moonlit window and walked to the doorway to look in at the sleeping body alone in the bed. She imagined an invisible bubble around Benny. She was permitted to pass through this bubble, but once inside, communication was strained, as though they were being watched.

The suit had been a floral one-piece with a weighty zipper the length of the back. Pink ribbons served as straps and also tied around the waist in a tired-looking bow. But it was so loose that when she tried it on the ribboned waist sat on her hips and her rear end was lost in the baggy seat. She had stood in the hall outside the bedroom, embarrassed by the bodice, which stood stiffly inches from her chest and might have been quilted, Heather thought now, and her uncle asked, What's the matter with that? while her aunt added cheerfully, You're all ready for the pool party now, dear.

At the pool Mandy swam happily and without shame in her transparent white underwear while Heather, fully clothed, sat in the shade. Fortunately, the fifteen-year-old daughter never appeared. The hostess, a tanned woman in an orange bikini that revealed a strangely corrugated belly, offered Heather the loan of a suit, but Heather, embarrassed, shook her head. She barely spoke the rest of the weekend, shunning her uncle altogether, and wrestled with an ache for her parents to return and to be reunited with her own house and family.

Heather got back into bed, careful not to wake Benny, then realized he was awake.

"Did I wake you?" she whispered.

"No. I was already awake."

"Sorry."

"I don't mind." He put an arm around her.

The next morning they awoke and, never touching, dressed and packed. They drank their tea in silence. She was paralyzed by his remoteness, by his inability to let her know more. It was unlike anything between them before. She was sitting with her legs tucked under her when he passed her, heading for the shower. He looked down at her, about to speak, then closed his mouth. He might have been concerned or, just as easily, irritated. She thought it possible that she didn't know him at all.

It was mid-morning when they left. Sunshine had returned. They decided to stop for an early lunch at the only restaurant in Spruce Cove. They sat inside at first, but on seeing there were tables in the back, facing the water, Benny wanted to move. Heather took up their cutlery and the saucer of coffee creamers and they went out. They agreed the view was spectacular in the sun, but still, it was cold and the wind was picking up. Much of the snow had melted as a result of the previous day's rain, and a treeless landscape was re-emerging. The restaurant was situated along one high arm of the bay, with a view onto the water and steep cliffs on the opposite side. The pack ice had moved out slightly, exposing water like a strip of belly glimpsed unexpectedly. Birds, possibly gulls, were calling from below, yet were not in view. Their cries rose up abruptly, then just as abruptly, faded. They seemed to be saying, *Look-at-me, look-at-me, look-at-me.* Heather thought they sounded hysterical.

They had both forgotten to pack coffee for the weekend and Benny was looking forward to a decent cup.

But the coffee was terrible. Heather figured it had been sitting there since early morning. Neither of them could drink it.

He said, "Shall I ask her to put on a fresh pot?"

"No," Heather said. She had seen the coffee pot. It was nearly full.

"Why don't I do that?"

"Better not."

With their cups of coffee sitting full before them, they both ordered tea.

But they agreed the fish and chips was fabulous.

"When she comes back, I'll tell her the coffee was too strong," he said.

"Who is your doctor, Benny? Will you tell me that much?"

"What's that flavour? Horseradish in coleslaw? That's unusual."

Heather said it was probably just the taste of cabbage, which could be sharp.

He said it again.

She said, "I really don't think it's horseradish."

He leaned towards her. "What is it then?" he whispered.

She shook her head, smiling.

"No, Heather, there's horseradish in this coleslaw."

"There isn't." She watched his face, thinking how much, now that their weekend was nearly over, she craved him.

"I'll ask the waitress," he said.

"Want to bet?"

"Five dollars?" His hand came up for the handshake. He was grinning.

"You're on." It was partly an excuse to touch him.

But when the waitress, polite and worried, said no and proceeded to list the ingredients — everything you'd expect — Benny looked so downcast Heather was embarrassed. The waitress left.

"Benny —"

"I don't want you to interfere."

Then he saw her face and said, "He's not a local doctor. He's not someone you grew up with, or I grew up with. I'd never met him before. Okay?"

"Okay."

"It will not improve matters to have you making calls."

"I wasn't going to."

"Everything is going to be fine. Can we just . . . be ourselves? Please."

"Of course."

But on the drive home they did not seem to be themselves. Heather knew the situation inside her head would be impossible to describe. She was not here and yet, she was excruciatingly *here*.

"The weekend went fast," Benny said quietly.

The sun was streaming onto their laps and torsos. She put a sweater over her bare arms, saying sunburns were worse through glass. Benny laughed and told her less UV light gets through glass. No, she was certain, she had read it.

"Heather, skin burns less through glass."

She glanced at him. "Bet?" she asked.

"Five dollars?"

"You're on." But this time there was not the same light-heartedness.

An hour later they passed an unmarked turnoff to the north.

"The turnoff to Isaac's Harbour," Benny said solemnly. They had been there together, two years ago, and had a wonderful time.

"No, it's still ahead."

He waited, then: "Yes, Heather, that was it."

"No it wasn't."

"It's very important for you to be right, isn't it?"

"I might say the same thing to you, stranger."

"What does that mean?"

They would be home soon, and they would separate. There was a tiny swollen pressure behind her eyes, deep in her optic nerves and across the bridge of her nose.

"I'm sorry, Benny. I don't know what's the matter with me. I feel as though I don't know what to say to you anymore."

"Hey, there's that new coffee shop up ahead. Let's stop, stretch our legs. I'm sure we'll have better luck with the coffee there." He paused. "I'm sorry too, sweetheart."

She turned to look at him, thinking they could somehow start the weekend over, but his expression was guarded. His eyes looked glazed. His smile was apologetic.

At the coffee shop they took a table by the window. It was late afternoon and colder. The wind had turned around and the sun was gone. The small harbour just below the parking lot was bottlenecked with ice.

He said the coffee was not bad and encouraged her to drink hers, but she knew it would only increase her agitation.

"I think I'll go for a long walk when I get home," he said.

"I think I'll pop in on my mother." She felt relieved; it was beginning to feel normal.

"Are you going to tell her about this weekend?"

It was then that Heather noticed the elderly woman sitting alone, directly behind Benny. She wore a black wig and a hearing aid like a wad of gum in her ear. Her face looked unbearably tired. She was resting her elbows on the table and holding her mug inches from her mouth between sips, as though to conserve the energy involved in lifting the mug from the tabletop.

"I worry about your mother," Benny was saying. "She knows a lot of people. I'm not comfortable with her knowing about my life. It's not her business. Can you promise me you won't discuss our weekend?"

"Benny, is that really so important?" She had almost said, *now*.

"You won't promise me that?"

She couldn't look at him. She was staring at the old woman, so that when the woman turned suddenly, her expression transformed from stoic self-preservation to alarm, Heather was looking directly into her watery eyes.

"Did you hear that?" the woman asked Heather. "Someone shouting?"

Heather turned back to Benny. "Don't do this," she said.

"Someone shouting?" the woman repeated.

Two couples approached an adjacent table. Heather was aware of them start to set down their food, then glance at Heather and Benny and move to a table farther away.

Benny was reaching for the ignition when he stopped and leaned against the steering wheel, squinting at the ice in the harbour below. "Are those seals?" he asked.

She had seen them, too. Her voice, when she answered, was faint. "No."

"What are they?"

They could hear the shouting now. And see the figures below at the edge of the pack ice. As they got back out of the car, they were immediately met with the frustrating impression of slow motion brought on by panic as a young man scrambled up the slope at the edge of the parking lot, waving his arms and shouting, Does anyone have a rope? while restaurant customers and employees were running out of the restaurant. Within seconds, ropes were hauled from the backs of trucks and cars and Benny had disappeared into a crowd of men rushing down to the ice.

Heather followed, then fell behind when an elderly man, anxious to help, appeared beside her and took her arm above the elbow. She slowed, but felt driven to the point of nausea by her anxiety to keep up with Benny, whom she could no longer see. She glanced at the man, trying to hide her impatience. He was unsteady on his feet and his hands were trembling. He wore a dark overcoat and a slightly grandiose leather cap.

Then, halfway down the slope, he seemed to grow furious with himself.

"Go on, maid, don't wait for me," he said, but Heather knew he would never be able to negotiate the rocky embankment alone. She would later remember thinking it was regrettable the day was ending, the light already beginning to fade.

As Heather reached the bottom of the slope, she saw a huddle of men along the shore. Benny was among them, stretched across a ledge of ice with another man locked to his waist. One end of a green rope was wrapped around Benny's wrist. The other end disappeared into the water. What had looked like an expanse of solid ice from the parking lot was a mass of ice chunks, none thick or stable enough to support a person for long. Swells were travelling through the slushy ice, lifting and dropping their cargo before crashing against the shore. With each wave the sea heaved closer to the men.

"I've lost him!" Benny shouted wildly. "Hey! Doesn't anyone see him?"

The man holding him straightened, though he kept a hand on Benny's back. "No, boy. And you'd better get back a bit." Heather could see a hardness around the man's mouth as he spoke.

More people were arriving, and in the distance sirens sounded. A waitress appeared, breathless, and asked, Was it children?

Someone nodded. Two boys.

"Why weren't the foolish buggers in school?" a man asked.

Heather turned and saw it was the old fellow she'd helped down the slope.

"It's Sunday, Pops."

"Come on," the man holding Benny said. "You're risking your own life now."

The man gave Benny a hand and pulled him away from the water. Benny stood and stared first at the old man and then at the growing crowd. A couple of men came up and touched Benny, but his expression was blank and unresponsive. He still held the rope. Heather moved to stand beside him.

"But he had the rope in his hand," Benny said.

People were moving jerkily along the shoreline, searching for some sign of a body, some colour other than the grey and white of water and ice. Heather knew that as the seconds passed it became more and more likely that no one would see those boys alive again. Yet only minutes ago — while she was picking her way down the embankment — they had been right here, with wet faces and flattened hair, in soaked, weighted winter jackets, reaching to Benny and thinking those inches to safety were nothing. That Benny would haul them out. She could see all this on his face and hear it in his voice.

Customers from the coffee shop, people like Benny and Heather who had only been passing through, began climbing back up the slope, while singly and in groups, townspeople came reeling down the embankment. Heather imagined the houses in the community above emptying as word went quickly around. Police, fire fighters and rescue workers appeared, bringing with them flotation rings, blankets, ladders, rakes and more rope — much of it simply tossed onto the ground. One woman, who had left the house without a jacket or coat, had to be held back from the shore. She wanted to leap into the water. Shouting, she didn't understand why no one was going in after her son.

Heather thought of the pack ice she and Benny had marvelled at two days earlier. At the time it had seemed majestic, bounteous. Now it seemed like trickery.

The day Justin Tucker came to Heather's house for her first date had not, in fact, been their first date. The week before he had driven her out to Torbay when the ice was in. She had never told anyone. She had followed him down across a sloping meadow and then onto the edge of the ice. The water had been still, not like this. She had seen seals a long way off. She knew of no one who had been out on the ice. Everyone knew it was stupid — stupid as taking drugs and stealing.

Justin had hopped from ice pan to ice pan, a kind of flight, and she had followed him. It was just the two of them in the universe, zigzagging back and forth in looping, preordained patterns. After an hour they hiked back up over the meadow holding hands, still full of the exhilaration, the shock, of having tempted disaster, of having pressed up against the unimaginable. Was that what these two boys here had been seeking?

Heather felt the concerns of her life — bad coffee, sunburns through glass, even Benny's illness — shrink before the horror of losing a child. She wondered if Benny's private, inexpressible fear was the fear of losing his son, should the worst occur. Benny would not be here to guide him, shelter him. To simply know him as he grew from boy to man. Heather glanced around. When she finally saw Benny, she recognized him first by his clothing. He was drifting among the crowd, not speaking, no longer offering advice or help, like a sleepwalker, a shadow.

She made her way towards him. It was like moving through a busy train station or bus terminal. When she reached him, she took his hand. It was icy cold.

"Let's get you home," she said.

He turned to her. He looked like a man who would never comprehend another thing in his life.

Chapter Seven

Heather's mother was crossing the backyard, trailing cigarette smoke and absently inspecting any new growth. Heather watched her bend down and ram the cigarette butt into the edge of a flower bed. Then she stood and lit a second.

When she came back into the room, she carried the smell of cigarettes caught in a layer of outdoor freshness. "Well, I'm gone."

Heather nodded, watching a large colourful bird fly up to the feeder like it was doing the breast stroke. It had a black crescent on its breast and was so distinctive she knew it would be easy to identify. Yet somehow she felt let down. Gradually birdwatching from her bedroom was losing its magic. And it never seemed quite as exciting as that moment with the red crossbills.

Her mother was watching her from the doorway.

"Heather, you have all these books about birds, but you haven't a single book about infants. You don't have a crib or high chair or diapers or anything. And that can be so easily remedied."

"Mom. I do not need a baby shower. Mom?"

"Okay, okay. Can I take you shopping then?"

"Not today."

"Heather, you should get out. Your feet have healed. Even just a walk. Everyone is walking."

"Everyone has quit smoking."

"It would be good for you. It would get you out of your head. And that old bathrobe."

Heather smiled, thinking her mother was a good example of someone for whom a little *Reader's Digest* psychology went a long way.

"You're stronger than you think. And actually quite normal."

"Mom. No more psychobabble."

"You're right. I'll stop." Her mother went to the window, scaring off the beautiful bird, and looked across the yard at a neighbouring house. "Did I tell you I saw Peg O'Keefe? She regrets painting her house now. Golden Radiance. Does that sound like a heritage colour to you?"

Heather shrugged. Sometimes her mother got started on questions. Benny was like that. Had been like that.

"Did you know all five of Peg's children are doctors?"

All those years, all those questions. He was always meeting her with a question, a direct look, an expectant pause.

"All tops in their class, Heather. Tops everything. Timmy. Dr. O'Keefe now. Eye specialist. A real crackerjack."

If she wanted, Heather thought she could remember every single one of his questions, where they had been, what they had worn, or not worn. Her eyes began to fill and she blinked quickly.

"Only one moved away. The middle boy. What was his name? Callum is a cardiologist and Grace is something. Susan is a dietician."

Heather looked at her mother. "Dieticians are not doctors."

"So you are listening to me. Well, she married a doctor. Tops in their field. You look pale, honey."

Years and years of questions, like kisses, tossed to her.

Are you a writer?

What made you choose that refrigerator? This bra, that blouse, this car?

*Does this relationship mean as much to you as it does to me?
When will I see you again?*

Her mother drew in a long breath. "Heather, many people face at least one serious hardship in their life."

"Please. You don't need to go on."

"Then how about names? Have you given any thought to names yet?"

"What if a person has more than one hardship?"

"Those people are unlucky."

Heather followed her mother to the door, then after she left, lingered there, taking in the view of the outside. She had hardly left the house in three months. Few people knew she was pregnant, a state of affairs that would be obvious to anyone now. She could hear birds, children, traffic, even the sound of her neighbour cutting wood. Was it Saturday or Sunday? He always cut and stacked new wood on the weekends this time of year and left it in his backyard through the summer to dry.

She began roaming through her house, tidying up, but for days still did not go outside.

One afternoon she was in the kitchen heating a can of soup. When it began to boil, she lifted the pot from the burner and remembered that once she had been happy. It must have something to do with the soup, she thought, reminding her of being over at Dad's when it was his week to have them and Mandy wasn't putting anything into her mouth except tomato soup. She had a sudden clear memory of who she was then, in her teens, a girl defined by frequent stabbing moments of happiness. Even the passage of time, the change of seasons, the very weather — wind, rain, snow, sun — had been sublime. They had protected her. She had been addicted to those moments.

Early the next morning, Heather rose and went to the window and looked out at her car, a red Echo. She speculated half a tank. She dug out heavy boots, an oversized coat, her new field guides and Mandy's binoculars. She looked around. As

89

soon as she was home again she'd take a shower and do the laundry. She'd go grocery shopping and thoroughly clean the house. She felt grand. It was the first time she had put something other than slippers on her feet in weeks, but she barely winced getting into the boots.

Outside she discovered it was a soft spring day. She squeezed her stomach in behind the steering wheel and was surprised by the cramped quarters. Her back immediately began to ache and she was breathless, but undaunted.

As she parked beside the dumpster behind the Canadian Wildlife Service building, Heather realized she felt almost hot under the spring sun. She dropped the visor and checked herself in the mirror. The woman who met her gaze looked alert, perhaps agitated, though frankly, the best word to describe that face, Heather concluded, popping the visor back up just as Darren exited the back of the building, would be deranged.

She watched Darren twice go back inside to collect something. He was wearing a T-shirt and loose jogging pants, an adaptation, Heather guessed, to the warmer weather. He fussed with the windshield wipers, though there wasn't a cloud in the sky, and checked the air pressure in the tires. His movements were uncharacteristically sluggish. As she started her car and pulled out behind him, Heather decided there were two questions she needed answered.

Was he married?

Did she *want* him to be married?

PART TWO

Chapter Eight

The storm petrel was in a box in the basement, which was the safest place for it, though they owned neither dog nor cat and a bird would be safe anywhere in their house. But it was so small, so much smaller than you might expect. Not even the size of a blue jay, barely that of a robin. And it was the second in a week. The first was found in the Virginia Park area by a woman. It was sitting on her doorstep and she almost stepped on it leaving for work. She screamed, thinking it was something else, a rat perhaps. The second one — the one in the basement — had made landfall at the Kidsville Daycare in Mount Pearl. The children found it beneath the slide and had been passing it around all morning. People didn't know what to do with them. It took a few seconds to realize they were looking at a bird at all. On rainy nights hundreds could be found stranded inland, having mistaken wet roads and parking lots for the black surface of the sea.

Darren knew not only what they were but that you needed to keep them sequestered until it was good and dark.

The Leach's storm petrel was the first bird Darren identified. He was twelve, on his way home from school, when he saw a queer-looking bird in an empty lot. It walked clumsily among the weeds and, in Darren's hands, gave off a sharp fishy stink.

He brought it home and in the evening his mother sent him to the library with his older sister, Jeanette, who flipped through magazines while he read about *Oceanodroma leucorhoa*. An abundant species of seabird, but one few people ever saw. It spent its entire life over the ocean, hundreds of miles from any shore, visiting land only to breed, and only at night.

He had hurried home, knowing exactly what to do, but while they were gone the dog had crept into his bedroom and swallowed the bird whole.

"That poor dog was only jealous," his mother said.

By ten o'clock the storm petrel was restless, its internal clock tuned to the arrival of night. From the kitchen they could hear it fluttering against the cardboard box, and Jeanette wondered aloud if it were not time for him to release the creature.

Darren put the box in the truck and drove it out to Cape Spear. When he opened the box he could see that the tips of the tail and wing feathers were severely frayed. It had been a trying day in the playground and a longer one in the box. The steep forehead gave the storm petrel a wise, pedantic look, despite its tiny size, while its slender black legs ended in webbed pads that looked impossibly soft. He imagined thousands of them running over the surface of the ocean at night, pushing against water as unyielding as concrete.

With the bird tucked inside his open jacket, Darren carried it down the boardwalk to the eastern-most point of North America and tossed it into the air. As long as it stayed airborne and resisted pitching on the water, it might survive, though it had lost weight and there was the sorry condition of its flight feathers. It was dark, and Darren lost sight of the bird almost immediately as, flying more like a butterfly than a bird, it vanished over the sea.

They had seen Mrs. Pynn infrequently, usually when the weather was mild. She would drift across the cul-de-sac at the end of Goodridge Place in her slippers and housecoat with the fallen hem. She had been chatty, and Darren avoided her, though Jeanette stood listening to the old woman, nodding and sometimes interrupting her with a benign question.

Mrs. Pynn disappeared in November. It was on Remembrance Day — fittingly — when Darren found her in the obituaries and discovered her first name had been Veronica. She would be sadly missed by her brother-in-law, Norman, and her nieces, Mary and Patty. Flowers were being gratefully declined.

"Well, well," he said, staring at his sister, who was reading the paper and may not have heard him. "Stayed in her own home till the bitter end. She always seemed a bit lonely, though, didn't she?"

He turned to look out the window at Mrs. Pynn's empty house. Above it, a water-laden blanket of cloud hung so low it seemed the peaked roofs circling the cul-de-sac were holding it aloft. It had been a spectacularly bad autumn. Thirty-two consecutive days of freezing rain, drizzle, fog or combination thereof, with only a hundred and fourteen minutes of sunshine clocked for the entire period.

Within a week Veronica Pynn's house went on the market, but it didn't sell until the end of the month. Darren guessed the house had seen few improvements during Veronica's life. Certainly the shabby exterior of the house gave one that impression.

It was a dim afternoon in early December when the new neighbours arrived, appearing first as a slew of skateboarders: boys of all ages, it seemed, the oldest rangy and bad postured, with bleached hair and broken expressions implying an extreme sport mishap was just around the corner. It was not clear how many of the youngsters actually belonged there. The arrival at suppertime of a parent — in this case, mother — did not shed much light on this, since they all ignored her.

The moment he saw her, Darren blurted out, "Not Isabella Martin." He almost groaned.

He had found Jeanette peering out the window of their front door. She had switched off the hall light, just in case anyone glanced over. It was at times like this that Darren felt a stab of concern for his sister.

"Who is Isabella Martin?" Jeanette asked, her face to the glass. "Have I met her, Darren?"

"Avalon Nature Club."

"So I haven't."

They watched the Household Movers truck pulling into the driveway and riding up across their yard as it made the turn.

"A little late in the day for moving, isn't it?" Jeanette said.

Two men in blue work suits jumped down from the cab of the truck and began to approach the house, slowly, as though still gearing up for the exercise ahead.

"Who is she, Darren?"

"Just give me a minute to think."

"Pardon?"

The moving men and Isabella Martin stood in the driveway talking. The outside light was on, allowing Darren and Jeanette a good look at their faces. Although he didn't know her well, Darren could recall her sudden, high-pitched cries of astonishment and slightly formal wardrobe. She said something to the men, who laughed. They were slapping their hands together because of the cold.

Jeanette cleared her throat and Darren glanced down at her. Her lips were slightly open, an unconscious habit of hers that indicated she was concentrating, or praying, though it was a while since he had accompanied her to mass.

"I don't know her that well," he said placatingly. "I'm sure she's nice."

Jeanette walked away. A period of silence between them

94

would now follow, so Darren lingered, observing the men as they began unloading the truck, then Isabella as she coaxed an elderly black dog out of her car, across the yard, up the steps and into the house. The dog fell across the doorstep and Isabella stood staring at it a moment before leaning down to gently shove it inside.

The unloading continued until well after Darren and Jeanette had gone to bed. Cars began to arrive, presumably parents collecting youngsters, around midnight. There was the sound of honking, cars idling, doors slamming. A light rain made the tires kiss the pavement grittily as they finally pulled away and went off down the street. At one point Jeanette knocked on his bedroom door, but he ignored it. He could hear the door to Isabella Martin's house open and close every few minutes, followed by shouts. Darren was hoping she *was* nice, because he was going to have to have a word with her.

He found the cigarette butts scattered across his front yard in the morning. Jeanette would hit the roof. He began to collect them, not knowing where to put them, when Isabella burst from her house, heading for her car. She glanced at him but didn't stop, pretending she hadn't seem him. Darren was relieved.

Then she changed her mind and walked towards him.

"Not a bad morning," she called to him when she got to the edge of her yard. It sounded as though it was the first time she'd used her voice that morning. "Off to work?"

He nodded.

"I'm Isabella Martin. I think we've met."

He stepped her way, the cigarette butts cradled in his hand.

"You're Darren Foley, aren't you? I don't know if you remember me."

"Avalon Nature Club?"

Her eyes brightened. "You brought in the assortment of bird eggs and stuffed penguins."

"Puffins. We don't get penguins in this hemisphere."

"Gorgeous creatures."

Yes. Her annoying habit of referring to plants *and* animals as gorgeous creatures.

"Before you go," he said, and she immediately crossed into his yard with an eagerness that worried him. "I just wanted to have a word with you about the commotion last night."

She was looking at his house. If Jeanette was spying from a window, he hoped she had enough sense to step back. He was trying to remember something he'd heard about Isabella Martin. There was still no sign of an adult male presence. A recent divorce perhaps.

He opened his hand to show her the cigarette butts. "My sister Jeanette would be distressed to see these."

He was conscious of the length of time it took her to focus on him again. She gave the cigarette butts an unsatisfactory glance.

"She's your sister?"

He nodded. "I'm not married."

Why had he offered that? It was the worst possible thing to say.

"My son has a lot of friends, but I never laid eyes on half those boys," she said. "I did think they were a hard bunch. I assumed they were from the neighbourhood."

Was that a clever insult? "They kept my sister up quite late," he said.

She produced an inscrutable smile. "These cul-de-sacs are ideal for skateboarding," she said. "But I'll talk to my son. He's only just turned twelve. He certainly doesn't smoke. He's a good boy. I don't even keep matches in the house."

She was looking back at her own house, as though making a quick comparison. The bungalow behind her was nearly identical to his own, yet her green siding was discoloured and faded, something brown had leached from the bottom corners of her windows, and other than a wind-battered dogberry, there was not a single ornamental in her yard. Lined up beside the front door were boxes that had not made it into the house the night before, dark and misshapen now from the rain and drizzle.

And she herself did not look too well put together either. The slacks she wore were in need of ironing and her raincoat looked as though she had taken it from the bottom of a box. Clearly, her hair had been shampooed within the past hour, but he knew enough about these things to know that she had not been concentrating during the drying process.

"I guess you're off to work as well?" he asked, thinking to wrap things up.

"Yes." She sighed loudly, staring at the ground. "I'm a substitute teacher. Vice-principal called last night. A teacher broke his arm. I suppose I should be more sympathetic."

This did not seem to be the same woman who had sat alone at the Avalon Nature Club lectures, occasionally raising her hand, as though it were a classroom, to calmly ask a question or make a comment. He released the cigarette butts, letting them fall back onto his lawn. He hoped Jeanette was not watching.

Darren found himself glancing at Isabella's hands on the steering wheel, then quickly looking away. There was a cute Doris Day air about her, and a suddenness in her attention to him that was disarming. At the same time he was cognizant of there being something odd and inexact about her, an impression somehow substantiated by the fact that she smelled of wine.

It had been her suggestion they share transportation to the Avalon Nature Club meeting, where December's guest lecturer had spoken on exotic flowers of the Portuguese lowlands. It was not well attended and the slides were all overexposed, which Isabella, who sat beside him, leaned over to whisper in his ear four times during the lecture. That's when the smell of wine was most obvious.

"Need anything at the Price Club?" she asked him on their way home.

He hesitated, alarmed. "Well, no, not particularly. Did you?"

*

Ardently.

He had been trying to find the best word to describe the way Isabella Martin shopped. That was it. She shopped ardently. He supposed she bought groceries ardently, too. A rib roast, a litre of milk, partridgeberry muffins.

She had waltzed into the Price Club, flashing her membership card. A Tuesday night and it was packed, which dumbfounded him, but then he remembered Christmas was only a week away.

Isabella slowed in electronics. Every television was on. "My husband couldn't bear this place," she told him. "All the noise drove him mad."

He noticed the comment had been delivered in the past tense. It reminded him to be careful. He followed her to linens where she fingered some towels and sheets.

"What did you get your sister for Christmas?" she asked.

Darren and Jeanette exchanged only one or two presents at Christmas and the day was often nearly over before they got around to it. There was always a bit of embarrassment and loneliness surrounding the exchange for Darren.

"Nothing. Yet."

"I've finished my Christmas shopping," she said. "Now this isn't bad." She picked up a baby-blue duvet. She slipped it from its packaging, flapped it open, then swung it around her shoulders like a cape.

"You look ridiculous," he said, smiling. "How much for something like that?"

"One hundred and eighty-nine." She handed it to him. "Gorgeous, isn't it?"

He did his best to scrunch it up. Though lightweight, it was fluffy and uncooperative. He cradled it against his chest and followed her to housewares, where she browsed, finally choosing a beverage set for $79.98. "I want to get rid of the old stuff."

"You're getting that too?" he asked.

She glanced at him, surprised, and he could see an endearing self-consciousness.

"I mean, you don't mind spending money."

She pressed a hand into the bundled duvet he held, but it was so dense he felt only a distant pressure. "That's like asking me if I don't mind eating chocolate."

Now they were at Home Depot, and Darren was beginning to worry that he might be on a date. No, shopping could never be considered a date. He liked Isabella, despite her peculiarities. He felt she was a decent person, though she didn't appear to have many friends. But she was single, and Darren didn't want to encourage her. That could be awkward, being neighbours.

There had been a time when Darren did his fair share of dating, particularly before, and even after, Jeanette began living with him. Tonight, briefly, he felt he was returning to a room he had forgotten existed.

But he was set in his ways now. He couldn't get his head around the idea of sharing a bed, closets, bathroom, all that personal space, with another person. And there was his sister to consider. It would be like feeding Jeanette to the wolves, to alter their lives now.

He followed Isabella down the wallpaper aisle. She was talking about renovating her son Cooper's room. In the meantime, Cooper needed a desk, reading lamp, shelf for books. Isabella held out a wallpaper sample for Darren's opinion. It was patterned with racing cars and basketballs.

"I suggest you steer clear of wallpaper," Darren said.

"Really?" She was looking directly at him.

He shifted. He held a reading light in one hand and a shelf awkwardly in the other.

"All right," she sighed, putting the wallpaper back. She took the shelf from him and sank to the floor with it. From a kneeling position she glanced up at him, her earrings swinging. "Do you think this looks stupid?" She was holding the shelf out in front of her, the support brackets resting on the floor. "Just imagine books and other stuff. Not many books, though."

"I don't follow."

"Does this look stupid down here?"

"You're putting Cooper's shelf on the floor?"

She stood and abruptly handed the shelf back to him. "Never mind. I'll just get it."

He followed her to the checkout. The irritation in her voice had surprised him. He was beginning to think it was crazy, this whole evening with her was crazy. Jeanette would be wondering where he was. And where, indeed, was he? First the Price Club and now Home Depot.

"What time is it?" he asked her. The incessant Christmas music was wearing on him.

"Didn't you wear a watch? It's close to eleven. Time to go home."

You got that right, he thought. She had seemed friendly, if not a little wacky, but now: petulant, almost contentious.

"Cooper did something to his ankle skateboarding," she began to explain. Her mood seemed to have completely changed again. "Twisted it. Bruised it. I don't know. The very day we moved. I thought a shelf with a low position would make it easier for him to reach his belongings."

"I suggest you take him to the doctor. Maybe they'd have some advice." He couldn't keep the patronizing tone out of his voice.

She spun around. "Of course I took him to the doctor. I took him to the children's hospital. I waited there half the day."

"What was their diagnosis?" he asked patiently.

"They said it looked fine on the X-ray."

"Then he's probably fine. Your turn."

"Yes, he's fine." She placed her items on the counter, staring at the young girl working behind it so long Darren began to feel ill at ease.

"I like your bangles," Isabella told the girl.

100

The girl blushed. "Thanks. My boyfriend gave them to me."

"He just can't walk," Isabella said.

The girl looked up.

"Darren?"

"Yes?" They were finally leaving the store.

"Do you think someone is following us?"

I'm not answering that, he thought.

The noise at night continued through Christmas. There was a mild spell and any snow that had fallen was gone quickly, apparently creating favourable conditions for twenty-four-hour skateboarding. A long metallic rolling sound from out on the street, something you might actually be able to sleep to. Not dissimilar, Darren thought, to the childhood sound of tree branches assaulting clapboard, a sound so constant no one heard it. A brief silence, during which Darren imagined the boys lifting into the black air, was followed by a series of startling smacks against the pavement, a jarring he felt in his teeth.

Darren parked the truck at the north end of Three Stone Pond. It was a four-kilometre hike to the beach through an un-interrupted stretch of black spruce forest. The air was cold, but not too damp. A streak of violet in the sky beyond the balled tops of the spruce lightened the landscape, lifting it up a little over the earth so that when Darren touched the ground his steps felt springy. Freezing rain in the night still clung to the twiggy new growth at the tips of the spruce branches and to the leatherleaf and sheep laurel along the track.

At the top of a rise he stopped to admire a stand of spruce, taller than most and more mature, draped from head to toe in tree lichen glossy with ice. The bark was heavily scaled and such a rich sienna brown that for several minutes Darren could not look away. The days were short this time of year. It would be dusk by four, but he was reluctant to go on. He looked hard at the trees again as he passed. He felt a longing to take them with him.

"I think it would be a good idea if someone spoke to her," Jeanette had said that morning, placing Darren's tea and toast on the table.

"I suspect she has little influence over those boys."

"God knows how many are hers."

"Just the one, actually."

"Yes, your little shopping excursion."

Jeanette brought him the phone and a slip of a paper on which Isabella's phone number had been neatly pencilled.

When Isabella's voice came on the line, it was clear she had been asleep. She was still in bed, perhaps under the baby-blue duvet. Perhaps her eyes were closed.

"Isabella? Darren here."

"Yes? Darren? What time is it?" Her voice was soft and forgiving, like a cushion.

"I apologize. I woke you. I'll call back."

"No. I was just having this dream." Her voice changed. He thought she might have sat up. "It was about my husband. He took me to this place. How strange."

Darren rolled his eyes at his sister.

"It was the size of the Grand Canyon. It was filled entirely with bottles of prescription drugs."

Darren was confused. "That sounds terrifying," he said.

"It was."

Jeanette was standing in the middle of the room, studying him. Darren tried to focus.

"Isabella, I need to talk to you."

"I was going to call you, too. I'm dying to invite you and your sister for dinner. How about tonight? That roaster does something divine to a chicken."

Boreal chickadees were following him. Their high-pitched chatter seemed barely within the range of human hearing. They could tag behind you a long time before you realized they were there, before you looked up and saw them flitting from tree to tree like a single thought. When he reached the clearing above the cliff edge, Darren left the chickadees behind in the forest, where their scolding grew briefly more emphatic before stopping altogether. He checked his watch and was relieved to see he'd made good time, then he quickly descended the scree slope to the beach below. The sun was out. Though not high in the sky, it gave the surface of the ocean a glistening pudding lustre. He crossed over the berm of polished cobbles at the back of the beach, heading towards a small patch of dark sand that looked rock-hard, but the moment he stepped onto it, it cracked and slid away underfoot, startling him more than it should have.

Jeanette was not aware of the second shopping excursion. She had been out when he'd run into Isabella last Saturday morning, when Isabella talked him into coming with him. She needed someone to help carry a new television, though in the end she hadn't bought one. They returned to the Price Club, where she did purchase a stainless steel roaster, durable enough to meet the most demanding of kitchen needs, for $219.99. Darren had tipped back on the balls of his heels with surprise, then followed her to the checkout, shaking his head.

There was no reason to tell his sister where he'd been. On the other hand, there was no reason not to tell her, either.

A small black and white heap lay at the far end of the beach. He went for it, guessing common murre. Darren could identify beach debris from several metres away. As he checked for oil and found none, then began to trim the tips of the wing feathers, he was reminded again of the roaster, the chicken and the invitation he had accepted without, as Jeanette pointed out the minute he put the phone down, consulting her.

He sat down on a boulder, still holding the murre in one hand. The head was gone — it always went first. The wing feathers were barely attached to the shoulder girdle and flopped from side to side as Darren inspected the carcass. He absently cut a notch in the edge of the wafer-thin keel where once the bird's powerful wing muscles had attached. He thought of his flight dreams, which he had been having since he found the storm petrel as a boy. But it was will power in those dreams, not physical effort, that gave him flight. He did not dream he was a bird, he dreamed he was himself, flying. He thought, *fly*, and up he rose over landscapes that were always tidy, verdant and foreign.

In the far distance he heard a car start. He jumped up. The day was closing in. It was a long hike back and an even longer drive.

"You were right," Darren said, nodding. Isabella beamed back. She had gathered her hair in two small ponytails, giving her a tidier, younger look.

"I was?"

"The chicken," he said. "It was delicious."

"Yes," Jeanette agreed. "I wouldn't mind the recipe."

"I told you when I bought it, didn't I, Darren? That roaster wasn't going to be a mistake."

Darren glanced at Jeanette as Isabella rose, carrying their plates to the counter, although he didn't see where she could possibly place them. It was obvious she was still in the process of unpacking. Plates and cups and wooden spoons rose out of a sink of wash water that looked suspiciously cold, its surface inert with soap and grease. A large box containing dozens of framed photographs and stuffed toys had been pushed into a corner. Beside that was a box for the recycling: mostly wine bottles. And a variety of objects had been pushed into a single pile on the kitchen table where they had just eaten: textbooks buckling with worksheets, a scarf with pink and orange pineapples, a toaster, markers, pencils, erasers, ketchup, a tub of yogourt.

Jeanette had no reason to be angry. Darren pushed back his chair, prepared to turn down any offer of dessert and coffee.

"Unfortunately," he said to Isabella, "it's been a long day."

Their hostess was standing at the stove, admiring her roaster. There was no evidence of dessert or coffee.

"Will you just look at the size of it, Darren?" Isabella said. Indeed, the roaster, large and oval shaped, easily straddled both her front burners. "Solid bottom. Gravy was a cinch." She grabbed the roaster by its double handles and carried it to him. He immediately swivelled in his chair to meet her. "Here. Feel this weight," she said.

As he reached out to take the roaster from Isabella, he glanced at Jeanette. Her expression had turned supercilious and aloof. Darren had known the look since childhood. It invited him to join her in an alliance that excluded Isabella, leaving her marooned with every person Jeanette had never liked or comprehended. But Darren was distracted by the pan, which *was* surprisingly heavy, and oddly comforting, though he wasn't going to say so.

Isabella said, "And the top can be turned over and used as a sauté pan. More wine?"

Jeanette put her hand over her wine glass and said, "I think I saw that very pot in the Zellers flyer last week."

"You save ten bucks? So what?"

Jeanette was returning the pan to the stove when the door opened. A boy with black hair and a million freckles was leaning heavily against the door frame. He was panting and looked unstable.

"Darling," Isabella said.

"I'm starved."

"I thought you said you wouldn't be home for supper."

"No, I never."

"We're just going," Darren said.

"Don't be ridiculous," Isabella said, not sounding herself.

The boy limped to the counter, then pushed himself along it until he reached his mother, knocking a half-eaten muffin onto the floor in the process. "What have you got for me to eat?"

Darren realized this was Cooper, of the damaged foot.

"Did you have a good time?" Isabella asked him, stooping to retrieve the muffin.

"No."

"You didn't. Why not?"

"I hated it."

"Cooper, I'd like you to meet our neighbours, Mr. Foley and

his sister, Miss Jeanette Foley. This is Cooper, my son. Unfortunately, he's injured his ankle."

"Hi," Cooper mumbled. For a moment he appeared shy. He looked in their general direction without making eye contact, then turned back to his mother. "What have you got for me to eat?"

"I'll put a plate together. Why don't you wait in the family room?"

Cooper hesitated, but his mother said, "Go on," and to Darren's astonishment, the boy dropped to the floor and began crawling out of the kitchen on his hands and knees, dragging his right foot.

"His ankle," Isabella said, frowning, "It seems to come and go."

It was disturbing, almost heartbreaking, and Darren felt the urge to go over and pluck the boy off the dirty floor, set him down and examine the mysterious leg.

Isabella turned her back to them, preparing Cooper's food, and said, "I made a frozen mousse cake. It's in the freezer. Can you hold on a sec?" The quirky confidence had vanished. He heard the television go on in the next room.

"No worries," Darren said, looking at his sister. "Take your time."

Isabella carried the plate out of the room. Almost immediately they heard Isabella cry, "Oh, Cooper. That was your father's."

Jeanette looked at Darren, alarmed.

"So what? He only cares about himself."

Isabella's response was a soft murmur.

"Darren," Jeanette whispered.

He nodded. "Just eat the dessert."

"Firstly, Darren, her house smelled like dog mess. Secondly, she's a very odd character. And thirdly, the boy."

It wasn't until they were home and in their kitchen having a cup of tea before bed that Darren realized how much the visit had disturbed Jeanette.

"I'm not going to jump to any conclusions," Darren said.

"What are you implying?"

"I'm only saying that I might not know what is normal in children."

"I can tell you that was *not* normal. Clearly, you don't know about the husband."

Darren sighed. "Not in the picture?"

"Well, Darren, he's dead — the boy's father is *dead*. He died very recently of cancer. Yet the boy spoke of him in the present tense and in a very disrespectful manner. And why was he crawling?"

Isabella's husband had died? She was a widow? Darren didn't know what to say. He was surprised by the news, yet realized it explained the vulnerability he sensed in both mother and son.

Darren resented Jeanette for holding out on this piece of information. Often her way. Her way of being diplomatic, delicate and grand. She was already dressed for sleep, though he could not see the nightgown or pajamas or whatever served as her first layer, since over it she wore a housecoat and, over that, a bulky sweater. Jeanette's indulgences were warmth and sleep. She reminded him of a mammal preparing for hibernation, which made him think of the black bear, or what might have been a black bear, and he nearly told her. But he wasn't certain and she might worry. Up the shore. He had just checked his watch and was about to remove his snowshoes when he'd glanced up to see a large creature come bobbing down the snowy slope at that very spot where balsam fir gives way to figwort and large-leafed goldenrod in summer. It was gone behind some trees within seconds. He had thought, no, black bears are rare on the Avalon, especially in coastal regions.

Whatever it was, it was not sure-footed.

"One other thing," Jeanette said. "She has a drinking problem."

Darren nodded — he had suspected as much — and rose to collect their cups and saucers.

"Leave those, Darren," Jeanette said. "I'll get them."

"It's no bother." He looked and saw her face had softened. He was reminded of their mother.

Darren took his laptop into the dining room where he would do a bit of work before bed. At the table he closed his eyes and immediately saw Cooper collapse to the floor and crawl out of the kitchen on his hands and knees. He smiled, suddenly understanding the argument for installing Cooper's Home Depot shelf at ground level.

Chapter Nine

It was still cold, but the sky was a distant creamy blue. Darren felt hollow, as though the memories of a thousand people had recently exited his mind, leaving only the space they once occupied and an evasive, baffling nostalgia. Nothing concrete; it was only a mood. The lengthening days, the sun beginning to feel stronger and flooding the woods, the world expanding. They would be done with winter soon. He felt optimism, relief, sadness. He could almost imagine how the future would look and smell and feel. At a familiar sound, he glanced up to see scores of crossbills hanging from the trees.

The skateboarding stopped as abruptly as it had begun. It was at this point that Isabella's ancient Labrador retriever started barking, much of the day and occasionally at night, during wind, snow, rain, and under clear conditions. Had Darren and Jeanette been so preoccupied with the skateboarding that they'd never heard the dog? Or was there a warped obsession with maddening sounds taking place in the Martin household? And where did the dog get its stamina? It could barely stand on all four legs simultaneously.

At supper Jeanette said, "That animal needs a mercy killing. Darren? If you ask me —"

"I heard you."

"You don't agree?"

She was smiling at him, trying to be gentle, but Darren was distracted. "Did we ever buy that new screen door?" he asked.

"Pardon me?"

"Remember? We talked about it last summer."

"Listen to it, Darren. It's moaning. It sounds like a grown man moaning. I find it hard to listen to."

"It's howling. Like a wolf, actually."

"Perhaps it's howling for a mercy killing. Why in the world is she keeping that poor creature alive?"

"I thought I might check out screen doors this evening." He felt an impatience for things to hurry up and change that was unusual for him.

"Isabella mentioned she was going to the mall this evening," he added.

"For heaven's sake, Darren. That woman is completely disrupting your life."

He wanted to tell her, Don't worry, nothing is going to change.

They had been back for a meal at Isabella's twice more. Despite her reluctance and near horror at the state of the house and Cooper, Jeanette went along.

Isabella was a messy, fabulous cook. When Cooper appeared he might display evidence of a setback with his ankle, causing him to crawl through the house, deaf to most questions his mother put to him. Or he might come tearing through the kitchen, yank open the door to the basement — where, apparently, he slept — and plunge down the stairs and out of sight. The sound of his quick, snappy footsteps on the stairs as he descended reminded Darren of a woodpecker rattling away on a tree or telephone pole. He wanted to stop the boy, strike up a conversation, forge some kind of understanding. But he would only watch him pass, knowing, on some level, that it was all the boy could permit.

And there was that dog, Inky. Isabella usually left him outside where he whined and barked, but occasionally he was there in the house, so enthused to see guests he only managed to circle the kitchen once before defecating right then and there. The dog seemed oblivious. The odour was deadly. Though Darren did not say so to his sister, he too, thought the dog's time had come.

Darren and Isabella attended the Avalon Nature Club meetings together and often stopped in at the mall on their way home.

You've got a soft spot for that poor soul, Jeanette had said, and Darren had not appreciated the condescension.

Isabella's purchases were not exactly frivolous, but they were costly and usually things she already owned but for some reason were not perfect: too slow, too old, too ugly. Darren began to wonder if her behaviour was a disorder. Was she a shopaholic? Was he an enabler? Were there such people? But he was unaccountably pleased when she made her purchases, or when she came over to the house carrying her new set of knives or pushing her new wheelbarrow, her calves pumping into the softening lawn. There was a freedom to her actions that he envied.

"Holds six cubic feet," Isabella announced, setting down the wheelbarrow.

"Has gardening always been a hobby of yours?" Jeanette asked.

"It's something I've always wanted to do more of," Isabella said, and Darren was surprised by her defensiveness. "In our other house we had a gorgeous big yard."

Jeanette shifted her weight and nodded, and Darren realized this was the same attitude she had taken while listening to the reminiscences of old Mrs. Pynn — Veronica.

Jeanette looked at Darren and raised her eyebrows. Darren ignored her.

"What happened to your car?" he asked Isabella. The hood and roof were covered in dirt and grass.

"Oh, yeah." Isabella didn't even turn around. "Cooper. He likes to get up on things."

They were wandering through Wal-Mart beneath the white lights when they saw the wading pools on special.

"It's a good idea to get these things now, ahead of the season," Isabella said. A box of tinfoil slipped from her arms.

The pools — Family Swim Centre Pools — were stacked at the end of an aisle, creating a bottleneck in traffic. Some of the pools were adorned with bright daisies, others with tropical fish. Darren retrieved the tinfoil, but as Isabella took it from him, a package of Pop tarts slid out. He retrieved that too but decided to hold on to it. He was reading about the pools on the side of one of the boxes. When inflated, they stood twenty-two inches high and were one hundred and forty-four inches long. Water capacity was over four hundred gallons.

Relax with your kids, it said, on a hot summer day.

He was thinking it would take half a day to fill one using the garden hose, when he had a sudden memory of summer when he was a boy. The scattered weeks of heat that were astonishing, as much for the change they brought to his parents as for the high temperatures themselves. Drained, his mother would permit him to stay out on the streets with Jeanette until nearly midnight. When they returned home their mother would be crouched in the open doorway — here Darren realized they would not have owned a screen door — smoking a cigarette. Normal rules of bedtime and appropriate behaviour, for both children and adults, seemed to have no place in that heat. Eventually she'd make up a bed for Darren and Jeanette in the backyard. In the morning they would awake covered in dew and to the promise of another hot, unorthodox day.

"$98.99?" Isabella said. "As much as that?"

Darren was surprised by her hesitation.

"Cooper would appreciate one of these when it gets hot," he said. "I would too for that matter."

"Sure, it never gets hot enough."

"What are you saying? Of course it does."

"One or two days, that's it."

"No. Several weeks. A month," he insisted.

"Then why don't we go halves, if you're so keen."

"Whose yard?"

"My yard, but you'd have full access."

"Daisies or fish?"

"I wasn't really serious, Darren."

"Hey, you might just find me in it."

Darren wanted Isabella to have the pool. That she wanted it, but had nearly showed some common sense, seemed disappointing. They put it on his Visa, and with some embarrassment, she handed him the cash.

"Cooper will be thrilled," he said. "Won't he?"

"I'm going as far as Trespassey and back up St. Mary's Bay," he told Jeanette the following morning. "I might be late."

"Am I to understand you paid for her pool?"

"I already explained. Isabella and I split it."

"I don't understand why you paid for her pool. Imagine the message you're sending that woman."

Darren thought of telling his sister, again, that it was his pool too, but the idea was sounding more and more ridiculous.

"You're letting her take advantage of you, Darren. That's not going to help that poor woman."

"I was thinking of Cooper."

Darren was running late. Embarrassment about the pool, combined with the sensation of summer that it had nevertheless stirred, brought on a terrible lethargy. Besides, the day was actually warm, the warmest this year. Darren would need to make good time in order to be back on the road by dark. He knew he should take the new bypass, since the alternate route crept through a string of towns — a congested, aggravating drive.

But Darren avoided the bypass because of the dead beagle.

The first time he took the new route it had been open only a day or two. It was November, frosty and clear, and Darren had swung onto the road with surprise as he left St. John's early one morning. The surprise was due as much to the fact that the Department of Highways had opened the road, as promised, before winter, as by the landscape it revealed: hills of fir and larch, fields laid out in rolling strips, bogs dotted with stumpy spruce. To Darren, it was virgin, unexplored. He passed only one other car in the five minutes it took to drive the length of the bypass.

But as he was coming down a long sloping hill, he spotted movement ahead near a culvert. He slowed as a German shepherd followed a beagle partway up the embankment to the new road. The beagle stood at the edge of the pavement, sniffing the air and looking first at Darren's stopped car, then back at the German shepherd.

Darren waited, hoping they would cross now while it was safe, but the German shepherd retreated several metres into the adjacent field and refused to budge. If not for the new road and occasional car, it would be like any morning, with visits to duck ponds, pig farms, garbage dumps, the homes of other dogs. Habit was hard to give up, but Darren sided with the German shepherd. After a few minutes the beagle crossed the road alone.

A week later Darren took the new bypass a second time. There was plenty of traffic and no opportunity to slow down. As he crossed the culvert he saw the beagle on the side of the road. Dead, it looked considerably larger than it had the previous week.

That was also the day he first noticed the red Echo.

Darren drove through the downtown and onto Pitts Memorial Drive. A minute later he exited to Kilbride. The speed limit was only fifty kilometres and he slowed, instantly regretting his decision not to take the bypass. He passed split-level bungalows, Chinese takeouts, convenience stores and service stations, then just before the junction with Old Bay Bulls Road, the view opened up. Pastureland dotted with ring-billed gulls was surrounded by bus lots, medical clinics and hair salons.

Halfway between Morry's Sheep Farm and Lees Vegetable Market, he watched a gull swoop towards an oncoming truck top-heavy with hay. The gull, perhaps realizing the approaching danger, flew to the other side of the road and directly in front of Darren's truck. It made a hard cracking sound as it hit his windshield, before being thrown upwards and out of sight behind him. In the rear-view mirror Darren saw the gull land on its back on the road, its wings flapping as it righted itself. A half dozen crows materialized over the treetops.

He pulled over. The bird would be either dead or seriously injured. It had looked like a herring gull. Thick as two bricks, he thought, yet the sight of it crashing onto the pavement was unnerving. Darren got out and walked back down the road. If only he'd taken the bypass.

The crows were silent, perched on wires and fences.

A subadult herring gull was standing in the gravel beside the road. Darren walked to within a few feet of it, but it didn't flinch. If it would just move, he'd be satisfied, he could get back in the truck and on with his shrinking day.

He waved his arm at the gull. Abruptly the gull turned and walked down into the gully and lowered itself next to a crushed pop can. It had showed no indication of limp or wing droop and looked relatively alert. Darren wasn't even sure it was the same gull. And it would be difficult to catch. As he was getting back into his truck, he glanced down the road. A red Echo was parked under the sign for Mullowny's Puffin and Whale Tours.

He stopped for gas in the Goulds, though the tank was three-quarters full. As he pumped the gas, washed the windshield — no cracks or blood — and paid, he kept his eye on the road. Nothing. Perhaps the car had turned off at Ruby Line or gone down to Petty Harbour. Perhaps it was owned by someone living in Petty Harbour, which would explain how frequently he saw it. Just a coincidence.

He got back in his truck and drove across the street to Tim Hortons and joined the drive-through. He was fourth in line with a good view of the road. But the line barely moved — what were those people ordering? After ten minutes he was both disgusted with the human race and concerned with his own sanity. It was almost noon, a ridiculous hour to embark on work that demanded a full ten-hour day. The thing to do now was return to town and get an early start tomorrow. He was manoeuvring the truck out of line when he saw the red Echo fly by, right there in front of him. It would not have seen him because it was going so fast.

He wondered what had delayed it.

Without allowing himself time to think, he pulled out onto the road after it. There were several cars between them. They passed Bidgoods, St. Kevin's School, Headway Hairstyling, Needs Convenience, and then the road dipped through a valley of scrubby empty lots, signs for dry wood and more widely spaced homes. Here he got stuck behind a van and the Echo disappeared ahead of him.

At this point he came to his senses. He would turn around at the next opportunity. But opportunities were being passed. Still no Echo. As he passed the van in a no-passing zone, he suddenly wondered whether the Echo had seen him hit the gull. He was thinking this when he realized the Southern Shore Animal Rescue Park was coming up, just past the pond.

He'd forgotten about Byron. Byron would have reminded him that you could never rule out the possibility of internal hemorrhaging. Byron would have done his best to rehabilitate even a herring gull. It had been a while since Darren had visited

Byron. His last visit to the Southern Shore Animal Rescue Park was the previous August when he'd brought in a harlequin duck. It had been so starved it died the next day.

The Echo and police car were pulled over onto the dirt shoulder right before the tiny sign for "Live Worms" that had been there for years and throughout all seasons. Darren slowed as he passed, trying to see the driver, but she was rummaging through her glove compartment and, to his disappointment, did not see him. He would have liked her to observe him driving on and out of sight. He was not surprised it was a woman, or that she looked like the lone female birdwatcher he had met that afternoon on Cape Broyle Head standing in the midst of a flock of red crossbills. Though he caught only a glimpse of the woman now, he could see she had the kind of curly blond hair that escaped easily from clasps, though hers did not look to be restrained in any way.

He had heard two people went missing out on Cape Broyle Head and, though rescued, had narrowly escaped calamity. She had told him she was alone and he had walked away from her. But first he had started going on about crossbills — what had come over him? His sudden frankness had alarmed and embarrassed him and made him anxious to get away.

Darren put his foot on the gas and both the woman and the gull out of his mind. He was heading in the wrong direction, but turning around now was out of the question. It was ridiculous to think he was actually being followed by a woman, whom he was certain he'd never seen before the encounter on Cape Broyle Head — if indeed that had been her. Did she blame him for her misfortune that day? For his walking away? He wasn't afraid of her, but it made sense to preserve some distance. Still, the situation surprised him. Until now, his expectation of human behaviour seemed unimaginative.

*

At three o'clock Darren parked the truck near the end of the beach but before getting out, paused to watch the silhouette of an ATV pulling its wooden cart across the highest berm. Normally he arrived early, before the handful of men came down looking for what the tide had brought in. They collected wood, though at one time, when they still fished, they'd searched almost exclusively for rope. Darren liked to think that whatever washed up got used, but that was difficult with all the rubbish in the ocean now.

At the far end of the beach fog was coming down over the hills, over the sheep, fallen fences and square houses. Darren got out of the truck and immediately heard the surf rolling onto the cobble beach, a rackety sound like applause. He thought of the wading pool, which now, with the distance of the long day, seemed an ill-considered purchase.

He crossed the footbridge that linked the parking lot to the beach and spotted a female red-necked phalarope in a pool of brackish water. Darren stopped to watch her spinning like a toy top, churning up tasty copepods with her feet. Her plumage was lavish and striking: a rich chestnut collar, pale throat, a white stripe above the eye as brazen as a geisha's face. It was the male — brown, drab, unmemorable — who sat alone on the eggs, keeping them warm as toast until they hatched. Then he raised the young. The female left shortly after egg laying to seek other males.

Polyandry. Atypical, given that monogamy was the rule of the mating game in most seabirds. As it was in humans.

Monogamy was hard work. It wasn't fair to draw parallels with humans, but Darren knew it was unavoidable. The offspring of monogamous species were demanding. They could be nearly impossible to raise — unexplained leg injuries in boys, insatiable appetites in birds — without substantial care from both parents. Monogamy required teamwork.

But even then there was the unexpected: death, desertion,

118

betrayal. It was not always easy to stay within the rigid confines of your own species' reproductive strategy. Darren thought of Cooper, the odds against him, being raised in a single parent nest in a chiefly monogamous context.

He patted his jacket pockets, absently eyeing a headless seal rolling in the surf zone, and realized he'd left his notebook in the truck.

He was just heading back across the footbridge when the red Echo came hurtling over the road. It stopped several metres from his truck, kicking gravel. The ignition was turned off; with it went some loud music he hadn't been aware of until it was gone. The occupant did not get immediately out of her car.

Chapter Ten

As Heather came over the crest of the winding road that led to the beach, she was remembering the dream. In it she was dead, lying on a mat inside a seaside hut, while in an adjacent room people were talking, Benny among them. Just before waking, she slipped out from beneath a block of white ice and came back to life. When she opened her eyes and found she was both awake and alive, her body felt heavy and luxurious, as though she'd slept a long time without fear. She'd had the dream that very morning.

She watched Darren cross the parking lot towards her, change his mind and head for his truck. He hadn't actually looked her way. She put on the huge coat she had brought, though it was probably unrealistic to think it would hide her condition, then grabbed the binoculars and field guide and got out of the car.

She walked directly towards him. There was nothing to do but pretend it was a coincidence. It was possible he wouldn't remember her. She found her heart was racing.

He said something she didn't quite catch. *Not you again?*

"Excuse me?"

But he shook his head dismissively, meaning it wasn't important. He was busy with something in the cab of the truck. A moment later he said, "Thought we were going to get some sun this afternoon. They've been predicting a nice day all week."

She glanced up at the sky. "I guess they were mistaken."

He laughed. "They're right every once in a while, but they really don't know anything more than a day in advance. When we're on the edge of the jet stream like this it's nothing but misery."

"I hear this is a good place for birdwatching."

He turned. "You haven't been here before?"

"No."

"Just so you know, don't wander over in that direction." He pointed down the beach. He could have been pointing at anything. "Tern colony. Pair formation is just underway. With the ATVs they get enough disturbance. I'm astonished they keep coming back."

They were crossing the parking lot towards the water. He had said nothing else about having seen her before. "Are you a birdwatcher?" she asked.

"No. I'm a wildlife biologist. And you?"

She was confused. "I'm a clinical social worker, but I'm on leave."

He glanced at her.

"And a birdwatcher."

They crossed the wooden bridge. "Some load of garbage, isn't there?" she said, surprised by how aggressive she sounded.

"It's shocking," he said.

Was he being sarcastic?

She followed him along a ridge of sand criss-crossed with the tracks of hundreds of passes by ATVs. In a row of distinct piles, as though an Alzheimer's patient had raked them up then wandered away, seaweed, sticks, urchins and shells lay tangled among a variety of garbage, from plastic bottles to car parts.

Closer to the water the sand gave way to polished stones. He hadn't invited her to tag along, but as he moved on, she followed him.

"What exactly are you doing? If you don't mind me asking?" she asked, stepping over a cracked toilet seat.

Heather found it difficult to keep up. The grainy sand sunk beneath her and she was unprepared for the tenderness in one of her feet, though they had told her she might have some permanent, though mild, damage. The small of her back was also beginning to ache.

"Looking for dead seabirds."

"Like this one?"

He turned and came back towards her. He seemed miffed. She pointed to a carcass nestled in a cluster of Styrofoam plates: two black wings linked by bone. He picked it up, shaking off the plates.

"Almost missed one," she said.

"I would have seen it on my way back."

"Go on."

"You're a bit of a pest, you know that?"

She couldn't tell if he was kidding around, or irritated.

"What is that, anyway?" she asked.

"Common murre. Code Four."

"Meaning?"

"Meaning only the frame is left. Not enough of the bird to know if it was oiled or not."

"So you're investigating oil pollution?"

"I'm trying to get an idea how useful this kind of fieldwork is in predicting oil-induced mortality rates in seabirds." He swung the bird back and forth in his hand as he spoke.

"Do you find a lot of birds with oil?"

"Depends what you call a lot."

Of course he would say that.

"Years ago, in the fifties and sixties, vessels were pumping oil offshore so regularly you could be knee-deep in oiled birds some mornings. A whole variety of species. The old-timers can tell you about that." He took a knife out and began shredding the tips of the murre's wings. "That would have been a lot."

She tried to imagine it. Up to her knees in waves and greasy dying birds.

"I'm cutting off the ends of the primaries," he went on, as though resigned to her questions. "To tag it. So I won't count this bird again the next time I'm here."

"Makes sense."

"One winter, seventeen thousand oiled murres washed up in Placentia Bay. Soaking wet. You wouldn't believe the weight on them when they're like that."

"An oil spill?"

"In that case, yes." He shrugged. "But sometimes all it takes is discharged bilge water. Routine maintenance."

His offering this information relaxed her, and she stopped trying to keep up with him. She walked slowly, watching the terns wheeling in the sky. Every once in a while he came across a bird and she nearly caught up with him, but he seemed determined to stay ahead of her. Then, at one point, he waited and held out a baseball he'd found. He rotated it in his hand and she saw the splat of black oil it had picked up from the sea.

"Better than an oiled bird," she suggested, but he just put it in his jacket pocket and walked on.

At the end of the beach a series of rock outcrops extended from the black peat embankment into the sea. Darren stepped up onto the lowest ledge, inspecting the top, then turned and gave her his first smile of the day. He said, "Once, in winter, I climbed up there and found myself face to face with an oiled oldsquaw. Drenched."

"What did you do?"

"Killed it," he said.

She was surprised. His look and tone had been almost fatherly.

Mercy killing, she decided. Well, I'm not going to ask him how.

He said, "Broke its neck."

She watched him make a vague, almost rude gesture with his hand and wrist. It reminded her of someone yanking at a difficult doorknob or knifing someone in the belly. She would have thought it easier to step on the bird's head and crush the tiny skull, but she didn't say so.

He was still standing on the rock ledge, facing the sea. A tuft of hair was caught between his orange cap and ear, sticking out comically. She imagined him getting oil all over his hands — or gloves — as he snapped the neck of the oldsquaw. Yet there was something admirable about his actions. Watching him, she sensed an opening, as though a window had been lifted, and she found herself looking in to see that essential part of him, something steady, good-natured, yet uncertain, that he'd been born with.

But now he was watching her too, the way he had on Cape Broyle: sideways, without moving his head. Like a man hurrying across a busy road with only his eyes turned to the traffic rushing towards him. The window had closed. He was taking the measure of her now. She glanced down and saw a rubber boot beside a comb.

"Let's head this way," he told her, walking backwards a few steps before turning in the direction of the tern colony. His pace was slower now and she was able to keep up with him. But when they got there, there wasn't anything to see. Every tern was in flight above their heads, producing, it seemed to Heather, cries of both excitement and dread.

"Where are the eggs?" She had to raise her voice to be heard.

"I wouldn't have brought you here if I thought they'd laid. Watch your step. They invest a lot of energy into those nests."

"What nests?"

He pointed to the ground, near her feet. "They're properly referred to as scrapes," he said, and then she saw them: slight depressions the size of saucers and defined only by a change in substrate. Some were smooth sandy patches among pebbles, others a collection of pebbles among cobbles. They were delicate and obscure. At first she had an urge to say something cynical, that an autistic child could have done a better job, but the mild regularity of these surfaces made her think of skin, of the dips and rises of the human body, from the indentations on Benny's buttocks to the oblong cups that formed in his armpits when he lay bare chested, his arms crossed behind his head.

Darren had left her and was ahead now, nearly to the parking lot. She watched him crossing the firmer substrate there and noticed for the first time his slightly odd way of walking: a light, playful bouncing. It occurred to her he was the type of boy who would have walked on tiptoe. This was once believed to indicate something, but she couldn't remember quite what: a slow reader, above average creativity?

By the time she caught up with him, he was getting into his truck. He closed his door, then rolled down the window and asked, "Was that you got lost out on Cape Broyle Head?"

She was aware of him assessing her figure, perhaps speculating how long she had to go.

She nodded.

"They said two people. Was your husband with you?"

"I don't have a husband."

"No? Well, you're some size, aren't you?" He was shaking his head.

She guessed she wasn't much more than a specimen to him.

He started the truck and pulled out slowly, giving her a perfunctory nod without eye contact. As she stood there, alone, it came to her out of the blue: The Bruce Effect. A crazy idea, yet she regretted not keeping her animal behaviour textbooks.

The following afternoon Heather was sitting in her doctor's office, avoiding a gruesome photograph of mouth cancer in the anti-smoking poster. It was just to the left of Dr. Redcliffe's head.

"My guess is you're perfectly fine," Dr. Redcliffe said, stepping back until she reached the wall.

Heather sighed. "I'm not myself."

"You're pregnant. All kinds of things are happening to your body. It affects your brain. Your moods. But we'll order some more blood tests." Dr. Redcliffe bent to scribble on a pad of paper balanced on a partly raised thigh. "Your blood sugar might be low."

"It's not my blood sugar."

The two women stared at each other briefly. They were the same age and had embarked on their careers at roughly the same time. Heather was one of Dr. Redcliffe's first patients and had witnessed her doctor's changing hairstyles, the parade of receptionists, the metamorphosis from tolerant and chatty to harried and direct.

"I've stopped gaining weight. Could I lose the baby?"

"I don't follow. The baby is healthy. The worst that can happen is a premature delivery, which, don't misread me, can be plenty serious, but you're nearly full term. So. Take it easy. Eat well and rest. Have you given any thought to names?"

"Something is wrong."

"Heather, might I say something?" The doctor took a step towards her, giving up the support of the wall. "I think you're reading too much into your symptoms. If you still feel this way after the birth, I'd be inclined to suggest an antidepressant."

"You're kidding."

"Let's wait to see how you feel after the birth."

"I'll keep it in mind."

"Are you all right? It might be wise for you to talk to some-one. It can't be easy going through this all by yourself."

"I can talk to myself."

Dr. Redcliffe smiled slightly. "You know that's not going to do you much good." She retrieved Heather's file from the examination table and pressed it to her chest like a schoolgirl. "Don't leave those tests too long. We might be going on strike. The hospital will be a zoo."

Heather waited in the room, though the door was open, inviting her to leave. She knew a throng of patients was anxious to be seen. Dr. Redcliffe was running an hour behind, which was better than usual. Heather found herself staring at the mouth cancer again but with less alarm. She was offended by the idea of antidepressants. What would Darren Foley think of that?

A woman carrying a baby in one of those things Heather had not yet bought was led into the examining room opposite Heather's. The woman set the thing on the floor and gazed down tenderly at her baby. Heather couldn't see the baby but she heard it begin to cough. It surprised her. It didn't sound human. Weak, rasping, breathless. It sounded like a mouse coughing. Yet it went on. The mother looked worried. Finally the coughing stopped and Heather was relieved to see Dr. Redcliffe enter the examining room and close the door soundlessly, the way she always did, behind her.

But Heather's door was still open and she could easily hear her doctor's cheerful voice. "Any better?" Heather heard her ask the baby. "Oh, let's have a look at you. *You were supposed to get better. You were.* His colour is good. This bug is going around. You need to let it work its way through his system."

The baby began coughing again. This was followed by some silence, then Dr. Redcliffe saying, "If I hadn't heard that cough . . . I want you to pop in at the hospital with him. He should have a chest X-ray for that. Hey, hey." The doctor sounded like she was laughing. "You're not going to fall apart on me, now, are you? The X-ray is just a precaution."

Heather placed a hand over her belly.

She checked her watch. It was not yet noon. Perhaps she'd call Darren at work. Why bother stalking him now, when a relationship, of sorts, had been established? Why not simply invite herself along, a beginning birdwatcher keen to learn more?

They were still over an hour from town when Darren pulled into an empty parking lot beside a closed kiosk. Heather, who had taken her own car, had no choice but to pull in as well; she had no idea where they were. Darren had not warned her he was going to stop, although there had been that nervous, almost cocky manner in which he had taken charge of everything all day.

Heather got out of her car and walked over to his truck.

"Do you find many oiled seabirds here?"

He turned off his ignition. "Of course not. Come on, I want to show you something."

"What about the loon?"

"It'll be fine." He looked at her. "It's a bird."

They passed a small sign announcing, "Geology Tours, Saturday, 10 am & 2 pm," then took a path that meandered away from the parking lot and descended alongside a valley comprised of pancake rock slabs cut by small streams. As usual, Darren walked on ahead, then dropped suddenly from sight.

"Darren? Where are you?"

Here and there the streams slowed to form paper-thin pools.

The orange cap popped up. He waited as she approached. "There's a bench here. Can you make it?"

A sitting area was just off the path beside a deeper pool. She lowered herself beside him.

"Did you notice the rock formation?" he asked.

"I did." She tried to sound interested, and he launched into an explanation, as she knew he would. She heard conglomerate, ancient beach, volcanic cobbles, sandstone matrix.

"I thought it might have been concrete," she said, joking.

"Christ no. It's five hundred and fifty million-year-old rock."

He grew quiet, perhaps disappointed. She grinned.

"What's funny about that?"

"Nothing." She saw that place of uncertainty in him again. The baby kicked and she automatically put a hand over her side, returning the pressure.

"Are you cold?" Darren asked. He moved closer to her. She sensed he wanted to put an arm around her. Was that why he'd brought her here?

Now would be an excellent time to ask if he was married.

She had already dated Benny twice, though they had not yet touched, when she learned he was married — he didn't wear a ring. That would have been the moment to ask herself, Do you really think this is wise?

They were having lunch and discussing pollution — the world filling with diapers and refrigerators — when he mentioned his wife. My wife is enthusiastic about recycling.

"You're married?"

He was halfway through the seafood pasta. He had said it was not that good. He laid his fork and knife across the plate and rested both his forearms on the table, enclosing his food. His arms were darker than her own, the knuckles pink.

He looked at her and said quietly, "I wasn't sure if you knew. I didn't want to ask. I've been a bit mixed-up about that. And guilty. I knew we had to get to this point eventually."

"You're married?"

"Heather, this isn't about sex. Did you think this was just about sex?"

"Of course not."

"Because it's not."

But when he leaned over to kiss her — an hour later in his car — she was relieved. It was, to some extent, about sex. He dropped her off at her office and she wandered into the dark building, dazed and happy. She had been longing to kiss him.

Two young girls lugging an assortment of handbags had emerged onto the rock bed above them.

"Are you familiar with the Bruce Effect?" she asked Darren.

She watched him look into the distance and squint as he searched his mental database. It was enjoyable to see. When he found what he was looking for, he looked puzzled. "The phenomenon whereby a pregnant female aborts her young when exposed to an unknown male?"

"Yeah. But I think it's reabsorb. Not abort."

"I think it's either. Pregnancy disruption. And I think it's chiefly been observed in rodents. Why do you mention it?"

She shrugged.

The girls' chattering voices could be heard as they drew closer.

"So that's why you were following me?" he joked.

It was the first time he'd referred to their previous meetings.

"I wonder if it's painful?"

He stared at her.

"The reabsorption? I wonder if it's painful."

He looked offended. "You're not reabsorbing that," he said, indicating her belly with his thumb.

"It was just something I thought of."

"You sound like you might not want that baby."

"Forget I brought it up."

They fell silent. Heather sensed Darren regretted his remark, though she already knew he was not the type to make apologies.

She turned and saw the girls standing only a few metres away, staring at them. It was obvious they had been heading for the pool. Surprisingly, they were wearing bathing suits.

"Heather, I want to ask your advice on something."

"Mine?"

"There's a young boy living next door to me. He's a good kid, just confused I think. His mother — a single mother — she worries about him. She's having a difficult time with him."

"Your neighbour?"

"Yes. I thought with your background?"

"I don't see children, Darren. And I'm on leave."

"I don't mean that you *see* him. Just observe him."

"Where?"

"As it happens, the mother is hosting a barbeque next weekend," he said. "It's the Avalon Nature Club's spring event. You could join us."

"I don't really think that's my thing, Darren."

"Anyone is welcome. It's not a big crowd. And the club is always looking for new members."

"Darren, that's foolish. I'm not going to be able to tell you anything — or the mother — by simply watching him at a party. And I don't see children."

"He does some unusual things. I think he'd be easy to observe. He chooses not to walk, for example."

The girls were engaged in a conversation that appeared humourless and unrhythmic, though Heather couldn't hear a word of it. It was soft and padded, like rain on a cabin roof. They were removing plates and utensils and containers of food, a jug and two glasses. Heather began to suspect their conversation was entirely food related.

"He doesn't walk? Do you mean he's delayed?"

"No, no. He's twelve years old and he can walk. But he crawls." Darren shook his head, smiling, as though it were too wild to believe. "He sprained his ankle six months ago. The point is, the leg is fine."

"But he doesn't walk?"

"Sometimes he gets up and walks, sure, but just as often he doesn't. You'd also have the opportunity to meet more bird-watchers."

"Darren, I don't think I'd be any help."

"By the way, where was the frostbite? Your ears?"

She turned quickly to him. He had been studying her ear, but now he was looking into her eyes. He would be justified in thinking her not only crazy, but ridiculous.

"My feet. How did you know about that?"

"Heard it on the news."

"Oh, right."

"So that wasn't you they interviewed?"

"No, my sister Mandy. "

"Mandy was also following me?"

"Yes. I'm really sorry about all that."

"I know your sister, don't I?"

"Yes."

"Maybe Mandy would like to come to the barbeque as well?"

They both knew she owed him. She looked back towards the girls, who were arranging themselves on beach towels, their naked legs sticking straight out before them with a demeanor girlish and prim. They slipped their bathing suit straps off their shoulders and then began fiddling with the height of their suits above their small breasts: a little higher, a little lower. They lay down, they sat back up, they adjusted their sun hats, they wiggled their bums on the towels.

"I can't believe those girls are wearing bathing suits," she said. "Surely they're not planning on swimming?"

"Come on," Darren said, taking her hand and shaking it. The touch surprised her. "You might like this crowd. You seemed enthusiastic about the crossbills."

Yes, the crossbills. That was true.

This would have to be her last meeting with Darren, who may have been scheming to extract a free assessment of his neighbour's child from her for some time. If he didn't have a wife, he had this neighbour. And yes, she owed him. She had been a complete stranger, appearing out of nowhere in isolated areas. She could have been armed, she could have been a serious threat. Yet he had put up with her. What she didn't get was why he would ask a pregnant nutbar for professional advice. Well, some people will take anything if it's free.

And maybe it was a way to score points with this neighbour.

"So I can bring Mandy with me?"

"Absolutely. As I said, the club is always looking for new members." He paused. "And I'll be bringing my sister as well."

Suddenly the girls stopped chatting. A third youngster had arrived: a boy alien-like in dripping wet socks and dry trunks, his naked chest pale and emaciated. The girls stared at him with disapproval and alarm, though Heather guessed they had been expecting him. He circled the girls without a word and then was gone at a run. The girls exploded into giggles.

At the parking lot Heather found she was winded. She leaned against her car and a sharp pain clutched her lower abdomen. She breathed deeply and waited for it to pass. Darren stood close by, visibly worried.

"Maybe I'm finally starting to reabsorb it."

"Finally?" he sounded as though he believed there was some truth to the idea. He pulled up the sleeve of his coat to check the time. "I need to get you back to town."

"I need food, actually. I think it's low blood sugar."

He studied her a moment, hesitating, then suggested they stop for supper on their way back. He had a place in mind. The Pearly Everlasting Country Manor. Heather said she'd never heard of it.

"Sounds like a funeral home," she said.

"Well, it's not. It's an inn."

Darren explained it was just past the nursery but before the Esso station and reservoir. She couldn't miss it. There was a short unpaved driveway on your left, maybe quarter of a klick, tops. They served dinner. She should go on, it was getting dark. After he'd checked on the loon, he'd be right along.

"Can you drive, Heather? I could leave my truck here."

Heather assured him she was fine to drive. But as soon as she started the car, she wanted nothing more than to go home and get into a hot bath.

She was the one who had found the loon. She had already decided she was better than Darren at locating the carcasses. The bird, which she had thought was either a swan or a goose until Darren set her straight, was massive. It was lying in the sand with its neck and head fallen across its flattened back.

"Found one," she had called to Darren, poking the thing with her boot. Its neck rose up and it stabbed her ankle and she leapt away.

Ten minutes later she drove past the entrance to the Pearly Everlasting Country Manor, braked and backed up. The name of the establishment was painted on a large elaborate sign, but it was partially hidden by alders. The driveway was not long, as

Darren had said, but the potholes were savage and Heather drove slowly. Just before a sprawling grey building surrounded on both sides by larch forest, the dirt gave way to gravel and a circular drive. Heather parked beside a jeep and got out and glanced behind her, hoping to see Darren's truck pull in. She approached the building. It was getting colder.

She was hesitating in front of a set of wooden doors at the front of the building, thinking it looked more like a terrible old orphanage than a place where you'd willingly pay money to eat and sleep, when the doors opened. A skinny woman wearing a red dress stood on the threshold. A paisley wrap, neatly folded lengthwise, hung over her shoulder as though over a clothes rack.

"Can I help you?"

"I'm looking for the Pearly something. An inn?"

"Pearly Everlasting Country Manor."

"Yes."

"This is it."

Another woman appeared at the door. Heather noticed her dress first — black velour with a satin-trimmed neckline — then noticed the woman herself.

"Rosemarie?"

"Heather?"

"You two know each other?" the first woman said. "Come in, come in."

The doors were fully opened and Heather entered a chilly entrance hall furnished with half a dozen derelict wicker chairs. Oddly, she and Rosemarie were embracing, as though they were old friends. Heather was immediately aware of Rosemarie's improvement.

"What a coincidence," the first woman said.

"Heather, this is my sister Brenda. She and her husband run the Pearly."

"What a coincidence," Brenda repeated. "Rosemarie is just back for a very brief visit."

Both women were staring at her. Though her coat was bulky,

Heather could no longer fasten more than the top few buttons because of her belly. She was conscious of her dirty pants and boots, not to mention the state of her hair now that she had removed her wool hat.

"So you've moved?" Heather asked.

"Alberta. I love it."

"Why don't you come in?" Brenda asked. "It's awfully drafty out here."

"Thank you. Actually I'm meant to meet a friend. "

Brenda gave a short nod to her sister and turned, and the two women began to exit the room, their heels clicking over the tiled floor. As Heather followed them, she glanced back and saw clots of mud falling from the cleats of her boots.

At the far end of the room they climbed a short flight of steps and entered a dark bar decorated with the usual fishnets, lobster buoys, barometers and miniature ships. Heather, who was beginning to feel winded again, was introduced to Rob, Brenda's husband and apparently the bartender. Heather hoped Darren would arrive soon.

"What can Rob get you?" Rosemarie asked.

It seemed imperative she order something. "Ginger ale, please," she said.

"Rob?"

Rob, who had been leaning against the bar chewing on a swizzle stick, reached up for a glass. He had a trim runner's body and thick silver hair.

"Actually," Heather said. "I'm meant to meet a friend, Darren Foley. He should — "

"Darren Foley, the biologist?" Brenda asked.

Heather nodded slowly.

"How is Darren?" Rosemarie asked her sister.

"But I can't imagine what's happened to him."

"The same," Brenda told her sister, and the two exchanged a look.

It occurred to Heather she could ask these women if Darren was married.

Rob was pointing to a drink on the counter. "That's yours," he said to Heather. He sounded a bit testy.

"Thank you. Perhaps he's stopped to call his wife."

"Who?"

"Darren."

Rosemarie turned to Brenda. "Darren got married?"

"Darren did *not* get married," Brenda said.

"That'll be the day," Rob said. He was looking at Heather.

"Don't be so hard on him," Rosemarie said to Rob. "Don't forget about Jeanette."

"Poor Jeanette," Brenda said.

"Poor *Darren*," Rob corrected, glancing up at the ceiling.

"Jeanette?" Heather asked.

"His sister, of course. She's afraid to live alone."

"Claims to be afraid of the dark," Rob said.

"Can we change the subject?" Brenda asked.

With that Rosemarie and Rob became silent. Heather was aware of the three of them watching her. Presumably they were wondering why she had never heard of Jeanette, and whether Darren could possibly be involved with her present physical condition.

"I haven't known Darren long. We were — "

"And he's never mentioned his sister?" Brenda asked.

"We were out birdwatching and he suggested — "

"If I were you, I'd be wondering if he's mentioned *you* to Jeanette."

"Rob!"

"Darren and I just met," Heather said quickly. "We were birdwatching and he suggested we have dinner on our way back."

"Here?" Brenda asked.

Heather nodded.

Brenda looked at Rob. "By the way, how many do we have tonight?"

"Not sure. Will Derrick come down?"

"I don't know if Derrick will come," Brenda muttered.

"But will he sit down?"

"Rob, I have no more idea than you do if Derrick will sit down." Brenda gave her husband a look that Heather was at a loss to interpret, then said to no one in particular, "Will you excuse me?" As she turned her wrap lifted off her back and hovered in mid-air behind her, as though fighting against all odds to keep up with her.

"She's mad now," Rosemarie said, as though she hadn't been quite mad enough before.

"What are you doing in Alberta, Rosemarie?" Heather asked, knowing she had somehow upset these people, yet genuinely astonished by Rosemarie's transformation: the black dress, pearls, makeup. There remained a mild edginess about her, but she had gained weight and smiled without effort. Heather told herself she had done the right thing by Rosemarie, sending her back to her psychiatrist. Prescription drugs had their place.

Then she remembered Dr. Redcliffe's suggestion.

"We moved west for work. The pay is unbelievable."

Had she overcome her counting routine? She wasn't eating at the moment, or drinking. She was doing nothing that could be easy to count. And how were those three children?

Rob reached an arm across the bar and asked Heather, "Can I get rid of that coat for you?" He sounded as though his intention was to take it outside and burn it. Heather was embarrassed, which was ridiculous. What was more ridiculous was that she was comparing herself to Rosemarie.

"Thanks, but I think I'll keep it with me."

Rosemarie said, "You better tell the cook what's up, Rob."

At this, Rob forgot about Heather's coat. He turned to his sister-in-law. "Brenda can deal with it."

"Brenda's left."

"I'm not having anything to do with it."

"Can I call her on the intercom?"

"I'll call her." He walked to the end of the bar. While he

punched the intercom buttons, Rosemarie leaned over to Heather and said, "He's never liked Jeanette."

"What's to like?" Rob called over his shoulder.

Rob returned and told Rosemarie he couldn't get an answer from Brenda.

"I'm really sorry about this," Heather said, wishing she could walk out the door. "Darren suggested we stop — are reservations required? Is that the problem?"

"Did you actually call her bedroom?" Rosemarie asked.

"I just said, she's not up there."

Rosemarie turned to Heather with an expression that was a combination of goodwill and fear — a flicker of Rosemarie's former self. "We're first cousins to Darren and Jeanette," she explained. "Brenda is a little protective of Jeanette."

"Protective in what way?" Heather asked. It was as though they were back in her office.

Rob cleared his throat, but Rosemarie cut him off. "I don't know how well you know Darren," she said to Heather. "But please don't let him know we were talking about him. He'd die."

"He wouldn't *die*," Rob said, sounding disgusted.

Rosemarie was becoming more familiar to Heather, as though bit by bit she was reverting to the woman Heather had known. She was avoiding eye contact with Heather now and fidgeting with her pearls, and Heather suspected that Rosemarie's family did not know about her days counting cereal boxes and candy bars.

"I'd never repeat anything," Heather promised, but as soon as she spoke she realized she had already betrayed Rosemarie to Benny, years ago, on the beach in Spruce Cove.

Rosemarie nodded but didn't speak. Heather glanced around the room, still expecting Darren any minute. It appeared they had run out of things to say.

"I haven't met Jeanette," Heather offered.

"Yes," Rob said. "You indicated as much."

Rosemarie sucked in a deep breath. "When we were kids,

Jeanette was a blast. But she could be odd. Just as easily talking to you a mile a minute as hiding in a closet. Still, she's got a heart of gold."

"She rarely leaves the house."

"Rob, she's a nervous person. Why can't you accept that?"

"She had a first-class fit when he went to university."

Rosemarie looked at Rob as though she'd like to clobber him, then explained to Heather, "Darren studied in New Brunswick."

"Nervous in what way?"

"It would be difficult for her to live alone," Rosemarie said, reluctantly. "Just for an example. Will you excuse me?" Then, to Heather's dismay, she was gone, too.

Rob immediately started inching away from Heather, moving glasses around and straightening out things behind the bar. He threw a tea towel towards the sink, missed and went after it. Where was Darren? He didn't have a wife — he had a sister. Who sounded agoraphobic. Surprising he hadn't asked Heather advice about *her*.

But she was in no shape to offer advice to anyone. Not to neighbours, not to sisters.

She was just slipping her coat on when a waitress appeared at her side and said Darren had phoned. He was on his way. The waitress insisted on taking her coat.

Rob returned and asked if she'd like another ginger ale.

Heather shook her head. She already needed to pee. Rob's restlessness was unnerving.

There was the sound of tires on the gravel outside and Heather said, "Thank god, there's Darren."

Rob sprinted to a tiny window meant to resemble a porthole and looked out, cupping his eyes with his hands. "It's seventeen shades of grey out there. No, that's not your Darren Foley."

"Are you sure?"

He came back, shaking his head. "Retirement party. That's all we get this time of year."

Someone touched her shoulder. It was Darren.

"Where have you been, Darren? What took you so long?" She was surprised by how rattled she sounded.

"I had some trouble with the loon," he said, sitting down beside her.

The retirement party spilled noisily into the room and Rob hurried off, fetching drinks.

"I never knew this place existed," she said.

"No. Many people don't."

"You didn't mention your relatives run it."

He shrugged.

"Who's Derrick?"

Darren looked around. "Derrick's here?"

"You tell me."

"Brenda and Rob's son. Cerebral palsy."

She felt the same sharp pain she had felt earlier. She ran her hand over her belly.

"He's their only child. What a heartbreak that's been. I can't imagine anything worse, can you?"

As Darren spoke he watched her sideways, something she was getting used to. She was relieved he was here.

He wasn't married. At least that mystery was solved. Then she felt a dizzying, formidable panic.

PART THREE

Chapter Eleven

During the last year of Benny's life, Isabella developed the ability to be everywhere in their house at once. To be privy to everyone's whereabouts, anticipate everyone's movements. Pouring detergent into the washing machine, she might hear footsteps on the stairs. The slippery, strangely wet-sounding steps were Benny's, moving so quietly she wondered if he had found out her sudden omniscience and was endeavoring to shake it off by sneaking into a room without her knowledge. But she knew. He might wander into the upstairs bathroom for half an hour, though no sound of running water or flushing toilet followed. What was he doing? He seemed only half present, as though he had become a figment of her imagination or memory, an illusion. She would wait for his next advancement through a large house that day by day grew smaller. When Cooper noisily exited through the front or back door, or climbed out one of the basement windows due to laziness or for some other more obscure reason, she knew. The emptiness that his departure created came careening down the hall or up the stairs like a bubble and found her, and for a moment she panicked. But she was adept at adjusting to the house's shift in population, its chang-ing moods.

Once, sitting on the edge of her bed folding laundry, three

baskets of wrinkled, clean clothes at her feet, she listened to Benny roaming through the upstairs rooms. Cooper was at school, and she heard Benny enter the boy's room. He might do this half a dozen times a day. A ball bounced, a closet door opened, papers rustled. He had started leaving notes for Cooper. "Don't forget I love you." "You're the man of the house now." "Don't do anything stupid." Finding these notes — usually on Cooper's pillow — made Isabella furious.

Benny was coming down the hall again, all the way to their bedroom. Seeing him now, her heart flip-flopped. His clothes hung from his shoulders and hips, his knees seemed slightly turned in, his hair had grown back grey above his ears. This was a man she had adored for a long time, though not, of course, at first. She hardly thought about that anymore.

He sat beside her on the bed, but for several minutes did not speak.

"There's a concern of mine I'd like to speak to you about," he said, and the way he spoke — authoritarian, almost magisterial — made her stiffen.

"Are those new?" he asked.

She ignored his question and snapped open a large towel. It gave her a remote pleasure to see it: fluffy, substantial, frivolous.

"I'd like to tell you this now because I don't want anyone — you or anyone — coming to me later with a drippy guilty look, asking me these questions. Because then there will be that awful moment of knowing, of really knowing, that I'm doomed."

"Ask you what?"

"I'm about to tell you."

This spark of irritability towards each other, given everything, surprised her.

"It's about my wishes. If *I* tell you, you see, I can pretend to myself that I'm not actually going to die. You can even pretend you don't need to hear what I'm going to say."

She stared at him.

"I want to be buried with my parents, of course. I want a closed casket. And by the way, I have always despised the idea of wakes. All those women crying, even children, even men. It's not about the dead person, is it? It's about the people in the room bawling."

He got up and left, then a moment later reappeared in the doorway.

"What?" she asked.

"You're not going to forgive me, are you?"

She finished her folding. She carried the folded towels to the linen closet in the hall, then returned to their bedroom. She went into the master bathroom and sat on the edge of the Jacuzzi and turned on the water. She looked out onto the park where the trees had only recently leafed, but although she had expected to, she did not cry.

That evening the phone rang just as Isabella was finishing the supper dishes. Benny was by the refrigerator, inches from the wall phone, scooping himself ice cream. Isabella struggled to free her hands of the hot, clammy rubber gloves. Benny had stopped answering the phone, and often Isabella answered it only to be met by a quiet, almost courteous click.

By the time Isabella had one of the gloves off and was reaching for the phone, she was ready to crucify the caller. It was Miss McCue.

During Cooper's early grades, self-doubt had characterized Lesley-Anne McCue, vice-principal of St. Margaret's. But now, telephoning to notify Isabella that Cooper was, regrettably, expelled from Sports Day, Miss McCue seemed to express an unequivocal, albeit grim, sense of right and wrong.

Cooper had thrown a water balloon at another boy, Daniel Merck, at 3:45 that afternoon.

"A water balloon? Where was this, Lesley-Anne?" Isabella asked impatiently. Soapy water was running off the remaining glove and down her forearm into her sleeve. She exchanged a look with Benny, who had been leaving the kitchen with his ice cream. He turned back.

"Was it on school property?" Benny demanded of the phone.

"This incident occurred on the corner of Rosebank and King," Miss McCue reported, then added apologetically, "You know how much I hate having to call you about this, with everything else you have to cope with right —"

"So it was *not* on school property?" Isabella asked.

"Mrs. Martin, we've been through this before. Our policy is that students be on best behaviour at all —"

"Tell that fascist I'm calling my lawyer," Benny said.

"My husband says you're a fascist, Lesley-Anne." Isabella watched Benny place his bowl on the counter with a surprised, trembling pleasure. Even so, Isabella knew that by speaking disrespectfully to the vice-principal, she had only shocked and wounded herself. The desire to apologize was already over-taking her.

"Mrs. Martin, you know I sympathize. If we had a letter of apology from Cooper by tomorrow morning which I could pass on to Daniel and his parents, we'd be happy to have your family join us for Sports Day. They're calling for a gorgeous day."

"I'm sorry," Isabella said. "I've got to go. There's someone at the door." She hung up.

Benny approached her slowly. He took her face in his hands, which smelled of ice cream. He kissed her forehead and said, "You're a genius."

"I regret that now. Cooper can't be doing that."

"It was a water balloon."

The phone rang.

"Mrs. Martin? Lesley-Anne again. Forgive me. It's been one of those days. It was Nick Hounsell who threw the water balloon. Cooper stood by and laughed. Mrs. Martin?"

"I'm here."

"You know we have a zero-tolerance policy for this kind of thing. By failing to intercede on Daniel's behalf, Cooper is as guilty as Nick. I wanted to give you the facts in case a letter of apology is written."

"Guilty?"

"Guilty?" Benny echoed.

"From what I understand, Daniel was more upset with being laughed at than he was by getting his shirt wet."

Isabella imagined the next hour or more, sitting with her son, toiling over a letter of apology. "Lesley-Anne?"

"Yes, Mrs. Martin?"

"I'll just keep Cooper home tomorrow."

"You have a safe evening, Mrs. Martin."

Isabella put down the phone and turned to see her husband giving her a spirited thumbs-up. But victorious was not how she felt.

Isabella's plan the following morning was to register Cooper for tennis. Though he had not been out of the house in weeks, Benny announced he wanted to go as well. He put on his old Adidas jacket and waited by the back door, much the way, she thought when she saw him, a youthful Inky once waited to be taken for a walk. She decided not to say anything about the slippers, and Benny followed her out to the car.

Spring had arrived. They passed lawns of fuzzy pubescent grass bordered by beds of tulips whose beauty was today, at best, shaky. Rain and time had done them in. Petals dangled upside down from flowers that two weeks ago had been flawless and intact. Still, it was a clean, washed day. The towering leafy trees looked to Isabella joyful and fresh.

Benny had always done the driving. Then one day he stopped. She had been driving ever since.

The last time he drove was the day she had come home from a morning of errands and found him, un-showered and un-shaven, casually dressed. It was clear he had not left the house yet. She could smell it on him: a perfunctory, stubborn paralysis. When he suggested they take a drive, she thought, *Now he will leave us.* Now he will tell me about that woman.

She had got into the car. She had buckled in. They set off for Portugal Cove, and along Windsor Lake he told her instead a different story. A story about pain, fatigue, tests, results, prognosis. He brought their car up tight behind another car, unable to pass, but unable to hang back and keep to a moderate speed. Benny had always driven too fast. She suggested he slow down. She had suggested this a thousand times. Her toes were pressed into the floor and she was beginning to feel car sick. The air seemed vacant. Looking across the lake, she believed she could identify individual needles and leaves, the glazed glint of a rocky shore, the iridescent feathers of crows.

As Benny came within inches of the other car, then released the gas and dropped back, Isabella's stomach lurched. Her anger did not surprise her. She reached for the emergency brake and wrenched it up. The car whined and bucked, but did not stop. Benny made a sound — not a complete word — slowed the car and pulled over, and Isabella found herself opening the door.

She crossed the road towards the lake. Behind her Benny called out, "What are you doing, Isabella? Where are you going?" She was aware he had rolled down his window, but not opened his door. She thought that of all the things he had kept from her, none would equal this: for months suspecting, followed by knowing, that he was gravely ill; then, in what must have been a dreadful, nearly impossible way, accepting it, preparing for it alone, without her. Was he God? Did he think he could make decisions for everyone? For her? For Cooper? She knew then, moving along the shore of the lake over rocks that in close focus were surprisingly bland and ugly, that this was the end of their marriage. We are finished, she decided, and she laughed at the irony. Then she was coming wildly back down along the lake towards him where he waited in the car, though she wouldn't cross the road, she wouldn't get that close to him again.

"Does *she* know?" Isabella shouted. "Have you already told *her*?"

He didn't turn his head, but she saw he was surprised. "Who?"

"Her! Heather, is it? Her name is Heather?"

"Come get in the car, sweetheart. Please."

"Never. Your driving habits are despicable."

He laughed, quickly turning to look at her. There was the way his laughter remade his face. I'm going to lose that, she thought; then, the world is going to lose that.

"I'm telling you first," he said.

A string of cars was passing.

"I didn't know you knew," he said quietly.

But Isabella could not tell him about Cooper and the camcorder. A telephone conversation in their kitchen that had awoken Cooper, yet not her. It made her so angry she was afraid she might hurt herself, or him, or someone.

She crossed the road, her shoes heavy on the pavement, and stood beside his door.

"Move over," she said. "I'm driving."

The River Valley Tennis Club was empty and cool, not at all like the day surrounding it. As Benny shuffled around in his slippers, inspecting the trophies, Isabella went out onto the courts. She wasn't going to wait around. The only person in sight was a stout, sandy haired young man hitting balls against the practice board. When he saw her he stopped and came back towards the clubhouse, once or twice breaking into a jog.

"I'm looking for Aiden," she said.

He nodded. He did not look particularly athletic or rugged, but he was, apparently, the new coach. He would be teaching Cooper this summer. Well, better than a coach who already knows him, Isabella thought. He looked quite likable. She briefly considered taking her son to the other club — for the coach's sake.

Inside she sat down across from him at the massive oak desk where registration had been conducted for decades. She noticed a strong chemical smell. Beyond a sofa upholstered in a shimmering orange synthetic, a television was on, the community events calendar set to mute.

"You'll have to give me a minute," Aiden said, flipping

149

through a box of index cards. He was squinting. It was dark in here, but she suspected he normally wore glasses. His face was freckled and fair. Behind her, Benny made a scraping sound and Aiden looked up.

"Didn't see you there, sir," he said. Isabella wondered how a mother brought up a son to be so polite. "Are you two together?"

"We are," Isabella said quickly, unaccountably embarrassed for the young man.

"Have a seat, sir, if you'd like. What's your child's name?"

"Cooper Martin."

"Okay, got it right here. I have him down for the beginner's group?"

Benny leaned forward. "Our son has been on the court since he was five. What's that smell? It's making me sick."

"Benny."

"Unfortunately, our son Cooper doesn't know his arse from a hole in the ground."

"Benny!" Isabella turned to glare at her husband, but when their eyes met there was that familiar twinkle. She spun back around to face Aiden, the muscles of her face tensing. She didn't know if she wanted to burst into tears or laughter.

Aiden looked startled, but recovered quickly. "As long as he wants to play, where's the harm? Personally, I'm thrilled to be back coaching. I was off for two years. Knee surgery."

Cooper hated tennis. Aiden's enthusiasm dismayed Isabella.

"Well, I've got cancer," Benny said. "Bad things happen."

"Indeed they do, sir. We just had the floors varnished. I apologize for the odour."

"I did my share of volunteering here," Benny said. "I was largely responsible for raising funds for that locker room, by the way."

"The locker room is definitely convenient. That's one hundred and fifteen, Mrs. Martin."

Isabella bent to write the cheque. Yes, a lot had happened in this dim, unremarkable space. A lot more would happen, though for other children, other parents.

"I used to be quite active here," Benny said. "I'm sure you've heard of me."

"No," Aiden said. "But then, like I said, I've been away."

Isabella handed him the cheque and he looked at her, then Benny. The smile he gave them now was more tentative.

Outside, the sunlight was a relief. As they strolled towards the car beneath the canopy of leaves, Isabella was aware of a muffled roar and wondered if it was the river, running past the parking lot. Then she realized St. Margaret's was holding Sports Day on the grounds just beyond the courts, hidden by a chain-link fence hung with nylon mesh — a windbreak and privacy measure Benny may, or may not, have played a role in securing.

Isabella got in the car, hoping Cooper was home, either watching television or playing video games. Benny was looking drained. She put the key in the ignition, then paused and turned, lightly placing her hand over his where it lay pressed into the seat as though supporting much of his body. He was staring out the window. Nothing registered on his face.

"My life insurance is not much, Isabella. I'm not prepared for this."

"Is that what you're thinking about? I'm not going to worry about that now. We'll be fine."

"The smell in there was making me sick. And I think that young fellow was lying."

Isabella nodded. Though she was anxious to get home, it seemed rude to start the car.

"He's heard of me."

Isabella thought it more likely that Aiden had heard of Cooper, who was often at the centre of mischievous goings-on. But she said nothing. She tried to imagine it. What would you most want to leave behind in the minds of others? That you worked tirelessly to improve your tennis club? Spoiled your son? Loved women? Or would the concrete evidence of these things be more important? Locker room and windbreak? A rambunctious, nearly uncontrollable child? Grieving women?

They had realized as soon as Cooper learned to walk that he was experimental by nature. A bottle of dish soap squirted into the dryer, plastic bags ironed, coloured markers sucked white for their unusual flavour. Matches held an irresistible allure from the get-go. Cooper was five when he scaled a bureau for a pack of matches and, alone in his parents' bedroom, lit them one by one. Isabella found him sitting cross-legged on the rug, his hands uncharacteristically empty and folded in his lap, the look he gave her pleasantly blank. There was the unmistakable smell of sulphur.

She wanted to remind Benny of that day. Of its adorable, happy ending.

"You've been lighting matches!"

"No, I haven't."

"Yes, you have. Don't lie to me. You've been lighting matches."

"No, I haven't."

"I've read you a hundred stories this morning and played a hundred games —"

The phone was ringing.

"Don't move."

It had been Benny on the phone. What had he wanted? She remembered launching into a tirade. She was close to crying, she was so fed up with finding that her son had nearly poisoned himself or burned the house to the ground or destroyed something irreplaceable. Benny, logical and calm, told her he would deal with it. In the meantime he wanted her to find all the matches and lighters in the house and get rid of them. She hung up and turned back to Cooper, who was on his feet now, staring out the window and looking as though he hadn't heard a word of the conversation, and carefully searched his pockets and the immediate area. She told him to stand still. But the phone was ringing again and he went for it. She sat back on her heels and took a deep breath and waited.

"Hell-o."

As she watched his face she felt a tug of worry. He was nodding and his eyes had glazed over. He lowered the phone and cupped the receiver with his small hand. She marvelled at his skill at mimicking adults.

"*Mom.*"

"Who is that?"

"It's the fire department."

Cooper's eyes turned inward again. He was rocking on the balls of his feet and nodding excitedly. "I know what he says. I know! I know!" he cried into the phone. "Sparky the Fire Dog says, *matches-and-lighters-are-tools-not-toys!*"

Somehow he bounced his way over to her, insisting into the phone that he knew what Sparky said, and onto Isabella's lap, where she hugged him tightly and closed her eyes.

Isabella doubted Benny would have been able to disguise his own voice. It would have been someone else from the office. She had never asked him who. She realized she would never know if she didn't ask soon. She reached for the ignition.

"Isabella, I want to talk about something else before we get home."

"What is it?"

"I don't want to argue about this in front of Cooper. It would only upset him."

"What is it?"

"I'm about to tell you."

She put her hands in her lap.

"Isabella, I know you're scheming to have Inky put down."

She turned, surprised. "I'm doing no such thing."

"Just hear me out." He paused and she knew it would be better if she said nothing. It was like a test. If she spoke, he would go back to the beginning.

"I love that dog."

"Of course you do."

"Just hear me out."

"I'm not going to have him put down."

"Will you just let me speak!"

Isabella watched a yellow Land Rover come tearing into the parking lot, driven by that thin woman whose name Isabella always forgot. She realized that for someone whose name she didn't know, she certainly knew her story. Or one of her stories.

"It would break my heart to lose that dog," Benny said. "He understands me better than anyone."

"I have no intention of getting rid of Inky. You have to believe me."

"Sometimes I don't know what to believe."

Although Isabella allowed for some distortions and embellishments, she did not doubt the central facts and thus carried a clear, disturbing image of the Land Rover woman slumped miserably on her bed, surrounded by friends tempting her with dainty sandwiches, fish and chips, turkey soup. No one had realized how hard the woman had taken her husband's desertion until a friend dropped by and found the children — unwashed but cheerful — still in pajamas at the end of the day, jars of peanut butter and jelly scooped clean, the blinds closed. The woman, dehydrated, docile and melancholy, was the main concern. A few of the friends were nurses. While the children were sent home with their aunties, the women got an IV into the house, hooked her up and had her talking sense in no time.

That would never happen to me, Isabella thought. I'd never fall apart like that. I'd always find a way to get through the day. She started the car.

When they got home, Cooper was watching television.

"How's Sports Day going?" Isabella asked.

"Word!"

Benny looked from Isabella to Cooper and back again, suspicious.

"It's just slang," Isabella explained. She was tired now.

"Well, I'm not sure I like it," Benny said, but he was leaving the room. He would be heading upstairs for the Pepto-Bismol. Yesterday, Isabella had placed a new bottle somewhere. She hoped it wouldn't be difficult to locate. She wanted to find it before Benny discovered the empty bottle in the bathroom and started a fuss. She was already in the hallway when Cooper called her back.

"Look, Mom. Wanna see something?"

Obediently, Isabella returned a few steps into the room.

"I got a nail up my nose. Like on *Ripley's Believe It or Not*."

"Where did you get that?" she asked, but she was turning away.

"It's a colossal nail too," he called after her.

The following week Benny discovered Cooper's DVDs and viewed them. He might have been at it several days, Isabella wasn't sure. She also did not ask what had initially prompted his interest in them. Most likely he simply came across them in his idle wanderings from room to room and had grown curious by the sheer number of them. It would seem later that Benny's discovery marked a turning point in their life, when Isabella began to notice the greatest change in him. She had read that boredom was a distant cousin to melancholy, and Benny not only had time on his hands, but the sure knowledge that this time, which he was at a loss to fill, was running out. She was aware of him moving further and further away from his family, becoming a strange, unpredictable man, a man who might spend days keeping his own dark counsel, then surprise her with a rambling chattiness.

Gradually she came to see, bitterly, that she would be robbed of retribution. Angry and unforgiving as she sometimes felt, she would not have chosen death as punishment for her husband's betrayal.

It had been over a year since Isabella had made the same discovery in Cooper's DVDs, and yet in all that time she had said nothing to either Cooper or Benny. She had allowed them to sit plain as day on a shelf in her son's room, almost as though she were hoping a different wife would arrive and deal with them. When early one evening the camcorder was retired — Benny standing on the second floor landing in his pajamas and throwing it down the stairwell — she was relieved, despite her recollection that it cost nearly eight hundred dollars — a birth-day gift for Cooper that Benny had been unable to resist.

She was just on her way out the door to the Avalon Nature Club lecture where it was her custom to sit by herself in the dark watching the nature slides and listening to the speakers above the whirr of the slide projector. Tonight someone was bringing in penguin decoys and talking about using them to elicit aggressive behaviour in other birds.

She was wearing new silk mules. She had looked down and watched the camcorder — it seemed surprisingly light — come bursting apart like a cheap, plastic toy around her. Bits split and shot away, while the green strap that had once wrapped around the back of her son's hand landed on the toe of one of her new shoes.

Cooper stood across the stairwell from his father, leaning too far out over the banister, screaming at him. Isabella considered the impossible odds of catching her son should he fall. Now Benny was snapping each DVD in half before furiously casting the pieces over the landing. Meanwhile, Inky was shuffling along the downstairs hall towards her, stumbling when he reached the edge of the rug. He sniffed the broken camcorder, defecated, then sat down, panting. The odour of dog shit rose quickly. Benny put his hand over his mouth and disappeared back into his bedroom.

Isabella knew it was unlikely she would get to the lecture that night. A gentle resentment began to fall over her. She hunted down Inky and grabbed him by the collar and dragged him out to the backyard, a large fenced-in space that had once satisfied him, but being abandoned there now elicited terror in the dog.

When Benny first stopped working, Inky would follow him from room to room, his toenails clicking on the hardwood floor. If Benny sat down, Inky would bring him things — a tennis ball, shoe, hairbrush. Later, when Benny began spending long hours on the living room sofa, Inky became more selective. Over the course of an hour the dog emptied Cooper's closet of stuffed animals, carrying them downstairs one by one. Isabella watched, fascinated, as Inky placed a teddy bear at Benny's feet, a kangaroo on his stomach, nudged a parrot against his neck.

Then, shortly after Benny's first chemotherapy treatment, Inky began defecating in the house, as though it were a way of protesting Benny's illness. Sometimes rising at night and stumbling to the bathroom, Isabella was greeted by the aroma of a fresh deposit hidden somewhere in the dark outskirts of her house. No amount of scolding from any of them seemed to affect Inky. Although he stood with drooping head and bent submissive ears, he was unable to mend his ways.

A year earlier Isabella had been passing through the dining room whose large bay windows looked out onto the park, and glanced out to see Cooper and another boy following a male jogger. Even from that distance, she suspected her son of harassing the jogger, whose halting gait and stiffly turning torso indicated a frenzied aggravation. Cooper was holding something out towards the man and they were running side by side, while the other boy held back, bent double with laughter. Isabella struggled to believe her son was a well-mannered, prudent boy, that whatever he was saying to this man was entirely reasonable, but the next moment the man had extended his arm to deliver a pseudo karate chop to Cooper's neck. Cooper stopped and the friend caught up with him. Isabella recognized the object in Cooper's hand. The camcorder.

It had taken several days to view all the DVDs. While Cooper was at school and Benny away on business, and after several calls to Future Shop where the camcorder had been purchased, Isabella had all the cables correctly plugged in and all the buttons set to the right settings. When she first saw her own body, or her body from the neck down, walk across the screen, she didn't recognize herself. The images were clear and sharp but the colours untrue. Her green linen skirt looked blue and hopelessly wrinkled — well, that was linen for you.

Her own voice asked, "For heaven's sake, Benny, don't you think I know when I've had enough wine?"

Watching this, Isabella's stomach turned. Had she really said that? Really used that tone?

Then the screen blurred as the images spun and there was Cooper's elfish face in close-up, dreadfully white and lacking freckles, whispering, "This is Cooper Martin bringing you another family fight."

Where had he been? Under a table?

She should have turned it off, but she was riveted with apprehension, with the shock of seeing an innocuous past — much of what she saw was boring — brought back to her. Disembodied figures were followed and forgotten, Inky's nostrils thoroughly explored, the contents of several flushing toilets observed to their end. She saw her own face occasionally in detail and wondered, was she truly so unlovely?

The time flashed in the bottom right-hand corner of the screen, 1:26 am, but Isabella would have known it was night by Cooper's blue pajamas slopping above his naked feet as he occasionally peered through the camera to find his way down the stairs. There was the jerking wall and all its family portraits, a window, the kitchen door, some murmuring and then a view of the kitchen table. There was Cooper's clipped breathing and Benny's voice in conversation, but only the kitchen table. It was simple enough: Benny was making plans to meet someone. He used the name *Heather*, and then he said *sweetheart*, as in, *Now sweetheart, I'll be on time but will you?* and it was 1:32 in the morning. Still, all she could see was the kitchen table.

The next day Isabella finished watching the DVDs. Towards the end she came to the jogger, who was asked by her son, "How's it going, uh? Don't want to get fat, do we?" Isabella had not recognized the man — a small miracle.

After hauling Inky out of the house, Isabella gathered up the dog shit with a plastic bag and collected the largest of the broken camcorder pieces. Then she pulled the vacuum hose from the wall inlet and ran it over the hall rug and bottom of the stairs. When she got to a small log of desiccated dog shit tucked behind the leg of the table in the hall, she plowed ahead and sucked it up. She knew that, for the next several weeks, using the vacuum would result in the scent of dog shit filling the house. But these were reckless, uncharted times.

As soon as she turned the vacuum off, she became aware of Cooper shouting and throwing things around up in his room. More than his camcorder would be broken by the end of this day. She was wondering how Benny was standing the noise when he emerged from their bedroom and began making his way down the stairs. He wouldn't look at her.

"Hungry?" she asked when he reached the bottom step and she realized he was neither going to stop nor speak to her.

He was walking away, into the family room.

"Grilled cheese?"

It was the challenge in her voice that stopped him, though he didn't turn. "I can see it now," he said. "I'm going to get blamed for this."

"You didn't need to destroy them all," she said to his back. "Do you want something to eat? I was planning on going out."

"Hey, don't let me interfere with your plans, Isabella."

In the kitchen she buttered two slices of bread and sliced the cheddar into thin sheets, the way Benny liked it. She felt lousy and wanted to pinpoint the feeling somehow, so she could erase it. She placed the sandwich in a frying pan, then dashed upstairs.

Cooper was on his bed, motionless. Most of his skateboarding and mountain biking posters had been torn from the walls. Books were off the shelves and the fish tank water looked muddy and unsettled. The bed itself had been stripped, the sheets and blankets dragged halfway across the floor.

"I didn't *do* anything," Cooper shouted when he saw her, pounding his naked mattress. "He did that for *no reason!*"

Cooper and Benny's relationship had been faltering for a while. Isabella did not question their inability to understand one another — one sick and the other a boy — yet when their arguments arose, the premonition came over her that her son's experiences with bad luck and unhappiness might be difficult to survive. She was noticing the rusty stains on Cooper's mattress, curious about their age and the likelihood of them being blood-related, when the smoke alarm went off in the kitchen. She rushed back down the stairs, imagining Benny in the family room, his hands over his ears and his jaw clenched.

The kitchen was filling with smoke. The sandwich, though still spongy and cool on the upper surface, was black on the bottom. She ignored the thought circulating at the back of her mind that she might want to take a deep breath and count to ten. Instead, she thought that if the rest of the family could throw things, so could she. She grabbed the pan and ran down the hall and into the family room. She yanked open the window and flung the pan out into the backyard. Fleetingly, she thought of Inky, but he was nowhere in sight.

"I'm going to go out on a limb here, " Benny began, trying to joke, but Isabella left the room before he could finish his sentence. She thought of the Avalon Nature Club lecture, but refused to look at her watch. Inside her head there was a funny sensation, *ping ping*, like both a sound and tiny movement inside her head. She wondered if it was the seed of insanity.

She began again: buttering the bread, slicing the cheese. She worked slowly, growing calmer, and eventually found herself appalled by what she had done. Had any of the neighbours seen the pan come flying out of the house? Might they see it yet? A small frying pan with its cargo of burned bread and cheese? She returned to the family room and approached the window slowly, afraid to face the consequences of her savage behaviour. Behind her, she heard Benny rise from the sofa. When she turned to him, he was grinning. He approached her and put an arm around her, and everything that was wrong fell away from her.

She understood, suddenly, her reluctance all this time to destroy the DVDs. Now that it was done, it seemed they were one step closer to erasing the family they had been, for better or for worse. As though Benny had erased memory: an autumn afternoon gone dusky in the park, a skim of snow across the yard in early winter, the powerful light of summer shooting through the house like an arrow. Happiness, disappointment, sorrow. Erased.

Inky was finishing off the sandwich. Isabella didn't see how he could avoid burning his tongue.

"Do you think Cooper knows?" Benny asked.

Of course he did. "I've no idea."

"I couldn't watch them all."

"I did," she whispered.

"You did? Why didn't you tell me?"

"You shouldn't have destroyed them all."

"But he was spying on me!"

"Benny."

"I'm sorry."

Was he sorry for breaking the camcorder and DVDs, or for betraying her, or both? She'd take the apology, regardless. She leaned against him and just for a moment, before he braced himself to support her, she felt him bend away from her weight.

"You're so familiar," Benny said, holding her close now.

They watched Inky lick the pan clean.

"Go on to your meeting, Izzie."

She looked at her watch. "It's already started."

"Go on."

That night, just before going to bed, Isabella asked Inky if he wanted to go out. He turned his eyes up at her sheepishly, his grey muzzle an inch from the carpet, and thumped his tail twice. He put a great deal of effort into rising, but made little headway.

"Never mind," Isabella said, giving up. "Stay."

When she awoke in the night she immediately smelled dog shit. Without turning on the lights she descended the stairs to the kitchen, got a plastic bag and gathered up the mess in the dark, for the first time admitting it was time to put the dog down. When she fell back to sleep she dreamed she and Benny were ascending a crisp, multi-levelled building. White light was everywhere. People were milling about and, like Benny, were dressed in white gowns. She was leading him up, level by level. Everything was set, she had made the appointment, the decision had been made. Then Benny turned to her and said sadly, "Goodbye, Inky."

Chapter Twelve

"Izzie? Izzie?"

"Coming."

"I was thinking about those boys."

"What boys?"

Benny opened his eyes. The rims looked dry and sore. He was having a bad morning and Isabella wanted to take him to the hospital. He kept saying they should wait a while yet and see. He spoke thickly. "Sorry. You weren't there."

"What boys?"

"They drowned. They were fooling around on the ice."

"Where?" She touched his sleeve. "Benny?"

He opened his eyes again to look at her, then closed them. "You'd never forget it. I'm glad you weren't there."

Isabella lifted her gaze from her husband's body and stared out across the park at the brown leaves of the oak trees. She imagined the tap-tap papery sound produced by the collision of dead leaves and rain.

"Sit up now so we can brush your teeth."

"Just past the turnoff to Isaac's Harbour, there's a new coffee shop that overlooks a small bight."

She nodded, helping him sit. His pajama legs were hiked up

to his knees, but he didn't seem to notice. As she tugged them down, she felt her eyes fill. His ankles and feet were swollen. He didn't notice that either. She handed him his toothbrush and a cup of water. The cup immediately teetered in his hand and some of the water sloshed out, but she had a towel folded over his lap. She took back the cup and held it for him.

"I knew I was sick then," he said, looking sideways at the toothbrush in his hand as though endeavoring to identify its use. "But I didn't really believe it." He stopped. "What?"

"Brush your teeth. You'll feel better."

He obediently bowed his head, popped the toothbrush into his mouth and began vigorously to brush his teeth. His method of rinsing, which dated long before his illness and which Isabella found slightly revolting, involved dunking the brush into the cup of water over and over while brushing. She slid a small basin below the cup to catch the spill. When he was finished the basin was full of bloody, pasty water. His gums were suffering badly under the assault of medications. The doctor had told her there wasn't much that could be done about it.

"Don't lie back down yet, Benny. We need to change your pajamas."

"I went back that night. After I dropped you off and had my supper with Isabella and Cooper. You didn't know that, did you?"

"Shhh, let's get this off you."

"I went back."

She had purchased him new cotton pajamas because he'd lost so much weight, but they'd become snug after the first wash. As she buttoned them up, she said, "You're busting right out of these, John Wayne."

He looked at her and grinned, distracted from his story. He lay back down, keeping his eyes on her, and said, "What's a man gotta do around here to get a woman?" She laughed. The accent was not bad, given everything.

Then he closed his eyes, tired again. She went out to empty the basin and bring back clean water for his face. As soon as she returned and sat down beside him, he opened his eyes and said, "I know it's you, Isabella. For a minute I was confused, but I know it's you. I know I'm in my house. In my bed. I know."

"That's okay." She had to whisper. If she spoke any louder her voice would crack. She stared at a teddy bear sticking out from under the bed.

"I want to tell you about it."

"All right."

"The place was mobbed," he said, then stopped and didn't speak for several minutes. She wondered if he had forgotten where he was again. Then he raised a hand and studied it as he spoke. It was a new habit of his, as though keeping an eye on his own flesh helped him think.

"People were everywhere, crying, hanging onto each other. The wind had turned around and the ice was moving off. People had flashlights, shining them on the water. He had the rope in his hand. Then a wave came and I never saw him again. A person doesn't last long in that water."

Recently he'd become more and more talkative, any time of day or night. She found it made her restless.

"They shot up flares and people saw something at the surface. But it wasn't a body. I never heard what it was. The next day they found both boys, close by. Caught up in seaweed."

Isabella stroked his arm over the pajama sleeve. "I'm going to give your face a nice wash now."

"We waited for him to come out from under. We waited. When I first got there I could only see his coat floating above him — a blue ski jacket. It was all so ordinary."

"While the water is still warm."

"Are you listening to me? I couldn't tell you, Isabella. The boy's eyes were brown, he looked right at me. He looked so cold, but there was that moment, before he was pulled under, when we both thought I'd rescue him."

She remembered. Just last spring. It was on the news for a while. Two boys on the ice. They should have known better. There had been a number of witnesses.

"You want to forget something like that, but it only goes away for a short time, then circles back to you. He reminded me of a friend of Cooper's. I think they moved away. A pleasant-looking kid. Peter something."

"Peter Hoddinott," Isabella whispered, imagining Benny and those boys. She dunked the washcloth into the water, then wrung it out.

"As long as Cooper doesn't do anything stupid," Benny said, "he'll be all set."

When Isabella was thirteen, she was asked to babysit for two children she didn't know. They were friends of friends who were in a bind. Although Isabella had already done a fair amount of babysitting, it was usually in her own neighbourhood and for families she knew.

The younger was still a baby. The mother said over the phone she would be asleep when Isabella arrived. She was an easy baby and never woke in the night. They also had an eight-year-old son, Benjamin. He was not allowed to eat anything sweet. He's sort of allergic to sugar, the mother explained. He'll get really excited if he has sweets. After the parents left, Isabella had a look through their kitchen cupboards and refrigerator. She saw it would be an easy rule to enforce since there weren't any cookies or cakes or ice cream. Nothing that would be considered sweet anywhere in the house.

It was summer and Benjamin was permitted to play outside until eight, when Isabella had been told he should be called in. Bedtime was at nine. Every once in a while, Isabella went to a window or stepped out on the back deck to search for him in his blue-and-white striped shirt, just making sure he was there. She didn't want to leave the house because it would be irresponsible to leave an infant, even one that was sleeping.

At ten to eight she called over to him. He ignored her shouts at first. She heard the other children stop and tell him he was being called in, and eventually he strolled over. She had liked him when she'd been introduced to him by his father. He was small but sturdy and had pretty eyes and a cute way of grinning at her. But she had called for him about ten times and was beginning to distrust him.

She told him it was time to get washed up for bed.

"What's your name again?" he asked, not budging.

"Izzie."

"That's so funny."

"It's a nickname. My full name is Isabella. I'm named after my aunt who was killed."

"You sound like my teacher from last year."

Isabella frowned. Her mother was after saying a million times she'd make a terrific teacher.

"Can I have a snack?"

"You can have fruit. Apple or banana. Or toast."

"Toast and a cup of tea. Please."

"Are you allowed tea?"

"Sure." They studied each other. His little grin was charming.

He showed her where everything was kept, though she already knew. She dunked a tea bag in his hot water for barely a second, just colouring it, then poured in an equal portion of milk. She began to enjoy his company and decided to have tea and toast as well. She brought the plates and cups to the table and he set them out. He buttered all the toast and while they ate, he told her about school, his baby sister, his friends, the game he had been playing. He grew more and more animated. It seemed he couldn't get the words out fast enough and a few times she wasn't sure what he'd said, he was speaking that fast. Bits of toast sprayed from his mouth. When he got on to ballroom dancing lessons and how silly they were, even his dad said he shouldn't have to go, he jumped up onto his chair and started dancing wildly. "Let's dance," he shouted. "Let's have a fine time!" He kicked his legs out to the side and hit the table. The dishes rattled and Isabella's tea nearly capsized. She felt her face grow hot.

"Hey. Sit down. Sit down right now, Benjamin!"

It was like when she tried to call him in from playing. If he heard her he wasn't showing it. She got up and went over and grabbed him, pulling him down, and then the two of them toppled onto the floor. She scratched her arm on something and released him. They stood up, staring at each other, both shocked. She was usually a calm babysitter.

"I just wanted to show you how we dance," he said.

"I think you better go get washed up. I'll do these dishes. Okay?"

"Sure!"

She watched him race out of the room, nearly hitting a number of things as he went. She'd never sat for a kid with so much energy. He was weird. She was bringing the plates and cups to the sink when she changed her mind and hurried upstairs after him.

But she couldn't find him. For nearly an hour she searched. She figured he was hiding from her, so at first she was annoyed, but not worried. She checked under every bed, in every closet, behind all the furniture and in all the rooms. She felt uncomfortable searching through his parents' bedroom. The room smelled different from the rest of the house — nicer, cleaner. She began to imagine that when she found him she would smack him, though she knew she would never actually do such a thing. She called for him, not loudly, because she didn't want to wake the baby. She began to beg him to come out and finally to offer him bribes. Cookies, candy, ice cream. She opened the back door, stepped out and shouted for him. It was dark now. She started to cry. She decided to call her mother, which she had been putting off. She was standing in the kitchen staring at the table where they'd had their snack. There was a sugar bowl on the table. It had small blue windmills on in. When she removed the lid, she saw there was hardly any sugar in it. She went over to the sink and lifted his tea and tasted it. It was revoltingly sweet.

She heard shouting upstairs.

When she entered the baby's room, he was standing over the

crib, gently cooing at his little sister, "You're some bad baby. Sure we're going to have to sell you." He glanced up at Isabella. He looked dishevelled and flushed. With a sinking feeling she realized he might have been outside after all. Then he leaned into the crib and shouted, "I LOVE YOU, BABY GIRL! YOU'RE THE BEST BABY GIRL THERE EVER WAS!"

Isabella rushed at him, just wanting to get her hands on him, but the baby was awake and bawling.

"Get out of this room," she hissed at him. She lifted the baby. She was exhausted and near tears again. Rocking the baby gave her comfort. She didn't care where Benjamin had gone. She would stay in this room with the baby until the parents came home. A rhythmic creaking sound started up in a nearby room and she knew he wasn't far.

When Benjamin's mother came into the bedroom, she looked at Isabella, who was still holding the baby. The baby had stopped crying but was hiccuping. Isabella could see she wasn't going to be in any trouble. The mother looked disappointed, but not surprised. She left the room. Isabella heard her call down-stairs for her husband. Then she heard her say, "Haven't I told you a million times not to jump on the beds? Benjamin!"

The baby heard her mother's voice and started to cry again. The mother came back in and took the baby from Isabella. "You go downstairs and Frank will pay you and see you get home safely. Thanks so much, Isabella. It was great to get out. I appreciate you coming over."

Isabella nodded and said goodnight. She swore she would never babysit for that family again and she never did.

While Benny napped, Isabella slipped into Cooper's rubber boots and put on an old sweater and drove over to Shoppers Drug Mart. It was Halloween and colder than she had expected, but she didn't bother buttoning the sweater, just wrapped it around herself so it overlapped at her breasts. She was waiting at the checkout, hugging herself, when she realized she wasn't wearing a bra. A man joined the line behind her. Her peripheral vision told her he was tall and overweight. Her bags of Halloween candy rang in at $12.38. Suddenly she was ashamed of herself. She hadn't been to the hairdresser in months and her nails were uneven and unpainted. She wasn't wearing a single molecule of makeup.

"Evening, Isabella," the man said, and she turned, aware of herself shrinking along her spine, knowing by the voice it was Rex Chafe, cosmetic surgeon extraordinaire.

"How're you getting on?" he asked.

Everyone was asking her this.

"Great," she said.

Rex was staring at her. No one believed her. They looked at her and thought, you can't be great. Your husband is dying, everyone knows he's been seeing another woman, your son is wild as the woollies and your dog is filling your glamorous house with feces. You can't be great, I don't believe it.

Rex placed a large bottle of green Scope on the counter and turned to study her.

"What have you got done to yourself, Isabella?"

"What do you mean?"

"Is it your hair?"

"Oh dear, I forgot the bread. Excuse me."

She scurried out with her candy, thinking, my god, I didn't even say goodbye, and crossed over to the bakery, though she didn't need bread, and joined the long snaking line, just in case Rex checked up on her. She was feeling that *ping ping* of insanity again.

She focused on the conversation of the couple in front of her. They were discussing their new home. It was then and there that Isabella decided to call a real estate agent, which Benny had been suggesting for a while.

She began searching for the new house in early November, just before Benny went into the hospital for the last time. It was a discouraging business, but she had done some investigations at the bank and with their lawyer and had come to terms with her limitations. But it wasn't only that: she knew she couldn't live another day in their house once Benny left it. She would be a different person. She was shrinking, her life swirling around her like the Bermuda Triangle or some kind of alien-produced humongous whirlpool that Cooper would know about, and she was at its epicentre. She and Cooper could let the rest of the world spin while they stood — quiet, oblivious, blind.

She never told Benny. On Saturday she went to the Bagel Café and thumbed through the real estate section. She contacted an agent and only gave him her cell number. The agent was discreet and never asked her anything he didn't need to know. She said two bedrooms with a backyard. She wanted to avoid the downtown. He assured her they'd find something suitable.

Already she was changing. She felt it.

She would return home, flushed, to her laundry, Inky's deposits, Benny's needs, a disappeared Cooper. Was this how it had felt to be Benny? Deceitful, untrue, fraudulent? She had never kept anything from him before. It seemed massive, crippling, destructive, and then she pinched herself: he was dying. What could be more destructive than that?

She didn't want him to die. Whatever he had done, whomever he loved, Isabella did not want him to die.

She found a house a few days after he went into palliative care. It was cold and the rain that fell was like ice. She had heard they were experiencing some kind of record: thirty-two consecutive days of bad weather. The agent seemed apologetic. He was wearing a red poppy in his lapel for Remembrance Day. But no house was going to be attractive right now, Isabella told herself, and she took the small bungalow. It was at the end of a cul-de-sac: Goodridge Place. It smelled of old woman. The next day she accepted the counter-offer on her cellphone, standing outside the hospital, shivering.

She immediately started to pack. She spent half her time at the hospital. The remaining time she spent packing, throwing out things, occasionally sleeping. She would stand up from taping a box and Cooper would be beside her, tugging at her sleeve.

"What's going on, Mom? What are you doing?"

"Everything is going to be fine."

"You're acting strange, Mom," Cooper whined.

Later she found him under his bed, covered in dust bunnies.

"Cooper?"

"I don't want Daddy to die."

"You're going to be fine, darling. Come here. Come out."

"I don't want to come out. You're acting strange."

She separated Benny's belongings from the rest of the contents of their home and put them in garbage bags to be picked up by the Salvation Army. After a while she realized she was keeping an eye out for something. What would it be? A snapshot, lock of hair, letter, receipt, article of clothing or jewellery? What kind of keepsake would Benny cling to? And more challenging, where would he hide it? She searched his pockets, desk and bureau drawers, tool box, glove compartment — she realized she would need to sell his car. How did one go about that?

There was nothing. The only evidence of betrayal had come via their own son, stored on DVDs. And Benny had destroyed those.

Then she found it: a white envelope with snapshots. The address on the outside was in Benny's handwriting but incomplete: Bridget Neal, 55 Baltimore Crescent, Toronto, ON. It was an address he had known almost by heart — except for the postal code — scrawled across an envelope he had once meant to send. Isabella had never heard of Bridget Neal. Was that an alias? The photos were old and stuck together. Perhaps they had been forgotten. Perhaps this was a woman Benny had known before their marriage. Isabella began to separate them, still expecting to find evidence of that *other* woman, the one she had known about.

Isabella still sometimes found it difficult to say her name, even inside her head.

But this other woman was a stranger to Isabella, and the photos were taken after their marriage because in many of them the woman — Bridget? — was wearing a scarf Isabella recognized. She had given it to Benny for his birthday.

Well, Cooper had given it to him. He had been only four, still round and sturdy with that low centre of gravity that seemed to give him a certain ruthlessness and power. She had taken him to the mall that afternoon and they'd selected the present. The scarf — grey and tan — had been delectably soft and irresistible to Cooper. The two of them had spent a long time wrapping it just so in those hours before Benny came home from work and Isabella still hadn't made the icing for his cake or marinated the lamb chops. She was standing in the kitchen chopping scallions, overheated from the day's busyness and the knowledge she was behind schedule, when Benny came into the house and Cooper, also flushed and revved, went flying towards his father, and Isabella heard him cry out, "We already wrapped your scarf, Daddy! We already wrapped your scarf."

Isabella had put the knife down and gone out to the hall and stared at her son in disbelief. Both her son and husband looked full of happiness. Cooper was on his toes, jumping.

"You don't *tell* Daddy what you wrapped. It's a surprise," Isabella blurted out. She hadn't meant to sound severe or speak to him as though he were an adult. She had just been so flabbergasted. She had thought that Cooper understood.

And then he did. Isabella saw it dawning on him: the purpose of shopping without Benny, then wrapping the scarf — *hiding it* — with the paper. A birthday present. Cooper got it, then burst into tears. Benny swooped him up and a lengthy session followed involving hugs and kisses and Benny's declaration that he'd not heard what Cooper had said anyway.

Isabella always felt awful thinking about that day.

Had this Bridget heard the story? Isabella bet she had. Benny

liked the story. He liked the way his son's face had been transformed by a sense of responsibility.

It's summer in the photos and Benny and Bridget are outdoors. It looks like Newfoundland: only a few deciduous trees,
a low sky, cobble beach. A few cabins appear in the distance, but
they are blurred in the photo, and there are no cars or identifiable
landmarks. That they are having an affair is not debatable. There
is a certain look on a woman's face in a photo that tells you she
is in love, and that she in love with the man with the camera.

But who was she? Long dark hair, dark eyes. Isabella flipped
over one of the photos and found the date, printed at the photo
shop: June 25, six and a half years ago.

In the last photo the woman won't look at the camera — that
is, at Benny. Instead, she is staring off into the distance, maybe
the sea. She is talking. She is sitting on a ridge of turf with her
hands in her lap and she is delighted with the moment.

Isabella thought the black smudge at the edge of the photo
was probably Inky's tail.

Her feelings of being crushed and heartbroken left her. She
was disgusted and humiliated. There was no telling if this was
before or even *during* his relationship with Heather Welbourne
— whose name she could now easily face — but either possibility
left her cold. She didn't want to know.

Although perhaps Heather Welbourne should know.

She recalled a way of Benny's when they made love, when he
seemed unable to endure another moment of foreplay. He would
look stricken and his movements would become sluggish but
deliberate. He would glance at her out of the corner of his eye,
as though he could not bear to be distracted from his single-
mindedness of purpose. The look on his face was the embodi-
ment of passion: pure, but impersonal. It occurred to her now
that in those last moments he had stopped recognizing her.

The envelope with the photos was inside a larger envelope
containing old receipts and warranties. If Benny had wanted
Isabella to discover the photos he could not have chosen a better

location. On the other hand, they were probably placed there so long ago they'd been forgotten. Certainly it was meant to be a temporary deposit. They were to have been sent. Isabella considered mailing them to the Toronto address. But mailing them to Heather Welbourne seemed a better option. She tucked them inside her purse and went off to the hospital.

When Isabella was twenty-eight, two friends invited her to a party at the River Valley Tennis Club. It was supposed to be a dance, but no one actually danced, unless they had too much to drink and then they just made fools of themselves. Isabella knew the crowd and said it would be boring.

"Won't they just be talking about tennis?"

Her friends laughed. "You need to get out more," one of them said.

"What odds what they talk about?" the other friend said. "It's better than doing nothing."

Isabella had known these friends from university. The three had graduated with teaching degrees and, except for Isabella, now held permanent positions. Isabella was substitute teaching. She had surprised everyone by her growing lack of interest in her career, and herself by discovering that she hated teaching. Some evenings she unplugged the phone so a vice-principal calling the next morning looking for a substitute couldn't reach her. She felt guilty and bored.

They arrived at ten thirty. There was hardly anyone around, though the music was so loud it prevented conversation anyway. They went back outside where there was the scattered crowd. The smell of weed wafted over once or twice. The dance was clearly not a success and Isabella wished she had not allowed herself to become associated with it.

One of her friends spotted someone she knew and they wandered over to another group. There was the awkward converging of two unfamiliar groups of people and half-hearted introductions. After a while someone suggested they go downtown to hear some live music.

"Will there be cover?" a girl asked.

"Marjorie, you tightwad, I'll pay your cover if it's an issue," a young man said.

Isabella felt too mature for all this and decided to go home. But she didn't want to draw attention to herself by announcing she was leaving and she didn't want to just wander off. She would wait until she was alone with one of her friends.

Everyone was strolling towards a couple of cars and Isabella allowed herself to go along. She got in the back seat between Marjorie and the loud guy who had boasted he'd pay her cover. One of Isabella's friends was in the front seat and the other friend was in another car. Isabella thought again that she should just go home.

The guy beside her was talking. She turned to look at him. He had a round, dumb-looking face, though, to be fair, she couldn't really see much in the car.

"Hi," he said, grinning at her. His whole face was involved in the grin. He seemed delighted to see her, though she'd never met him before in her life. She thought maybe he was drunk or high and mistaking her for someone else.

"Hi," she said.

"How are you?" he asked eagerly.

She turned to look at him again, to see what his expression was now. It was the same. He looked young and short. His grin wasn't really all that unpleasant.

"Do we know each other?" she asked.

"I don't think so. What's your name?"

"Izzie Parsons."

"I'm Benny Martin."

"Nice to meet you."

"Yeah."

They were downtown now. The driver was looking for a parking space and Isabella's friend was telling him to just park anywhere, it wouldn't kill them to walk.

Finally, Isabella asked, "Where did you grow up?"

"Bonway Place."

They had not grown up in the same part of town and had rarely crossed paths. There had also been the age difference. After a while Isabella had forgotten about him and about the guilt she felt for despising him. The incident between them seemed like something she'd read or seen on television.

"I babysat for you once," she announced.

"I think I remember that."

"You were awful."

"Really? Come on." He seemed genuinely surprised.

"You don't remember?"

He shook his head.

So she told him: the so-called sugar allergy, how he saturated his tea with sugar when she wasn't looking, then went into hiding for a full hour.

He laughed. "I was a sugar junkie when I was a kid. It's true. My mother kept all that stuff away from me because it made me wild."

Isabella could not believe this easygoing young man had been that boy. "Are you still?"

"Wild?"

He thought she was flirting with him, but that hadn't been her intention.

"No. A sugar junkie?"

"Of course not. Don't kids grow out of that?"

"Where were you hiding?"

"I have no idea. I don't even remember that, though I do remember you. I liked you. I thought you were nice."

"I don't think I was."

"I used to beg my mother to ask you to babysit again, but it didn't happen."

"I refused."

"Go on. You're kidding."

She nodded, grinning. "It's true."

"I was that bad? Christ. My apologies."

They had found a parking spot. She was aware of him as they walked to the pub and stood in line to pay the cover. He was talking to someone else now. The group spread over two tables. She sat with her drink among people she didn't know, but it didn't matter because the music was just as loud here as it had been at the tennis club, making it difficult to understand anything anyone said.

He was too young for her. He would be twenty-three, twenty-four. Though maybe that was okay, she wasn't sure.

When the band took a break, the guy sitting beside her got up and Benny came over and took his seat. She wasn't surprised. She was expecting that.

"Isabella. That's your real name, is it?"

She nodded.

"What do you do, Isabella? Do you work, Isabella?"

She was delighted with the way he spoke her name. "Apparently, I'm meant to be a substitute teacher."

"Not your thing? What are you meant to be?"

"Not sure."

"Isabella. Isabella." He shook his head.

She felt an uncontrollable urge to grin.

"Rather a grand name."

"I was named after my aunt. She died a few months before I was born."

"How?"

"Hit a moose. She wasn't wearing a seatbelt."

"They didn't then, did they, Isabella?"

"No. They didn't." Suddenly it was becoming an insipid conversation. She was boring him.

"That's a heavy legacy for you to shoulder."

"What do you mean?"

"It's like you're expected to have a safe and happy life. To make up for your aunt's tragedy."

"Of course not." She felt that whatever he was thinking about her was wrong. She felt he was assuming she was a woman who played it safe and never took chances. The band started up again and he turned to listen to it.

She stayed another half hour, then gathered her things and stood. He reached out and touched her elbow. She wasn't expecting that.

"Maybe I'll phone you sometime," he said. "Maybe we can get together and do something?"

She had to look down on him because he hadn't stood. It indicated laziness or slightly bad manners on his part, but she probably wasn't one to talk. She nodded. "Sure," she said.

He grinned. "Maybe I'll phone you next week then, Isabella?"

But he didn't. He didn't phone for weeks, though she was anticipating it and kept her phone plugged in. She found herself called in to substitute more often as a result.

Chapter Thirteen

The movie Cooper had rented was nearly over and Isabella checked the level in the wine bottle. It was empty, a surprise and disappointment. She would have liked one more sip. The movie, which Cooper had assured her was a classic, was a recent release lavish with blood and gore: a woman's severed head, a girl stomped to death, dresses and petticoats and bedding sloppy with pink, pretty blood. Neither Isabella nor Cooper thought the blood looked believable. It was too bright.

"I suspect that was the point," Isabella said.

"What do they make it out of, Mom?"

"I'm not sure. I think they used chocolate syrup in the old black and whites. Yum, yum."

"They couldn't use that now." Cooper was digging items out from between the sofa cushions. A pen, stapler, hemp bracelet, monopoly shoe, tissues.

"No, I wouldn't say."

"Look, Mom."

"Don't be pulling all that stuff out now, Cooper."

"Just look."

He held out a small dark object. Isabella bent to have a closer look, but even before she knew what it was she knew better than to touch it.

"Well, that's unfortunate," she said, which Cooper found funny. A dried-up bit of dog shit. "Put it in the garbage for me, please, then wash your hands."

She sent Cooper to bed, promising she'd be right down to say goodnight. The two of them had been in the bungalow on Goodridge Place several months, but she still wasn't sure how she felt about Cooper sleeping in the basement. He seemed too far away, perhaps because she couldn't hear a single sound he made. She went into her own bedroom and remembered for the umpteenth time that she had intended all day to change the sheets on her bed. She tore the top sheet off and was appalled at the crud that had accumulated at the bottom, presumably transported via the soles of her feet. Were they equally dirty? She would check in the morning. In particular, she noticed a lot of dog hair, which led her to consider the whereabouts of Inky.

She returned to the kitchen and opened the door and leaned out into her new neighborhood. Jeanette's car was in the adjacent yard, behind Darren's truck. It was a warm night. Spring was here. Inky would be fine and he wasn't barking. There was only, in the distance, someone speaking in a harsh, clipped manner, making a point.

She closed and locked the door and decided a bit of toast would help her sleep, but was surprised to find herself weaving on her way to the refrigerator. She didn't realize she'd had that much to drink. She put her hands on the kitchen table and nearly fell onto it, her face lurching to within inches of the mahogany-stained pine. She saw the words "Danny sucks . . ." but couldn't make out the rest of it. She exhaled impatiently. She was forever reminding Cooper to write over several pieces of paper to protect the soft tabletop. Yes, toast would be just the thing, toast with the blueberry jam she'd bought that day, and a glass of milk. This time crossing the kitchen she made a conscious effort to follow a straight path, and thought she did quite well. She was careful pouring the milk and pleased with herself for finding things so quickly and easily in her new ugly home.

She carried the toast into the living room, eating it as she wandered around, absently looking for a place to sit. The lights were off, and through the window that faced her front yard, the single dogberry caught her attention. The recent addition of leaves seemed to make even such a puny tree worth admiring, though in the light from the streetlights it seemed reduced to two colours: black and green. She wanted to sit by the window and more closely examine that tree, but there was a stack of unpacked boxes there. She turned, thinking to drag the armchair from the opposite side of the room across, and was on her way towards it, when she heard the voice again. Somebody making a point.

Her clumsiness vanished. She quietly placed her plate and glass on a nearby table and made her way to the window facing the side yard. The drapes were drawn. She dropped to her knees and surfaced between the glass and drapes.

She slid the window open a few inches and heard Jeanette ask, "When did you decide this, Darren?"

She was crying. Sweet Mother of God, Jeanette was crying. Through the wooden lattice enclosing her neighbour's deck, Isabella could make out two figures: Darren sitting, his back to her, and Jeanette standing.

"Mom?"

"Shhh! Don't turn on that light!" Isabella whispered, pushing the drapes away.

"Why's it so dark in here, Mom?"

"Shhh. Don't turn on that light."

"What are you doing?" Cooper was looking in her general direction but couldn't see her yet. "Mom?"

"Over here. I think the neighbours are having an argument." She ducked back under the drapes.

Jeanette was asking, "When are you moving out, then?"

"I didn't say I was moving out. I just said — "

Cooper popped up beside her. "You're bad to the bone, Mom," he whispered in her ear.

"Shhh."

"Darren, you know I don't like to sleep alone in the house. You know I'm afraid of the dark, Darren."

"I haven't made any decisions. It wouldn't be the end — "

Jeanette's next comment was broken and muffled.

"Do not mention that pool again, Jeanette. Please."

Isabella sat quickly back on her heels and put a hand over her mouth. She was surprised by the sharpness in his voice, by the hint of cruelty. By the mention of that bloody pool.

The pool was still in its box in the den. There had been a distancing in her relationship with Darren since its purchase, a purchase she regretted. Shopping with — or without — Darren had distracted her, and she knew it for what it was: a way to get through her day. But when he had pulled his Visa from his wallet, insisting the pool be bought, she'd felt uneasy.

Perhaps she had been looking for control, a stabilizing influence, someone to reach a hand out to warn her off her extravagances — though, if anything, Darren had encouraged her purchases. He was kind, and she appreciated the way he accepted Cooper without giving her any parenting suggestions. But the pool had been a mistake.

She returned to the window. Through the lattice she caught a glimpse of Darren's hand as he lifted a can of Coke and squeezed it. There was the sound of metal crunching, followed by a noise like a burp.

"It wouldn't be the end of the world, Jeanette," Darren said, rising.

Then the light went off, the door closed and there was silence. Isabella watched Jeanette descend into her backyard and fade from view; perhaps she was inspecting the potentillas she'd been pruning the other day. Isabella rose and collected her glass and plate and tottered into the kitchen. Cooper had vanished. Glancing down, she was mortified to see her white blouse spotted with blueberry jam the size of bullet wounds. Though she had never seen a bullet wound except on television.

The following morning Isabella lay on her bed listening to a repetitive thumping coming from the bathroom. She was dressed, but had returned to bed after breakfast, careful to dangle her feet over the side because untying her laces and removing her shoes seemed out of the question. Her head contained a familiar constituent difficult to label: at times it was definitely pain, then it flipped and became regret. Lately, she had been drinking a little too much wine. It was something she was going to have to keep an eye on.

"Cooper?"

But there had been an element of thrill, you couldn't deny that, spying on the neighbours, although now she recognized another feeling for what it was: shame. If only Cooper had not come up from the basement and caught her. If only he'd stayed in bed where, of course, he wasn't sleeping. She wasn't sure what he did at night after she'd gone to bed, but she was fairly certain he wasn't sleeping.

Or reading. Or doing anything at all she would approve of.

"Cooper?"

"Word?"

He was just outside her closed door. "Cooper, what are you doing?"

Cooper's answer came in a high-pitched voice that was not unmelodious and reminded Isabella of the Supremes. "Somebody's going to get hurt," he sang.

She knew he wasn't talking to her, not per se. And she detected no malice, no real threat. She was thinking he was really perfectly well adjusted when he delivered a horrendous kick to her bedroom door. She thought how much she hated the hollow, cheaply made doors of this house. If she opened or closed a door in one end of the house, all the others rattled.

Isabella could use Benny on a morning like this. When Cooper had been a sleep-resistant infant and she, exhausted, had wished for anything other than getting up, Benny would take Cooper to Tim Hortons or out to feed the ducks, leaving her alone in bed to catch up on her sleep. But, ironically, she had been unable to resist the temptation of an empty house on those mornings, and rarely fell back to sleep. There would be the commotion of the two of them leaving, the murmured string of bribes and extensive explanations on Benny's part, followed by the sound of car doors shutting, the engine starting — a period of warm-up on winter mornings — and then, at last, the car was pulling out of the driveway and Isabella would turn over onto her back and open her eyes. There was the smell of coffee, the kick and whirr of the furnace and the profound desire that they not return for hours. Ten minutes later, exploring her own house as though she'd never before seen it, barefoot and carrying a mug of tepid coffee, she would be struck by the vast emptiness of those rooms. But though empty of people, of movement and talk, she would feel the presence of love, like a liquid poured into every nook and cranny of her home.

"Cooper?"

"Mom, were you pissed last night?" He was still standing just outside her door.

"Of course not. And I've asked you not to use that particular word."

"We thinks you were, Mom."

Regret.

"Mom, some missus called."

Isabella sat up on an elbow. "Come in here, Cooper, so I can see you."

The door slowly swung open as though of its own accord; Isabella was reminded of that exhilarating haunted house in Disney World. Cooper had not seen it because he was too frightened, so Isabella had gone in alone, leaving her son and husband to wait for her outside.

Cooper approached her bed and stood stiffly before her.

"Who called?"

"Don't know."

"Did she leave a message?"

"No."

Isabella sniffed. "Have you been lighting matches?"

"No."

She studied him. He looked far too restless. "Why don't you invite someone over today?"

"Can't."

"Why not?"

"Lewis is grounded. It's Stuart's dead uncle's birthday and he's at church. And Andrew is at Lewis's house."

"Stop. Who's grounded?"

"Lewis."

"Then why is Andrew there? Are you sure Lewis is grounded?"

"Yeah, I'm sure. His mom even told me."

"But Andrew is at his house? That doesn't sound grounded."

"Mom, you and Dad don't know what grounded is. Grounded does not mean staying in your room. Grounded means staying in your *house*. Grounded means you can still watch TV, play Xbox and have friends over. Are you laughing? Shut up, Mom."

"I'd appreciate it if you didn't speak that way to me."

And Dad died six months ago.

"Mom, can we buy some Kool-Aid?"

"Certainly."

"When?"

"When did you need it by?"

"One hour. Please."

"Oh, honey, there's the phone again. Could you get it for Mommy?"

"If they don't have black cherry, I want strawberry."

"Get the phone, please?"

Isabella stared at the ceiling. There had been a leak in one of the corners, staining the ceiling a cloudy urine colour. She was thinking about what she overheard last night. It was a relief to hear Darren speak that way to his sister. He needed to stand up for himself.

But do we all possess the capacity for some cruelty? Benny? Herself?

Isabella had wanted to hurt Heather Welbourne, but in the end it was Benny who hurt her, backing away from her after he became sick. Retreating, moving inside himself. Isabella had been grateful for this, for what appeared to simplify her life and protect her dignity, but she could not escape the knowledge that there had been elements of cowardice and cruelty in Benny's actions.

"Think of murderers," she said aloud, thinking of cruelty in general, which led her to listen for Cooper. Where was he? Had he answered the phone? Was he still in the house? Was he safe? She was forever imagining him getting himself beaten up, kidnapped or murdered. Dropping him off at school, which she did two to three times a week when he missed the school bus, Isabella had developed the superstitious habit of glancing back to get a last look at him before he entered the building. She felt that in some way this glance protected him, yet the action always inspired the alarming thought, what if this is the last time I see my son alive?

Cooper returned with the phone. "It's some missus," he said loudly and Isabella gave him a severe, pointless frown. She took the phone.

"Yes? Oh, yes, hi Cindy. Barbeque this Saturday. Darren Foley said it was potluck. But I'm new to all this. Yes, see you then."

Isabella handed the phone back to Cooper. "Did I sound nutty? Did I sound like I was in bed?"

"Mom, you worry too much about what other people think. And you *are* in bed. Listen, pop quiz: how do you know if a Newfie's gay?"

She was having second thoughts about the barbeque, which she had offered to host. It was a few years since she'd had a real party, and this house . . .

She had brought the old barbeque with them when they moved, but the truth was it looked like a fire hazard. She wondered what Home Depot had in stock. She lay back down and closed her eyes. Not too expensive, but new. She felt a slight surge of pleasure at the thought. She and Cooper might go have a look that afternoon. It was a minor hangover. She would get up in a minute.

Isabella's first hangover was her worst hangover.

It was at an end-of-summer outdoor party, she couldn't remember where. She had been restless all that summer. There had been a band and lots of people. Had it been a park, or someone's yard?

She and Benny had been seeing each other for nearly a year, but not on a regular basis. Weeks would go by and she wouldn't hear from him. She wondered what he did on the weekends when she didn't see him. Was he dating other girls? Those his own age? She had heard he was spending some time with that girl Marjorie.

They had made plans to meet at the party. No specific time. He was like that: vague, casual, which left Isabella feeling hijacked. She didn't know if underneath his flirting and foolishness, he was actually humble and shy, incapable of recognizing something — or someone — that could be his, or whether he was insecure and cruel, a person who lined up admirers to count them. She often felt anger towards him stirring inside her.

She and her two friends bought a litre of milk and flask of Kahlua and mixed sombreros in the car before going into the party, which they had heard would be alcohol-free. Isabella's friends talked about how hard it was to get their heads around going back to work. September was only a week away. Isabella added little to the conversation. She knew they were pretending to bemoan the end of summer for her sake. In truth, they were looking forward to teaching again.

It didn't really matter to her, though, because she was daydreaming about Benny.

Isabella drank most of the sombreros. Normally, she did not drink. She knew enough about herself to know that there was a part of her that was different from other people — ruthless, confrontational, eccentric — and that drinking released that part of her. When it was time to get out of the car, her friends had to pull her onto the sidewalk, where she stood swaying. But they were all giggling. They linked their arms through hers and ran up across a lawn. The sun had set, though there was still light, and a breeze had come up. The air did not feel like summer anymore.

It was not a dry party after all. There was a cash bar with beer and wine. The band was inside a tent, where people were dancing, but from the bar the music was muted and hard to identify. Her friends told her to slow down. Have a Coke instead, they suggested. Isabella didn't like the insinuation. She wandered off, searching the crowd for Benny. Her longing for him intensified. It seemed hours had passed by the time she made her way back to her friends.

"Where have you been? We've been looking all over for you."

"Do you see Benny?" She stepped on someone's toe.

"Wow, is she ever loaded. Should we take her home?"

"There he is. Isabella. Look. He's just coming now."

"Where?"

"Right there!" Laughter.

She turned and there he was. In her memory he was standing with a sweet guilty smile in a clearing devoid of other bodies.

He looked as though he was half expecting her to step up and embrace him, and for a moment she thought she would do just that. Instead, she felt anger lift inside her. She slapped him across the face, then fell backwards, hard on her rear end. Her last memory was of herself sitting on the grass like a rag doll, her legs stuck out before her in an unladylike manner. Gasping sounds buzzed about while hands came down to get her. She never asked whose hands.

"I can't believe you did that," her friend said to her over the phone the next day. "He's so nice."

"What did he do after?" Isabella asked in a small voice.

"He spun on his heels and marched off." Her friend sounded satisfied, as though: what did she expect?

Isabella's self-loathing went on for weeks, though it was worse that first day, when she was so hungover she couldn't move from bed, yet had to keep her head elevated or else it would swell to the size of a pumpkin and burst open.

Benny never called. He lived with his parents, so she was afraid to call him.

He could have left the province, or gotten engaged.

She missed him, and eventually she went to his house. She was let in by a teenaged girl — the crying baby, Isabella assumed — who disappeared in search of him. Isabella stood in the foyer, between the two sets of doors, and waited.

Later she would look back at the young woman she had been and see a hollow, lonely person. She would shudder, relieved by the miracle of her life changing course as it had.

She waited ten, fifteen minutes. She assumed Benny was refusing to see her, yet she couldn't budge. She hated herself. She was certain she was shaking from head to toe, but when she glanced down at her hands, they were hanging motionless at her sides.

She was still there when his father came home, bemused to find a silent young woman in his foyer.

"Everything all right here?" he asked her.

She nodded, but wished now she'd left the house. This was beginning to involve too many people.

She heard calling from inside the house, unmistakable confusion. The sister sounded apologetic and defensive.

When Benny appeared he looked surprised, but guarded. Her impression was that there was no hope at all for them.

"I wanted to apologize."

He seemed to be thinking about how to answer that.

"About time."

It was not what she expected him to say. It gave her hope.

"Have you been waiting for my apology?" she whispered, incredulous.

He crossed his arms over his chest, grinning at her reaction. "My sense was that I deserved one."

He was kidding with her now. She adored him.

"I was so drunk, it's no excuse, but I didn't know *what* I was doing, Benny. I'm so sorry."

"You were in the bag, all right, missus. You. Were. In. The. Bag."

Isabella and Cooper were watching television: *Just Shoot Me, King of the Hill, Grounded for Life*. It was midnight when Isabella finished the bottle of wine. A movie was coming on. Isabella sniffed. "Who made that smell, I wonder?"

"Wasn't me."

"Wasn't me. Are you drinking plenty of water?"

"Maybe it was Dad."

Isabella stared at the television. The movie was beginning with a murder.

"Maybe it was," she said.

Ping ping. Now we're both crazy, she thought.

Cooper rose early. He was counting on his mother to sleep late, which she usually did if they'd watched a movie the night before. In their new house, the kitchen was not far from her bedroom, making it essential he not slam the cupboard doors or toss dishes into the sink or drop a spoon on the floor. The more orderly he kept the kitchen, the faster he could clean it up when he heard her begin to stir. These days she did a lot of talking to herself, so he would be amply warned. It was whispering mostly, primarily in the bathroom, though occasionally in the car with him sitting right there next to her.

It's just a way to get through the day.

Why did I agree to that?

Think of murderers.

Nothing alarming, but the idea of her talking to herself around other grown-ups was humiliating. Like around the bird man next door.

He measured the water and flour and mixed them together in a large pot. The directions said to stir thoroughly before heating, and he was very attentive to this. Lumps would spoil everything. He turned up the heat and, once the mixture had come to a boil, waited three minutes, then removed the pot from the stove and dumped in the black cherry Kool-Aid and stirred some more. It was a little thick, which pleased him, and the colour was dark and realistic. He tasted it, then let some run down his chin and wished he still had his camcorder. That had been some awesome piece of machinery. But, thanks to Dad, it was wrecked.

Dad. Where did Dad go to exactly anyway? Since his departure, Cooper had been considering the ramifications of thought. Is a person dead once they stop thinking? On the other hand, perhaps they are just not born yet. Cooper believed he not only remembered his first thought, he remembered being born. Everything was black as night and he was moving towards something — something round with some swampy mottled light to it. It was only now, after being born and going to school, that Cooper figured it must have been Earth. But back then, he wasn't really himself, Cooper, because he didn't have a body. He was travelling away from the black everything to something he had forgotten he knew really well. He never knew anything so well as this thing he had forgotten he knew. Now that he was born, Cooper wasn't exactly sure what it was he had forgotten. Memories were like that, like dreams, they were always one step ahead of you. But Cooper thought it might just have been Life. He had forgotten Life and was going back to it after being away.

His first thought had been, *Oh, I remember this.*

Cooper would like to know what his father's last thought had been. He wondered if it was the same as Cooper's first thought. *Oh, I remember this.* Perhaps not. And what if a person dies suddenly without warning? What about the elimination of thought when you are right in the middle of having a thought? It made

193

the thought seem pretty pointless. Say you eat a poisonous plant, get a whiff of poison gas or burst into flames. You might have been thinking it was time to buy a new fishing rod for your kid, or how lucky are we, another fine day — a comment adults were always making. You might have been in the process of looking forward to something, perhaps your favourite food because you could smell it cooking — spaghetti and meatballs. You're feeling warm and happy and then suddenly you're dead.

Of course, his father had been in la-la land by then. It was unlikely he was thinking about fishing. Or the weather. Or eating. And he probably was not thinking, *Oh, I remember this.*

A door opened and closed and Cooper froze. Luckily, there followed the sound of the bath running. Cooper removed the pitcher of juice from the refrigerator and emptied it into the sink. He poured in his own mixture, still steamy and sweet-smelling, and tiptoed downstairs with it.

Chapter Fourteen

Darren had come home early from work and was in the living room reading the paper. Occasionally he glanced up to see Cooper roaming around outside, possibly looking for another stump, though Darren had already told him one would be enough. It was great to see the boy walking. He was wearing several T-shirts but no jacket or coat. Although it was spring, it was still cool. The wind had come around from the northeast and was cutting. It was important to dress warmly this time of year with the weather so unpredictable, especially if you were out in the woods. Especially if you were pregnant. Darren had been trying to guess how far along Heather was. He didn't want to ask. He had also been wondering who the father was. He watched Cooper disappear behind his truck, which worried him slightly.

He heard a noise from the bathroom. Jeanette. She had returned home from doing errands earlier and immediately disappeared. All was quiet again. Evidently she had not opened the shower curtain.

There had been three herons initially. The crew saw them flying low above the twenty-five-metre high whitecaps, heading for the tanker. Darren imagined it must have been quite a sight, five hundred miles northeast of the Azores and there they were:

three long-winged creatures with folded necks and trailing legs, their bodies rickety as they battled eighty-knot winds to reach the tanker. From the bridge, the crew watched the birds make a sloppy, unimpressive landing on deck, briefly looking more like blue-grey tumbleweeds than birds. They were placed in a storage room, but one died almost immediately and was cast overboard.

The tanker was another week reaching Conception Bay due to headwinds and some nasty weather. A second heron died within a day of Newfoundland, but by then, superstition had set in and none of the crew would approach the storage room. Darren had taken custody of both the dead heron and the lone survivor, who was now in the bathtub, an hour and a half ago. The dead bird was in the freezer between the ice cream and fish patties. Jeanette wasn't going to like that either.

When she emerged from the bathroom, her face was shiny and scrubbed and she was in her pre-bedtime layers.

"Retiring early?" he asked.

She sat down across from him and took some of the newspaper. He wasn't going to be surprised if she didn't speak to him. Not after the other evening when he'd brought up the idea of moving out.

Without looking up, she asked, "Who's that in the bathtub?"

"A heron, but it's not a great blue. I think it's a European species. A grey heron."

"Is that significant?"

"It's unusual. It was on the ship a week and those clowns never even tried to feed it. I might have to take it down to Byron in the morning."

"You haven't been doing much shopping lately," she observed.

It was none of her business, but he didn't want to argue with her.

"And the dinner invitations have dropped off," she added.

He'd forgotten to tell her about the barbeque.

"I did think her cooking was too rich."

"I was only being neighbourly, Jeanette. You made too much of it. She's lonely, her and the boy. I was just trying to help."

"A lonely soul. I agree with you there." She snapped the newspaper. "If the doctors go on strike they're not getting any sympathy from me."

"Were there many goldfish left?"

She glanced up. "Where? In the bathtub?"

Darren slowly drew back the shower curtain, and sure enough, all the goldfish were gone. He had purchased a dozen in at the mall on his way home from the tanker. Half he'd dumped into the tub. The other six were in a clear plastic bag under the sink.

Visiting the tanker had consumed his entire afternoon, though he hadn't been surprised when the crew insisted he come aboard to collect the birds himself. He was ferried out via longliner to the ship, which was enormous and freshly painted bright pink. A group of crewmen followed him as he was taken to the rope locker, a spacious room lined with gleaming yellow lockers where Darren guessed the ropes were stored, since there was not a single one in sight. A handwritten note posted on the door warned, "Live Birds Inside." Although the crew had grown fearful of the herons, someone must have been coming in to clean up because the floor was spotless. It was unusual, Darren was made to understand, that they had kept these birds. The normal practice was to toss them overboard.

The live heron was standing on one leg, beside the dead one. The crew hung back as Darren seized the heron and put it in a box, then slipped its dead companion into a garbage bag. Back on deck, while the crew debated who would carry what down the ladder to the longliner, Darren marvelled at the size of the ship. Its deck was the length of a football field and its total height at least six stories. Birds lost over the Atlantic often sought refuge on these vessels. Darren imagined the birds' attraction, not only to the ship's almighty size and excessive pinkness, but to its sheer presence over the unyielding seascape, as though it had been invoked not through chance, but necessity.

Now the heron was standing in the bathtub beside the stump he and Cooper had dug out of Darren's garden shed. Its neck and head were sunk to the level of its grey wings, which were folded in such a way that they resembled a cloak draped over the bird's back and shoulders, lending it an elegant Count Dracula air despite the lavender-coloured tub. Minutes passed, during which neither the heron nor Darren moved, and then the heron lifted its head high on its serpentine neck and with its right leg made a few leisurely attempts to scale the side of the bathtub. Darren backed away and the bird defecated. The feces was projected the length of the tub and Darren saw that among the otherwise dazzling yellow matter there were some black bits — indicative of bleeding in the guts.

He knelt beside the tub and dumped in the remaining half dozen goldfish, but knew he would be bringing the heron to Byron the next day.

When he returned to the living room, Jeanette was gone.

The heron survived the night, but had rejected the second course of goldfish, which were either floating belly up or moving sluggishly through the dirty water. While Darren scooped them up with a drinking glass and flushed them down the toilet, the heron stood oblivious, its black and white crest rising and falling like a toy whose batteries are running low.

For nearly two decades, Byron Murphy had run the Southern Shore Animal Rescue Park. Southern Shore Concentration Camp was more like it, Darren thought to himself. Sure, half the animals brought to it perished. Nonetheless, he called ahead and left a message with Byron that he was bringing down an unusual heron.

He took the Goulds bypass without giving it a second thought and eventually passed the very spot where Heather had been pulled over for speeding. He wondered what she was doing today. He thought about seeing her at the barbeque on the weekend, then worried she might not show up. A few miles on, he turned in at Byron's and was concerned when he saw the parking area vacant. Byron lived alone in a bungalow that Darren had the misfortune to visit only once; the medley of odours resulting from fried meat, sour clothing and sick birds had been alarming. Darren didn't like to think about the things he and Byron had in common, especially the fact they were both bachelors.

The birds were kept in a long shed beside the house. But here too the lot was empty. The Southern Shore Animal Rescue Park, as its name suggested, served as both hospital and nature park. It was through the latter role that Byron made his meagre income. The place was looking more rundown than Darren recalled, though it had never been particularly shipshape, and then the door to the Rehabilitation Centre, as Byron called the shed, opened and Byron stepped out and waved. As usual, he was wearing shorts.

Darren had first met Byron after spending a summer as field assistant for a renowned seabird biologist, which meant Darren spent three months sitting in a dark cabin on an offshore island blowing eggs for that biologist's illegal personal collection. He came back to university disillusioned and in bad spirits. Byron had worn his intelligence openly and, Darren thought, arrogantly. Competition between the two had been spontaneous. It took all the years of graduate school for this to wear off, though Darren remained childishly vigilant of Byron's excessive knowledge.

Byron was smiling as he crossed the lot. He seemed happy to see Darren.

"Where are the school buses?" Darren asked.

Byron made a dismissive gesture with his hand and said, "Let's have a look at that heron."

Darren opened the back of his truck and watched as Byron leaned in to have a peek. He still wore his brown hair parted

199

down the middle, an antiquated style that took some getting used to. His dark eyes were enormous, round and perpetually startled. They reminded Darren of a tree-clinging bush baby.

"How long has it been without food?"

"I gave it some goldfish last night."

"How many?"

"Half a dozen."

"And before that?"

"At least a week."

Byron was shaking his head and frowning. "The goldfish were a disastrous idea." He lifted the box and Darren followed him inside.

The "hospital" smelled of feces, dead fish and antiseptic. They entered the small operating room where an aluminum table folded out from the wall, similar to a changing table in a public washroom. Byron placed the box on the table and stood blinking.

"You'll have to excuse me if I seem a bit slow off the mark. I was up all night with an owl. Normally, first thing I do is leave the bird alone. Do nothing. Don't touch it. Put it in a dark room with the temperature a few degrees above the comfort zone. Birds come in, no meat on them — "

"I'm not sure that bird can afford to be left alone, Byron." Byron's friendly lecturing always made Darren defensive. He put up with it because he was the one who had landed the secure government job, while Byron was stuck here becoming yearly more eccentric and less respected.

"Second thing I do, after leaving it alone, is hydrate it. More important than food. But you know that." Here he shook his head again. He went over to a small table and picked up a large syringe and filled it with Gatorade. "If we can stabilize the electrolytes . . . . Would you mind holding this?"

Darren took the syringe and rubber tube, then stood obediently back a few feet as Byron opened the box.

"Too late, Darren."

"What?"

"It's gone."

Darren approached Byron and the two of them stood silent for a moment, gazing in at the crumpled heron. Already, it seemed, its colours were fading.

Byron took a deep, catching breath. "When you said unusual heron, Darren, I thought maybe you had a cattle egret. But now this is something. This *is* something." And he lifted the body out of the box and laid it on the metal table. "Venture a guess?"

"Grey heron?"

Byron looked disappointed. He turned the heron over onto its back and spread the wings. The keel was clearly outlined. There was no doubt the bird had been consuming its own muscles for days. Here was a body crying out for forced hydration.

"Grey heron. Yes, indeed." Byron stroked the bird's feathered thighs. "White thighs. White headlights. Very diagnostic."

Byron looked at Darren.

"You see what I'm getting at? These white patches on the leading edge of the wing, just past the carpel joint. This is a grey heron, Darren, absolutely no question. Congratulations."

"Well —"

"Would have been an improbable sighting only a few years ago. What you've got here, of course, is a ship-assist. One other thing. Greys tend to curl their toes in flight. Not as leggy as our great blues. Something to keep in mind should you see a great blue that doesn't look quite right, Darren. When you're out and about. Doing what you do."

As Byron spoke, he fiddled with the heron, patting down its feathers and pulling its legs straight, then doing the same with its neck and head so the body was stretched several feet across the table. To have come all this way, Darren thought, only to die in a box in the company of two well-meaning but essentially ineffective humans. But he was not surprised the bird had died. He had been expecting it.

He placed the syringe on the table. He was more interested in Byron's excessive knowledge of other things.

"Listen, Byron," he said casually. "Have you ever read of the Bruce Effect being observed in humans?"

"What? How did we get onto the Bruce Effect?"

"Seems a bit unlikely, doesn't it?"

"Quite."

Byron laid the heron back in the box and closed the lid. Darren could see that Byron's mind was elsewhere.

"They're shutting me down."

"What?"

"Operating without the proper permits. Not licensed for veterinary medicine. A few other infringements. I thought you knew."

"I had no idea. Have you been fined?"

"Good heavens, no."

This explained the empty parking lot, the lack of school buses. And, come to think of it, the hand-painted sign hadn't been there at the edge of the road.

"I'm sorry to hear that."

Byron shrugged. "Want to have a look around? It may be your last opportunity."

"You bet. Who's in the recovery room?"

"Boreal owl." Byron opened the door partway and Darren leaned in. The room was dark, but in an elevated wire cage Darren could see a kitten-sized bird racing around, startled by their entry. It wore an orange figure-eight bandage on one wing.

"It was hit by a car and found on the side of the road," Byron said. "Broken humerus." At the sound of Byron's voice, the owl stopped and huddled in a far corner. Darren had watched Byron set bones a number of times. Byron could feel the break with his fingers. Like a piece of cloth laid over gravel, he explained, he could "hear" it with his fingers.

"There's also a gannet in the closet. It keeps getting out and scaring the owl. Maybe you could take it with you? It just needs to be released."

Darren followed Byron into the rodent nursery where normally rats and mice were housed in stacked drawers. Most of the drawers stood empty. But the truth was, Darren was not surprised by this turn of events.

"Have they said what they plan to do with the birds?"

"They'll be donated to the museum," Byron said. He opened the freezer and spoke through a cloud of condensed air. "Didn't know what to do with these fellows. Might be of use to someone."

Darren peered in at the heap of frozen rodents. The bodies were coiled around each other as though they had died huddled together for warmth, though certainly Byron would have killed them first.

"A hundred and thirteen." Byron spoke absently, as though he were speaking to himself. Darren figured he normally did a fair amount of that anyway.

"I think I have time for a quick tour of the park, Byron."

"Hey, excellent. I'll grab my coat. Don't let me forget the gannet when we get back."

Darren nodded, knowing he wouldn't forget, but hoping Byron would.

They exited the Rehabilitation Centre and took a shortcut through a boggy gully to the nature walk proper, which was similar to the shortcut but wider. Here and there, in response to seasonal wetness, planks had been laid down, though many had sunk below the level of water and moss and shifted unpredictably beneath their feet. Various plants were labelled, as with a card marked "Lambkill, *Kalmia angustifolia*" wrapped in translucent plastic and tied to a plant with string.

Darren remembered an argument that had taken place between them nearly twenty years earlier, when he made one of his first, nosy visits to the park. Byron had incorrectly labelled black spruce as white — or was it white spruce, black? — but when Darren corrected him, Byron's sulking, uncompromising reaction had been surprising. Darren wondered where that tree had stood and for the first time entertained the possibility that he, rather than Byron, might have been mistaken.

Although the sky was cloudy, when they emerged onto open

field, the bronzed brightness blanketing the landscape was a relief. A raised boardwalk snaked several feet above the barrens and into a compound enclosed by a wire fence. They stepped up onto the boardwalk and entered the compound through a gate that swung unevenly and whose hinges, Darren saw, were loose. Once they were inside, Byron fiddled for a moment with the gate, but it wouldn't catch and he gave up.

"I always made a show of closing the gates when we had visitors," he said, "but frankly, it's not necessary."

A series of whistles, descending note by note and called out so clearly they made the air seem hollow, sounded nearby. Three snowy owls were emerging from behind a stand of shrubs, half hopping, half walking, while a fourth did not approach but stood his ground, whistling at them.

"The male," Byron said. "Been here fifteen years."

One of the owls jumped and spread its wings, and the wind carried it a few feet.

None of them could fly and Darren vaguely knew their histories. One was a wing amputee. The others had broken bones that had mended, but imperfections in the healing process prevented true recovery of flight. There was also the problem of permanent wing droop, a condition that made the birds cosmetically unviable for public viewing. Real zoological parks did not want them. Displayed inside a glass case was the most anyone could hope for them now.

The owls were densely feathered, even on their legs and toes. They were splendid, but also preposterous. For years they had been fed dead rodents that Byron first prepared by whacking their skulls against the edge of a table. As the hopping alternated with clumsy walking, Darren thought they looked more like children waddling around in snowsuits than magnificent white owls. Indeed, they were like children — children placed and forgotten in a bleak refugee camp. Or children locked up in closets and discovered at eight years of age, unable to speak or make eye contact.

"Missing one," Byron said, looking around.

Even so, a closet, a camp — wouldn't those be better than the provincial museum?

Byron was scanning the perimeter of the enclosure. "Now and then one gets carried over the fence if it's gusty. Or it walks out the gate. But it always hangs around outside and waits for me. Oh, there, look."

Several hundred metres away, beyond the enclosure, an animal was coming over the hummocky ground and, like the ones inside, occasionally jumping up and attempting flight.

Byron went back out the gate to await the returning owl. Seeing Byron, the owl hesitated, then continued towards the compound. It reached the fence and pressed up against it, as though there was the possibility it would give way, and Byron circled out a short distance before coming back for it. The owl turned over onto its back, its huge wings falling open, and presented Byron with its black talons. Byron tugged a glove out of his back pocket and handed it to the owl as one might hand a favourite blanket to a sleepy child, and with a motion that seemed almost gluttonous in its speed and readiness, both talons reached out to clasp the glove.

Byron leaned over and grabbed the owl's legs and carried it like a farmyard chicken back inside the compound.

It was time to go. Darren headed towards Byron. When he reached him he laid his hand on Byron's shoulder, lightly, and Byron flinched, as though it had been a long time since he'd been touched.

They returned to the Rehabilitation Centre in silence. Byron's reaction to his touch left Darren feeling lost, disoriented. He thought of Heather and their first meeting in the woods, her blond hair wet against her cheeks, the wild expression in her eyes.

"Coming to the barbeque this weekend?" Darren asked. He was anxious to get back in the truck and be gone.

"Still having that, are they? Tenacious bunch."

"They're always asking about you," Darren said.

"But there was one report. Strictly anecdotal, however."

"Huh?"

"The Bruce Effect in humans."

Darren stood still. "Do you recall the details?"

"I do. It was in a remote village somewhere in South America. I believe the location was withheld. An isolated group of closely related individuals, numbering in the hundreds. They carried a sex-linked blood disorder that resulted in a high rate of fatality in young males, just past puberty. But a strictly monogamous society. As a result, young impregnated women were frequently left widowed. Someone working in the area — on something else entirely, a botanist I believe — observed that when a widowed woman took up with another male, in a number of instances her pregnancy vanished. Until, of course, she became pregnant by the new male."

"They weren't aborting them?"

"There was no evidence to support that."

"I suppose this was restricted to the first trimester?"

"Heaven's, yes. I can't see it happening any later than ten weeks. Can you? Fetal reabsorption? This isn't science fiction, Darren."

"No."

"Now hold on while I fetch the gannet."

It was nearly midnight by the time Darren got home and dropped the tailgate, so he was surprised when Cooper materialized at his side.

Darren dug out his spotlight and trained it on the gannet, which was opening and closing its bill and producing a plaintive, raspy two-syllable cry. Its thick neck was mobile, curling and uncurling snake-like above its body, but its torso and dirty leathery feet were clearly paralyzed. There wasn't much hope for the creature and Darren was annoyed at Byron for passing it off on him. Perhaps Byron simply wanted to avoid seeing another bird die.

Darren looked from the bird to the boy and wondered if he should suggest Cooper go home to bed. But was Isabella even there? Perhaps she was out shopping? No, that was impossible. What would be open at this hour?

"Cool eyes," the boy said, and Darren nodded. He had to agree. They were perfectly circular and of a colour like no human's: the orbital ring was cobalt blue and the iris a pale, cold grey. The eyes of a goddess, he thought. He hoped Cooper hadn't seen the bright orange feces dripping from the tail feathers. He switched the spotlight off and reached in for the bird. It was the weight of a dressed turkey.

"That's a sin," Cooper said in a soft, admonishing voice and Darren figured not a whole lot got past that boy.

"Can I have him?"

Darren laughed. "I don't think so."

As he walked towards his house, Cooper yelled out, "Are you sure I can't have him, Mr. Foley?"

"I'm sure," he yelled over his shoulder.

His foyer was dark and he nearly tripped over a pile of shopping bags. Jeanette was sitting in the living room, dressed for bed.

"I didn't know if you were coming home," she said.

"What is all this? Why would you think a thing like that?" As he stepped around the bags, the gannet began struggling and he almost dropped it.

"What have you got there?"

"Gannet. I'll put it in the basement for the night. Why didn't you think I was coming home?"

She shrugged. "Brenda called. She said you stopped in at the Pearly a few days ago with a woman. I thought it must have been Isabella, but Brenda said the woman was pregnant."

He didn't know what to say. He felt guilty and disloyal for not having mentioned Heather to his sister before. He had wanted to. The gannet was growing impatient. He squeezed it with his forearm and it went still.

"Jeanette — "

"I bought some new clothes. But when I got them home I discovered none of them fit. I'll return them tomorrow."

"You didn't try them on at the store?"

"There wasn't enough time."

But he knew his sister would have trouble undressing in those small change rooms. He had nothing to say to that. It was how it was done. He carried the gannet downstairs and lowered it into the old cardboard box that served as an overnighter for seabirds. The gannet looked comatose. Even if it were not doomed, it would be several years before its transformation into a white adult, brilliant in the sunlight.

Darren sat back on his heels. He considered the bird's oceanic journey since leaving its nest last September. And before that, there would have been all those weeks of summer, the lone occupant of its increasingly filthy nest, the sole object of its parents' immense reproductive investment. All those minutes, hours, days — nothing to do but wait for its next meal, flap its wings, test and build its strength. The unimaginable promise of flight. But when that moment came, many leapt from the cliff and fell directly to the sea, somersaulting over its hard surface, sprained and broken. No second chance.

Yet others left as though they were only daydreaming of doing so: one or two moments see-sawing in the air before instinct engaged, and they were gone for years.

While his mother slept through the second half of the movie, Cooper slipped outside. It was a dark night, but after a while he could see everything he needed to see. Mr. Foley's truck was not in the driveway.

Sometimes Cooper felt the impulse to break something: someone's glass door or lawn statue. How easy would that be? You could sneak out in the night and under cover of dark pick up a rock and aim it in. Then run. How would they ever catch you? By the time the police were there you'd be back in your bed. No one would know. Unless they got hold of your thoughts.

The door to the shed opened easily. It was unlocked and the hinges worked smooth as anything, not a squeak. Cooper switched on his flashlight. On one side of the shed was a pile of wood. This was where Mr. Foley had found the stump for the heron. It was meant to make the bird feel more comfortable in Mr. Foley's purple bathtub, but how retarded was that. On the other side of the shed was the lawn mower and work table. Under the work table was the can of gasoline for running the lawn mower. Mr. Foley had suggested hiring Cooper to mow his lawn. When Cooper was a bit older, he had said, but Cooper figured it was the type of thing that would never happen. Plus, he was old enough now.

The gasoline can had a long neck and was easy to tip, without having to be lifted, and Cooper went straight to work, filling his largest Super Soaker canister. He got a few drops of gas on the floor, but knew they would evaporate. He had experience with gasoline and engines because he and his father used to go on fishing trips with another man — a client of his father's — and the man's grandson, who lived in Grand Falls-Windsor. The grandson's name was Danny and Cooper liked him, but the only time he ever saw him was once each summer.

Cooper and his father would meet Danny and his grandfather at an Irving station along the Trans-Canada Highway, then they would all get into Danny's grandfather's truck and drive an hour down a dirt road. Cooper would fall asleep during the drive, but wake in time to see them approaching a lake and the cabin belonging to Danny's grandfather. They would get out of the truck and the grandfather would yell, Hey, boys, give us a hand with this gear! A smell that Cooper had forgotten all year would come off the lake. It was fishy and rank, but at the same time fresh and soft. It was a feeling on his face as much as a smell in his nose.

The four of them would go out in the boat right away to fish before it got dark. Danny's grandfather would make sure the engine had gas and they would motor out across the lake to a special spot they knew was good for trouting. Just before getting there, Danny would reach over to cut the engine and they would glide quietly across the water. They spoke in whispers.

They fished, concentrating on the water and where their lines disappeared into it, and the boys would beg not to have to go in. But Danny's grandfather would remind them there was all of tomorrow and that he needed something more substantial than air to swallow, and Cooper's father would laugh and say, That's right, it's getting dark.

Cooper liked Danny, and he envied him for having a grandfather with a fishing cabin. But Danny never stopped talking and moving until he fell asleep. The cabin had its own smell too, like dirt and garbage and rot, but after the first night Cooper didn't mind. The boys had their supper and the two men would sit and have their drinks. Cooper's father would talk about things Cooper did not understand and had never heard him talk about at home. Every once in a while he would catch Cooper watching him and give him a big grin, and Cooper would remember they had a whole day of trouting to look forward to.

Meanwhile, Danny would be crawling all over his grandfather, who would just laugh and say, Mind the drink now son, mind the drink.

Danny hated gutting the fish, so after the first year Cooper got into the habit of doing it. He knew he was good at it and he liked the responsibility of handling the sharp knife. One evening they came back in with dozens of trout, more than they'd ever caught. The other three went in the cabin but Cooper stayed outside to gut the fish. He wanted to get right at it. There were promises of help, but he didn't mind. He knelt down and began removing the fish from the two baskets. He worked carefully and steadily — cutting off the head, slitting the belly, removing the guts — aware that he was getting faster and more efficient. Each time he reached for another fish he briefly examined it, thinking about who had caught it. He placed the cleaned fish in a row on the ground beside him.

The door opened and his father and Danny's grandfather came out with their bottles of beer and stood a few feet away, watching him work.

"He's a real crackerjack at that," Danny's grandfather said after a while.

Cooper didn't look up.

"He's my boy all right," his father said.

Cooper had a feeling then of bursting. He concentrated on preventing any kind of expression from showing on his face. He wanted his face to look like stone. He didn't want anyone to know what he felt. He wasn't really sure himself what he was feeling.

He heard Danny's grandfather take a long swallow of beer, then say, "My oh my, what a day," before going back inside the cabin.

His father bent down to gaze at the gutted fish. "We'll have some feed tonight, won't we?"

Cooper nodded, but still could not look up.

He felt his father's hand tug playfully at his hair.

Cooper pushed the gas can back under Mr. Foley's work table. The moment he was outside he saw the truck pulling into the driveway, so he hid his canister behind a bush to retrieve later and went out to see what Mr. Foley had in his truck.

Mr. Foley was just letting down the tailgate when Cooper came up.

"What is that thing?" Cooper asked.

"Christ. Where did you come from?"

"It's making a sound like a puppy," Cooper said. "What is it? What are you going to do with it?"

"Northern gannet. A type of seabird."

Its cries put Cooper off a little, but he couldn't resist getting closer to it. Mr. Foley was shining a deadly powerful spotlight on it and Cooper could see how the tip of each chocolate-coloured feather bore an identical streak of white. It looked as though a big dark bird had been dusted with white powder so evenly it had been measured. It looked like a math exercise. And its eyes were perfect circles and as beautiful as marbles or sea glass. They looked like the eyes of someone gone crazy.

"What are you going to do with it, Mr. Foley?"

"Let it rest a few days, then let it go. It might just be bruised, or have sprained something."

"Can I have it?"

"I don't think so."

Mr. Foley turned off the spotlight and the bird became colourless.

"Will it find its family after you let it go?"

"Unlikely." Mr. Foley leaned towards the bird and placed his forearm right in front of the bird's face. The bird immediately latched onto his wrist. "But you never know."

Cooper stepped back. "Careful."

"Not to worry," Mr. Foley said. "If he grabs my arm he won't get my eye, right?"

Mr. Foley placed his other hand over the gannet's face, covering its spectacular eyes. The gannet released his wrist and Mr. Foley scooped him up under his arm, his hand still shielding the bird's eyes.

"Are you looking forward to the barbeque this weekend?" Mr. Foley asked.

Cooper shrugged.

"Why not? It'll be fun."

Cooper stood beside the truck, watching Mr. Foley carry the bird upside down into his house.

Cooper had choked on a candy once. His father had come across the room and picked him up so quickly Cooper didn't even know what was happening. Suddenly he was upside down and his father was shaking him. Cooper coughed the candy back into his mouth where its sweetness was so familiar, but his

212

father was still shaking him. Finally Cooper spit it out on the carpet, and his father spun him around and hugged him. After a while his father said, Better not tell your mother.

PART FOUR

Chapter Fifteen

How long has it been since she put words on paper? Weeks? Months? Mandy doesn't remember. She's been writing her stories in her head, in bed with her eyes open in the middle of the night, Bill wrapped around her and so snuggled in she thinks she might leap from her skin.

Lying beside him in the dark she has been writing a story about anger. A surprising thing for it to be about because when Suse Hayes starts out looking for that lost cow she isn't angry. She is a big girl, already her full height and bearing hefty, beautiful breasts with black areolae, though she doesn't know this is the name for them. Suse's legs are strong and the hair on them is thick and soft. She would have married a man who picked on her because she was so rugged and unassailable. She would fill a bucket with partridgeberries in fifteen minutes, talking to her companions all the while. She talked non-stop and often repeated herself. Some would have avoided her. Others would have said she was the finest kind. There was something of the little girl that stayed with the grown woman. You thought that when she smiled. Alone, she slipped her hand through the buttons of her dress and lifted one of her breasts, always astonished by its weight.

*

The leaves are out, some flowers, but what a miserable spring. And now, a barbeque. Bill could take it or leave it. But they had made up their minds, they'd promised Heather they would go. In fact, Mandy had been quite insistent about it, and now she's doing this dragging-her-ass routine, stopping at Shoppers to grab a few things, moving as slowly as she can across the parking lot like she's Miss Depressed Newfoundland and Labrador.

Yes, they'd promised Heather, who had emerged after months of recovering from frostbite about to have — *surprise* — a baby, though no one will tell Bill who the father is.

"What's the matter with you?" Bill asks. "Writer's block?"

Mandy stops in front of the doors. He figures she thinks they're automatic and is waiting for them to open, but then she gathers up all of today's strange anger and says, "Guess again."

He follows her inside and then as she tromps up and down the aisles in her boots, collecting the telltale evidence: can of Coke, bag of Doritos, box of tampons, bottle of Advil. He realizes she is giving off that aura: her lank hair, pale forehead, that complex, irrestible body odour. He stands behind her in the lineup, inching his way closer, pretending he's never met her, doesn't know squat. She spins around and scowls up at him.

He steps back into someone.

"Hey, how's it going, old man?" It's Rex Chafe, cradling a bottle of green Scope.

"Great. Just off for a barbeque."

"First barbeque of the season, is it?"

"First one." Has he seen all Mandy's purchases, the nosy bastard?

"Sure, they're calling for snow."

Bill shrugs.

"What's a barbeque without snow?"

"Right on."

Back in the car she starts in again about Suse Hayes.

216

"All I want you to do is admit to the possibility of foul play. Just admit to the *possibility*."

"I can't. I don't believe it happened. I believe she got lost in the woods. That's all I believe. That's one hundred percent all I believe."

"And she just died? People don't just die."

"Yes. They do."

"But there has to be a reason."

He doesn't have an answer to that. He knows he's being pigheaded, but doesn't care.

"You can't admit to even the tiniest possibility?"

"No."

"Well, fuck you."

"Are we picking up Heather?"

"Stop worrying about Heather all the time. She's got a car, mister fucking helpful. Oh, perfect, it's raining."

"I'm not worrying about her. I thought you were worrying about her."

"Not me."

"Then let's not go to this thing."

"Shut up, Bill. We're going, okay?"

"Are you sure Heather is coming?"

Silence.

"A get-together with the granola crowd is not my idea of a good time."

"It's not the granola crowd, it's the nature crowd. You're so out of it. Where are you going?"

"Making sure Heather is coming."

Bill pulls into Heather's driveway and parks behind her Echo. They sit and look at the house. Though it's late afternoon, all the blinds are closed. It had been sunny earlier and the sky is still partly blue. A solid grey cloud is closing over it like a lid over an eye. Bill, who grew up in a suburb similar to this one, hates the hollow look of them this time of year. The yards, trees, houses, cars — all seem stripped down to their skeletal essentials. Everything is rigid and inflexible, like metal, and the wind, which has been gaining force, can only tease free some paper scraps and old leaves.

Mandy gets out of the car and walks up to the house. Bill watches her press the doorbell, knock, then try the doorknob. She turns her back to the wind and the few spits of rain. She looks young.

She returns to the car. "It's locked. She must already be there."

"But her car is here."

"So?"

Bill gets out and hurries up to the door. He's prepared to pound on it, but when he tries the doorknob, it opens. He steps in. It's not until he's inside that he realizes how fierce the wind was outside. The foyer is dark and still. There is a pleasant smell, like tomato sauce.

"Heather?"

"Hello?"

He doesn't know the house well, but it's small and he finds her in her bedroom, sitting in a large armchair. Her face and neck are drawn and thin. She seems to have lost weight, except for that protrusion. The place is not as tidy as he would have expected.

"Hey, Heather. What's up?" He's surprised he doesn't feel more awkward.

"What do you mean?"

"All set for the barbeque?"

"Well, I was just sitting here thinking about that. I don't know if I can go, after all, Bill. Where's Mandy?"

"Car."

Heather nods. For a moment it looks like she can't speak. "Is she mad at me?'

"Mad at everyone."

"You know, I can barely move with this stomach. And I hate barbeques."

Heather is slowly running her hands over her stomach, as though she is caressing herself, but it's not really her, Bill thinks, it's somebody else — the baby. "Barbeques? The great social leveller? Come on."

She laughs.

"Are you cooking something?"

"It's potluck, right?"

"What?"

"The barbeque. You're supposed to bring something. I made a casserole."

Bill realizes he and Mandy will fail to make a contribution. "Well, then. Better get it. We're not leaving without you."

Heather pushes herself to the edge of the chair. "I guess Mandy is insisting you go?"

"Come on. We're all going."

"I promise to meet you there. Bill, I promise."

"Should I believe you?"

"Yes."

Mandy walks Suse across a cobble beach where a man is hunched down repairing his boat in the fog. Seeing the girl pass, and how late in the day it is, the man thinks, That'll be some job, to go looking for her in this fog. Mandy glares suspiciously at the man, but Suse continues on. There is one cow that always wanders away from the others. It can take half a day, sometimes, to find her and bring her home. But Suse likes cow hunting. She likes work in general. She sings as she walks, stepping briskly. Some say they can hear her singing as far as Admiral's Cove. The air is cold and wet, and all day the fog hangs over a landscape that is open and mixed — not the dense fir forest that will have grown back when two sisters become lost.

Twenty-three years after Suse disappears, a father and his son are out in the woods cutting firewood. Mandy recognizes the place. When the father announces it's time for a break, the son sprints down to the river to fill the kettle. On his way he finds her. In the months to come he will hear it going around that she was in a sitting position, but to the boy, who sees her first, she looks like a pile of animal bones. He comes back up the slope with the water, not mentioning to his father until they are boiling the kettle that he's found one of their missing sheep. But when the father goes down to have a look for himself, a part of him goes cold. The hair is still on her head. They put her bones in a wooden box and bring her home.

Bill finds the cul-de-sac — Goodridge Place — just as the rain turns to hail. He shuts off the car and he and Mandy listen to the sound on the roof and windshield: like someone flinging handfuls of gravel at them. They run to the house, then wait several minutes at the front door before a boy lets them in, saying only, "They're out back."

They make their way through to the kitchen where a woman is standing at the window, looking out onto the deck where a second woman and a man are stooped over a barbeque. Bill can see the hail bouncing on the deck floorboards.

The woman inside turns and says, "She's not having much luck getting the thing started. And it's brand new. My brother Darren is helping her."

Bill doesn't have a reply for this woman. He is surprised that after only a few seconds in her company, he doesn't like her.

"I'm Jeanette Foley," she says. "Another disappointing day, isn't it?"

"This weather's cracked," says the boy, behind them. When they turn, he is crawling into the kitchen on his hands and knees.

"Cooper, get up off that floor," Jeanette scolds. "Your poor mother is trying to have a party."

Bill flinches. He'd like to leave and wishes he hadn't gone out of his way to convince Heather to come. Mandy is grinning at the boy, her hands on her hips, and Bill has the crazy notion she's about to get down on the floor and roll around with him, like a pair of puppies.

The boy stands and shuffles out of the room and down the hall.

"Honestly," Jeanette says, shaking her head.

It develops into one of those parties where most of the women are unfriendly, the men are asleep-standing, and no one really drinks enough. There is an odd assortment of people and the kitchen is cold. Bill hears the hostess, Isabella, announce it's nearly June, she will not turn on the furnace. He is standing with Mandy, who is talking about being stuck in an elevator, and Jeanette, who is talking about the cost of a new screen door, when he notices the snow. He says nothing, as though he is responsible for it, but after several minutes everyone has seen it coming down and there is a communal moan.

"Perhaps there won't be a summer this year," Isabella remarks. She and Bill are the only ones drinking.

"That's cracked," the boy says.

"Yes, my darling, it is."

"A year with no summer," Jeanette says. "God help us."

"You know, it's happened before," Bill says. "A year with no summer."

"When was this, Bill?" Mandy asks, stepping directly in front of him.

"1820s. Maybe."

Strangely, both women laugh at him.

"Go on with your story," Mandy says.

Bill's lost interest. It's a long story. To get the full impact of it, it's a long story. "Heather's arrived," he points out.

"Finally. So go on with the story, Bill, for fuck's sake."

He sees Jeanette register shock. "It was cold. Snow stayed on the ground all summer. I mean, in Canada. Fish died. Plants turned black. Very crappy, miserable weather."

"Imagine."

"Could it happen again?" Jeanette asks.

"No, it's not going to happen again," her brother, the Darren fellow, says. "I wish everyone would just relax. There will be a break in the weather by the weekend."

Mandy has swivelled in Darren's direction. Bill watches Darren recognize her and smile warmly.

"Who's our hostess?" Bill asks Jeanette.

"That's Isabella Martin. Her husband died last year. Forgive me for saying so, but sometimes you wouldn't know it."

Heather, Bill realizes, has not come all the way into the room, but is hanging back a few feet, gripping her casserole dish as though it's either red-hot or explosive. He is about to go to her, but Darren gets there first — another warm smile from the man — and takes the casserole.

Bill looks around, searching for Mandy, but she has left the room. The bathroom, he figures, given today's biology. She is so fixated on the Suse girl. If only Suse this, if only Suse that. What's going on with her? It's possible she decided to walk home without telling him.

But he finds her in the living room with the boy — the crawler. The two are sitting together on the sofa with Mandy's bag of Doritos, like teenaged boyfriend and girlfriend. She looks up at Bill and does that thing with her eyes: squeezing them together and briefly staring at him hard. It's a far cry from an expression of love and warmth, but he takes a seat beside her anyway.

"I've always had an amazing imagination too" she is telling the boy. "All kinds of crazy stuff."

"Sweet."

"I think it helps with my writing."

Bill sniffs covertly. He smells something tangy and sweet. Could it be coming off the boy? Perhaps he needs a bath.

"For example," Mandy tells the boy, "when I was a kid I had a problem swallowing. For like three years the only thing I could eat was Campbell's tomato soup."

"Hardcore."

"Poor Mandy," Bill says, thinking she would do better to confide in him, so that it is with good reason, he believes, that she turns to him now.

He reaches out to rub her shoulder, but she immediately turns back to the boy and says, "No one knew. Except for my sister."

"Holy crap. My father can't eat shit."

"Which one is he?"

"Not here," the boy says.

Bill wants to press close to Mandy's body flooded with its hormones. He tries to recall the sharp, pinpoint smell of her underarms. He imagines lifting her arm and pressing his nose into that soft hidden tissue.

But he wants to tell her something. What is it? That what happened to that girl, Suse Hayes, could have happened to anyone. That's been his point all along, he realizes. Foul play or not, it could have happened to anyone. There is no promise for anyone that life will go well. She's taking it too goddamn personally.

"Mandy, let's go."

"Do you want to know how to make fake blood?" the boy says.

"Why? What time is it?" Mandy asks Bill.

The boy lifts a bony wrist and inspects an invisible watch. Then he looks at Bill and says, "Half past, kiss my ass, quarter to your hole."

Mandy laughs. "Did you hear that, Bill?"

"Do you want to know how to make fake blood? I got an awesome recipe."

"Hi, Heather."

Heather has come partway into the room. She stops and stares at the three of them. She looks around and slowly lowers herself onto a box. "I was looking for the bathroom," she says to the boy.

"What's wrong, Heather?"

"You're crushing our new pool," the boy says.

Bill watches Heather get to her feet as quickly as possible. She lurches left, then right.

"You okay?" he asks, feeling guilty that he talked her into coming.

"Perfect." She sounds winded.

When Mandy begins talking about Suse Hayes, Bill wants to groan out loud. But she is ignoring him, speaking exclusively to Heather and the boy. He listens to Mandy confirm what he told them that snowy night driving back from Cape Broyle, but she is embellishing and after a few minutes Bill finds himself spellbound. She explains that Suse knows where that old cow will be. Suse never just gets lost. Her first spasm had come earlier in the day. It was mild and distant but she knew what it was. Suse has not menstruated for months. And remember, Mandy says, she's clever. Cow hunting so late in the day is no accident. Now the spasms involve everything God has placed in her abdominal cavity: uterus, ovaries, intestines, bladder, vagina and rectum — though Mandy admits Suse probably doesn't know these are the words for them. When Suse emerges onto the edge of that meadow, she sees the cow. It's always in the same spot. She sits among the goldenrod and purple asters, still blooming this late in the year, and takes off her sunbonnet and wipes her forehead. She tells the cow she'll be back for it as soon as she can, though maybe not until the next day. She knows it won't be long before people are out looking for her and she is eager to escape any attempt to rescue her. She stands and walks a while until she trips and slides down a gully. At the bottom, she curls onto her side and realizes she left her sunbonnet with the cow. It's a whopper of a pain and it will last for hours, well into the night, obliterating the world.

Heather is still standing. She looks at Bill and he can see how upset she is by the story. He wishes the boy hadn't heard it.

"How do you know she was pregnant?" Heather whispers.

"She doesn't," Bill says. "She made it up."

"What a terrible, sad story," Heather says.

"It's possible," Mandy says.

"It's possible she just got lost," Bill says.

"Hardcore," the boy says.

Bill can hear the hum of the not-so-lively party in the kitchen and a gravelly, exhausted barking from the basement. He feels old. Much older than Mandy. And he feels the differences between them becoming too important. It shouldn't be that way, but it is.

Heather says, "Excuse me."

"Just who was that?" Cooper asks.

Mandy turns back to the boy and explains, "My sister Heather. Her feet got frostbitten. I was with her when it happened."

But the boy is up and reaching for a huge orange and purple Super Soaker at his feet.

"Do you need help with that, Cooper?"

The boy ignores the question. He staggers slightly under the weight of the thing, then straightens and marches out of the room.

Heather found the bathroom and locked herself in. Darren had asked for her diagnosis of the boy — Benny's boy — and instead she stood by while her sister provided that horrific story. Her abdomen tightened. Not now, she thought. She leaned her head against the back of the door and closed her eyes. So Darren's neighbour was Isabella Martin. And now she was in Isabella's bathroom, surrounded by Isabella's things. Heather hadn't known she and the boy had moved, but how would she? It was a long time since she had driven by their house beside the park.

She thought of Suse's sunbonnet on the bog, of herself — months ago — wandering through the woods in her stockinged feet, of her desire to dart off the path and deep into the interior of the headland. To run and run until no one could find her. She thought of coming face to face with Darren under the canopy of crossbills.

She would only stay another few minutes. If she never saw her casserole dish again it would be just fine. She'd make excuses to Darren later. She opened the door and went into the hall and hesitated. Left or right? She was confused. Her cell-phone vibrated in her jacket pocket, but she ignored it. Carrying it around was habit. Whoever it was could leave a message, though she'd been ignoring those, too. She knew the callers and their messages: Darren reminding her of the barbeque; Mandy backing out, then changing her mind, then backing out again; a few clients who had managed to get her cell number wondering when she would be taking appointments again.

Why didn't they just see someone else?

She eventually made her way back into the kitchen. Isabella was at the other end of the room talking to Darren. Heather was aware of Darren glancing at her, trying to get her attention so he could introduce her. She was certain Isabella had recognized her. And the son — she sensed he had as well. Just then he entered the kitchen with something on his back. He began to approach his mother, then veered away from her. He looked as though he hadn't grown at all since she saw him in the kitchen that day with the pancake sandwich, when she realized Benny's love and attachment for his son were overriding. Heather knew she had become derailed that day. She had felt a sudden looseness, the beginning of falling.

She was standing beside two men in conversation. She inched closer to them, trying to avoid being seen by Benny's wife and son.

"Question for you, Byron," one of the men was saying. "Decades ago there was a grad student working for Tom Brookes out there on parasites. Using mist nets."

The men had not — through eye contact or body language of any kind — invited Heather to join their conversation, but she stood with them, watching each talking face in turn.

"I was looking through the data," the man continued. "They caught a lot of mourning warblers. You'd be hard pressed to find a mourning warbler now."

"Right."

"But it was all cut-over then. Give it another twenty years."

"A fire."

"Right. Now my question is this. They also had a lot of Lincoln's sparrows."

"Misidentification."

"That's what I was thinking. So what the heck were they catching?"

The second man — Byron — was wearing shorts and had hiker's legs: sculpted and strong. Heather had a fleeting moment of self-disgust, remembering that her own hiking experience had gone so poorly. She noticed that Cooper seemed to be circling her and the two men, and fiddling with something.

"I think I saw a bananaquit," Heather announced, though even before they turned to her, she knew she'd made a mistake. She was stepping from side to side in order to keep the men between her and Benny's orbiting son. The men looked puzzled.

"Excuse me?"

"Bananaquit."

"In the Caribbean, were you?"

"No. No Caribbean for me. St. John's. At my feeder."

"I doubt that very much."

"*Cooper!*"

Heather waited for the other man's comment, the one with the legs, but he did not get beyond opening his mouth. It happened so quickly — the fabric of his white shirt flooding a dark crimson — that had she still been looking at his legs she would have assumed, as did a few people, including the man himself, that the substance had originated from his bloodstream and not from the long rope of red fluid ejected from the Super Soaker backpack worn by Cooper.

"Someone grab that kid!"

Cooper had opened fire on the room, but Heather knew he was aiming at her. He never looked directly at her, but certainly she, and the people nearest her, were receiving the brunt of it. It was fruity and sweet smelling, heavy, gluey. The backpack was leaking and dripping onto the kitchen floor behind him.

Although mortified — as the seconds passed it was obvious she was his primary target — Heather was relieved to think that once Cooper was finished, she could go home. She also registered that there was nothing wrong with his legs. He was standing there erect as any little soldier amidst the growing puddle.

People shouted and cursed, jostling each other into corners then out of the room. As Isabella came across the room, she slipped, and if not for Darren, who put a hand out to steady her, she would have fallen. As soon as she reached Cooper she stopped. She looked dumbfounded.

It was Darren, saying "All right now," who lifted Cooper up. Heather saw the boy close his eyes as the Super Soaker backpack slipped off and clattered onto the floor, and Darren carried him out of the room.

Heather took a few steps backwards, away from Isabella, and bumped into the man in shorts who had suffered the initial attack. She was surprised he was still in the kitchen. She apologized but he stared at her blankly. Behind him she saw the liquid dripping off the cupboard doors and pooling on the countertop. She could feel it across her belly and thighs. It was sticky. She was also beginning to cool off; the room had been chilly to begin with. It was then the dog came in, snorting and wiggling his rear end, though his movements were stiff.

"Inky," Heather said, without thinking.

He had become an old dog.

Finally, she was forced to face Isabella. Almost everyone else had left the room. She could hear the commotion in the hall as people prepared to go home.

"I had no idea," Heather said, meaning she had not known Isabella had moved. But she wondered if Isabella thought she meant she had no idea — at first when it might have made a difference — that Benny was married.

"I had no idea you lived here."

Isabella nodded. Heather could see she was struggling with the knowledge that Heather was pregnant. Estimating her due date. Tallying the months. There was no reason to stay on, but Heather knew Isabella didn't want her to leave yet. There was something Isabella wanted to say.

She moved quite close to Heather, and Heather froze. Isabella seemed shocked and fascinated. Heather didn't blame her.

Suddenly Heather smelled Benny. It was the laundry soap, dog, cooking, Isabella herself — all those things Benny would have carried with him.

"Can I ask you something?" Isabella asked. She was barely audible.

Oh, God, Heather thought. What will I tell her? She nodded.

"How long did you know him?"

She stared at Isabella and tried to focus. Was it a trick question? Never had she imagined standing so close to this woman. As close as lovers. This was a face weighted by disappointment, curiosity, long nights.

"It was six years, until he got sick."

"What time of year did you meet? Do you recall the month?"

"June."

"Is that his?"

Heather wanted to ignore this question. A look of anguish crossed Isabella's face.

"Did he know?" Isabella asked.

"No."

Isabella's expression seemed to soften and fall. Heather thought of the boys on the ice and for the first time it occurred to her she might have done a kind thing by not telling Benny she was carrying his child. Not a terrible thing. She could see this on Isabella's face. The relief made her feel light, then bold.

"How was he . . . ?" Heather asked.

"How was he at the end?"

Heather nodded. Did he ask for me?

"They kept him comfortable."

They stared at each other, as though they might learn a little more about Benny from each other's face.

"He was cremated," Isabella added.

Heather had not wanted to know that. His body destroyed. Burned. His arms, fingers, mouth, hair.

There were sounds behind them: a thud and a yelp. The man named Byron was on the floor. He lifted himself onto one elbow and blinked. Isabella turned and went immediately to his side, as did Inky, and Heather left the room.

Darren was standing beside her car. It had stopped snowing, but a thin layer had settled in the cooler zones: car roofs, hedges, walkways. The house had emptied quickly. Cries of disgust at the snow were followed by car doors slamming and engines starting. She had no idea at what point Mandy and Bill had departed. Hers was one of only a few remaining cars. She began to shiver.

"There you are," Darren said. "Are you okay?"

"I need to get home."

"The way you were walking, I thought you'd gone into labour. Can I drive you?"

"I have my car. Thanks." Then she remembered. "That boy will be fine, Darren."

"Oh, right."

"I better go, Darren. Excuse me." He was blocking her car door.

"You know, he talks as though his father is alive."

"But he does know the truth?"

"Yes. I've heard Isabella tell him, more than once. And the man was dying in their house for months."

"If Cooper's mother is interested in counselling, I'm sure it would be an excellent idea. People respond to grief in different, sometimes peculiar ways. It can take a while to accept that something bad happened. He's only a boy. He's taking his time."

"That sounds too simple."

"It's not simple at all. It's complicated. That's why it's hard to understand. How can it be so goddamn cold this time of year?"

Darren sighed, and to her dismay she realized he was taking her question literally. "Strictly speaking, it's a southwesterly," he said. "But the fact is, it's a northern system that's looped back around. It's the coldest southwesterly you'll ever get. I just wish everyone — "

At that moment someone began calling to them from the house.

It was Byron. He came quickly down across the lawn, holding the side of his head. He stopped and glanced back and forth between them, but each time his eyes sought out Heather's she looked away. She was too tired to make eye contact with this man.

"Darren, I fell. I slipped and fell against the stove and hit my head. I can't tell if I'm bleeding or not, I'm so covered with that kid's fake blood."

Fake blood? Heather thought. *Fake blood.* It hadn't registered.

"Of course, the brain can be injured without penetration to the skull."

"How do you feel, Byron?" Darren asked patiently. "Do you feel dizzy? Drowsy? Confused?"

"I should be checked. I'm developing a brutal headache. I thought I'd been shot."

"You're probably right. But you shouldn't drive, Byron. I better give you a lift over."

"Good point. I shouldn't drive. Another thing, that woman in there — awfully nice, by the way — she's a bit upset."

Heather could see Darren hesitating.

"You realize you're going to have quite a wait, Byron," Darren said. "Because of the strike?"

"What strike?"

"The doctors in the province are on strike," Heather told Byron, hoping, for Darren's sake, the plain facts would persuade him to wait until morning.

"They're not."

"Where have you been?" Darren wanted to know. "Everybody and his missus will be in for a sore throat."

"It'll be packed," Heather said.

"Although I heard on the news they expected worse."

"Darren, it'll be packed."

"Nevertheless, I am feeling woozy."

"I'll take him," Heather said. "It's on my way."

"No, Heather."

"You better check on your neighbour. It's a mess in there. I'll drop him at emergency."

"She said it's on her way, Darren."

"I don't mind."

"I'll be right along," Darren promised. "I'll see he gets home."

She nodded as though she were sleepwalking. She was excruciatingly tired and the five-minute drive to the Health Sciences Complex felt like something she'd been at for days. As she brought the car to a crushing, lethargic stop at each intersection, she couldn't understand how such a short drive could last so long. Byron was blithering on about concussions and skull fractures, which was irritating and helped keep her awake, but it was so incessant and pointless she grew concerned that he had, indeed, injured himself.

When they arrived, she parked the car and told him she'd accompany him inside. Just in case, she explained.

"In case I collapse. Good point."

They passed through the emergency doors where a small, easily overlooked sign forbidding entry to the media had been posted, then into a corridor of tiled walls and columns. Heather immediately noticed the abundance of haphazardly arranged chairs, nearly every one of which was occupied.

Heather and Byron approached admittance, passing a number of women all looking grey and tired and either angry or defeated. One woman sat with her elbow on the arm of the chair and her sweater pulled up over her mouth and nose. Many looked asleep. Some clearly had a bad flu.

The first thing the clerk wanted to know was whether Heather realized she was in the wrong part of the hospital. "I

232

can let you through this way, but you should have been told the entrance is — "

"I'm not in labour," Heather said coldly. "We're here for him, not me."

The second thing the clerk wanted to know was whether that was real blood.

Strangely disappointed, they had to admit it was not real blood. Heather glanced down. While her clothes were wet, it was Byron's white shirt that most obviously bore the ruddy evidence of Cooper's initial assault. The clerk's question was not unreasonable, given this was an emergency department, but perhaps because it was also doubling as a twenty-four-hour walk-in clinic and because neither Heather nor Byron seemed excessively distraught, the clerk said, "I didn't think so."

"It's only paint," Heather explained.

"It's not paint," Byron said.

"Well, it's not blood."

"It contains a number of ingredients. I can't identify all of them, but certainly Kool-Aid is one. Corn syrup another."

The clerk had turned her attention to her computer screen. "Hospital card?" she asked.

"How long will this take?" Heather asked.

"There's no telling. Either one of you with a hospital card?"

Heather stepped back. In a moment she could leave. A few chairs and wheelchairs lined the short hallway connecting the emergency department to the rest of the hospital. Space had also been made for two stretchers: on one a blond woman wearing sunglasses reclined; on the other a dishevelled, confused-looking man appeared to have just sat up. Heather remembered this area being stark and empty at the time of her visit for the frostbite.

Primarily women occupied the two hallways, while the men had taken possession of the waiting room, where, along the farthest wall, a string of young men in soccer uniforms sat, every one of them with his head resting against the wall and following the least movement with his eyes. The few women in the waiting

233

room sat alone, one beside a vending machine. Heather could see the back of her neck and shoulders, her caramel hair recently set, and still with the absent air of a sleepwalker and under the watchful eyes of anyone whose eyes were open, Heather wandered away from Byron and into the waiting room.

Her mother had made a good seating choice, Heather could not help thinking, as the vending machine gave her less contact with other patients. And on her other side, her large leather handbag stood upright, occupying the seat. She was wearing her white rayon skirt and beige cardigan, a youthful, summery combination that dimmed her blue eyes and drained her face. Heather picked up the handbag and sat down.

Across her mother's face a flicker of relief was followed by consternation.

"You're having the baby. What do you want me to do?"

"No, I am not. Sit back. What are *you* doing here?"

"Good lord, you finally got my phone message."

"What are you doing here, Mom?"

"Do you answer *any* of your phones?"

Her mother had never left a phone message in her life. "Did you try Mandy?"

"Who?"

"Mandy?" Heather's throat began to feel funny. She was awake now.

"Oh, I know who Mandy is. But I'm not calling her. My God, if I have to hear one more question about cow hunting."

"But what's wrong?"

Her mother stiffened. "It's personal."

Heather looked up. Just a few feet away, a woman knitting a misshapen yellow square was listening to them. Beside her, a pale-faced burly man was breathing loudly and leaning on her. He was sweating profusely.

"Is he all right?" Heather asked the woman.

Her mother gave her the softest of nudges.

The woman nodded. "He's after whining and complaining

234

all day," she said, the knitting needles clicking furiously in her hands. "He's the mother of all sorrows, he is."

Heather suspected the woman had been saying this to people all day. She looked over her shoulder and scanned for Byron, wondering if he had seated himself elsewhere.

"Heather," her mother said, taking her handbag and reclaiming her daughter's attention. "I already mentioned Timmy to them at the desk. Surely he can get me seen more quickly. It's all who you know in this town."

"Who?"

"Timmy O'Keefe. Dr. O'Keefe now. You might want to go back up there and spell his name for them, Heather. Nurses aren't the brightest crowd."

Embarrassed, Heather looked across at the woman, who at that moment gave her shoulder a fierce shake, rousing her husband. He lifted his head from her shoulder and blinked dully. He looked very sick. "I think I'll just have a little lie-down," he told his wife. He slid gingerly off his chair, landed lightly on his knees, and curled up on the floor.

The woman stopped knitting and stared at her husband, but it didn't take long for two nurses to arrive and get the man on his feet. As they led him away the woman finally stood. They told her to stay put.

One of the nurses looked briefly around the room and noticed Heather.

"You're in the wrong part of the hospital, love."

"I'm not having a baby!"

The nurse froze, taken aback, then laughed as though it was the funniest thing she'd heard all night. Heather's mother put a hand on her arm, a cautionary gesture that seemed to suggest they save their energy.

"How long have you been waiting?" Heather asked the woman.

"We're after coming in about two this afternoon," the woman replied loftily.

"That's nine hours," Heather said. "Mom, how long have you been here?"

"Certainly not as long as that." Shifting slightly, her mother pressed her lips together.

"Mom?"

A man leaned out from the row and said to no one in particular. "I've been here thirteen hours." He glanced around, looking to make eye contact with someone, and settled on Heather. But then the blond woman with the sunglasses put some change in the vending machine and he turned to her. Heather was surprised the woman had abandoned her stretcher, but when she peered down the hallway she saw it was gone. Rooted out of it, Heather figured, for a more deserving customer.

It was at this point that Byron spotted her and came straight over. He took the seat vacated by the sick man and said, "What a scene in there. I got as far as the duty nurse, who checked my vitals. Nothing alarming."

"That must be a relief," Heather said.

"Yes. Even a minor head injury can result in severe brain damage."

Her mother nudged her again. Heather realized she would not be able to keep from her mother the fact that her arrival here was entirely on behalf of this man.

"Mom, this is Byron," she said. "Byron, I'd like you to meet my mother —"

To Heather's astonishment, they both stood, as though being formally introduced. Byron held his hand out, but Heather's mother ignored him.

"I'm going to the ladies' room," she said. "I'll be back in a moment."

"You know where it is?"

"I do."

Byron sat back down.

As soon as her mother returned, she asked, "Did you ask them to page Timmy O'Keefe for me, Heather?"

Heather hesitated, glancing at Byron. "They said they would do what they could."

"That doesn't sound promising."

There followed a period of silence occasionally broken by Byron's comments on head injuries in humans, then in birds, which expanded into bird diseases and injuries of all kinds. The woman beside him, listening attentively, began another yellow square, or what Heather assumed would inevitably resemble a square. Heather's mother amazingly offered the information to Byron that Heather had a new bird feeder and a number of bird books. To Byron's question whether Heather was into birds, her mother responded by saying it was only a passing interest. At this, she rose for another visit to the ladies' room.

When she returned Byron was discussing the various objects that could be used to set broken bones. A stainless steel bar from a rat's cage was as good as anything, just sharpen it and boil it. Heather's mother interrupted to ask whether or not he was married.

The question was so thoroughly outside Heather's future reality or interest, she ignored it. She checked her watch. It was 2:37 am.

"No, I'm not married," Byron told her mother.

The woman beside him knitting the yellow square nodded and drew her breath in sharply, signalling this came as no surprise to her.

Heather found herself resenting this. The man was a crackpot, but he didn't need to know others thought so.

She wondered what had become of Darren. He had promised he would be right along. It didn't matter. She was staying anyway.

Near dawn her mother said, "You can't imagine how much I'm looking forward to having a grandchild."

Heather was surprised. It was the first time she'd heard her mother express this sentiment. She placed her hands over her stomach. It was of an unbelievable size and tautness. Some women were happiest when they were pregnant. Some women were *only* happy when they were pregnant. Heather realized that the more she looked forward to the baby, the less she missed its father.

"Are you happy, Mom?" Heather asked.

"I suppose so. Yes."

Heather was aware of both the woman knitting and Byron listening. She didn't care.

"But it's odd that I would be this woman," her mother said.

"What do you mean?"

"It's odd that I ended up being alone all these years. A single woman."

"Why?"

"Because when I was a girl all I wanted was to love, and be loved. I waited and waited for it, and then when I got it, it didn't last." Her mother sighed and patted her handbag. "But I'm happy enough now."

Heather didn't know what to say. She told her mother she was going outside for a moment to get some fresh air. As she walked slowly past admittance, a nurse looked up and asked if she was all right. Heather nodded.

She took a seat on a bench and breathed in the out-of-doors air, so fresh and oxygenated she began to believe she didn't require sleep after all. Bunches of clouds were forming high in the sky. The colour was impossible to name. Not grey, not white, not pink exactly. Lower in the sky, a bright streak of light intersected the nearby wooded hill, which seemed incompatible with the helicopter pad at its base, the plateau of parking lots and finally the hospital with its golden machines capable of passing a narrow beam of X-ray photons straight through human tissue to see broken bones, swallowed objects, congested baby lungs.

A figure was coming across the parking lot. A man with a bouncing, deliberate walk. She thought he looked rather handsome. She tried to rise.

"What are you doing out here, Heather?"

He stopped in front of her.

"You should have gone home hours ago."

"I was waiting for you."

A look crossed his face: uncertainty, hope, pleasure, then worry she'd seen it.

"Sure, Byron's a big boy."

"I know that. But I also ran into my mother."

"Here?" He sat beside her.

"Bladder infection." Heather was finding it difficult to breathe without making a lot of noise. "She gets them. Chronic. She's fine."

"Are you okay?"

"A few minutes ago," Heather said, panting and arching her back. "My water broke."

Chapter Sixteen

By the first week of August, most people could no longer remember when the hot weather had started. Everyone was complaining of a lack of sleep. Heather had been hearing it for days, since she returned to work, and knew it was, like Christmas, a formidable psychological stressor — humidity, heat and sleeplessness.

She was working two days a week. She had been anxious to return to her office, to her clients. She had forgotten how much she liked her job. How much she liked the anticipation of what the day might bring.

She purchased a fan at Canadian Tire to combat the heat and poked it in a corner of her office. It created a bizarre environment, just moving the heat around like that. She suspected it was only an illusion of cooler air.

She was surprised the Quigleys had made an appointment at all. She assumed they would have moved on, disgusted — particularly Derm — with her sudden, unexplained disappearance.

But when the Quigleys arrived — promptly — Derm was not with them. Donna and Tracey seemed confused with the three empty chairs Heather had stationed in a welcoming crescent. Eventually they sat, side by side, looking vulnerable and nervous.

"We were wondering what happened to you," Tracey said and Donna nodded.

For several minutes neither would look directly at her. Both were wearing tank tops and cut-offs, which struck Heather as far more sensible than her own cotton sweater set and skirt. She realized they were saying they'd missed her.

Then Donna sucked in some air and said, "We don't know where he's to."

"Toronto."

"We don't know that for sure, Tracey."

"Derm is gone?" Heather asked.

The women nodded.

It seemed impossible. Although he had been overbearing and full of himself, he had made the trio what it was. Heather would never have predicted this.

Now even the illusion of coolness was beginning to fade. Both women had been carrying lit cigarettes when they entered the building, held covertly at their hips. Heather pictured them stepping off the bus — the car would have been Derm's — and without delay lighting up. The smoke joined the swirling heat of Heather's office and she imagined it settling into every nick and cranny of her clothing, every pore of her skin.

"Tracey here — well, I never — she's after looking for a job," Donna told Heather.

For a moment Heather couldn't remember which of these women had been Derm's wife. But wasn't this symptomatic of what had always been the real dilemma?

Tracey produced a shy smile. "I'll need to, won't I, if I get a divorce?"

"Now she's talking about divorce."

"That comes as a surprise to you, Donna?" Heather asked.

"I don't understand," Donna said. "He hasn't even called us. He might be in trouble."

Donna finished her cigarette, then dropped it on the floor and ground it out with the toe of her flip-flop. "Did we do something wrong?"

"Jesus, Donna," Tracey said quietly. "Do you even know where you're to?"

Donna looked like she was near tears. She leaned down and retrieved the squashed butt, then held it in her hand and looked at Heather. There were no ashtrays in sight.

Heather stared at the flecks of tobacco on the hardwood floor and remembered her last rendezvous with Benny.

Could she really have been so heartless?

"Miss?"

"I'll take that, Donna," Heather said gently. "Not to worry." She opened a drawer and pulled out an ashtray.

Could she really have locked him out of the car in the rain and driven away?

"If she gets a job," Donna said, "I don't know what I'll do. Sure, he did everything for us."

"I tried some of them tricks you told me," Tracey announced. She sat back. She was clearly pleased with herself.

"I'm happy to hear that. And you're staying on your meds?"

Tracey nodded.

"Staying on your meds is essential."

"I know."

After the tragedy of the boys on the ice they did not see each other for a while. It had been in all the papers and on the news and Benny had felt exposed by the attention to the event, although there was never a photo or mention of him by name — only a reference to those bystanders who had been first on the scene and who made a courageous attempt to rescue the boys.

But after that Heather had trouble reaching Benny.

By the time they met again, it was late summer, a year ago. They had been out in the woods and returned to his car just as a light rain started. It blurred their view of the stand of poplars and patch of ocean visible from inside the car.

243

"Heather," he had said. "It's not possible for us to continue seeing each other."

"Don't you dare say that to me now."

"I have a family." He sounded tired, as though he'd been trying to explain something to a child for hours.

She closed her eyes. He was dropping her like a hot potato. She wondered if she had always known he would.

"I've been clear about that from the start, Heather."

When she opened her eyes and saw the rain on the windshield, she was briefly unsure of their whereabouts. He was watching her.

"This can't come as a surprise to you, sweetheart."

He tried to take her hand but she pulled away.

"I'm going to be having a number of procedures over the next month or so," he went on. "New procedures. A new line of attack." His laughter was brief. "I wish I had the guts to tell those doctors to fuck off."

What procedures exactly? The idea of them was dreadful, chilling. She realized his life was shrinking. There used to be a place for her in it, but his illness would soon be shutting people out. One by one, doors would close on everyone who had known him.

Not only that, there would be an order of priority that made her desperate.

He was waiting for her to say something. When she looked at him, she saw that he was scared. Well, he couldn't have it both ways.

"Right."

"Is that all you're going to say?" He sounded incredulous.

She thought again about the procedures. Then about his wife beside him or in a nearby windowless waiting area. "What do you want me to say?"

He looked hurt, then angry. She hated it when he got angry with her and for a moment she wished she could stop herself.

"*I'll be thinking of you?* Is that what you want me to say? Or, *good luck?*"

"Why are you shouting?"

They sat without speaking for several minutes. She was surprised by herself, by her emotional unpredictability. They had been lying together in a clearing just a short while ago, but now, as she considered leaning over to pick the debris from his back and hair, she found herself frozen by something akin to homesickness.

He began searching for his keys. He arched his hips as he checked his pockets. He slapped his coat and rifled through the CDs and gum wrappers and tissues in the compartment between them. "Dammit, there's so much junk in here. Would you mind tidying up this stuff?"

She stared out the window.

"Have you got the keys, Heather?"

Although it had been overcast and misty all day, this was the first rain.

"Heather, are you sure you don't have the keys? Didn't I hand them to you before crossing the river?"

She shook her head. She couldn't forgive him for getting sick *or* having a wife.

He stopped, then opened the door and stepped out. She could hear the rain first-hand now and feel the warm, close air as it surged into the car. Before slamming the door, he leaned in and said, "I just wanted a little sympathy from you."

The path to destruction lay right in front of her. She couldn't step away from it. She leaned over and hit the button that locked the car doors. Hearing the locks click, he swung around and looked at her with disbelief. He was standing in front of the car and getting wet. He lunged back to the door and tried to open it, yanking on it several times. If he spoke she didn't hear it. For a moment she felt a bubble of laughter, as though they were only kids playing. A happy life would be returned to her, surely — it was just around the bend. Then he turned away from her, walking back out across the meadow. She didn't know where he was going or what was going on anymore, either with herself or with him. Did he really think he stood a chance of finding the keys out there?

Everything between them seemed wrong. He wanted to talk about his illness now. She had wanted to talk about it in Spruce Cove.

She reached out and lifted her hat from the dash. The keys were tucked inside, where she'd put them. She knew and she didn't know. She climbed into the driver's seat and started the car and backed out and up the gravel road away from the coast. She drove slowly, not checking the mirror to see him standing at the edge of the meadow, getting rained on, abandoned, surprised. Like the act of driving was one long, careful interruption of self-awareness, an annihilation of thought and time.

At the top of the lane, she stopped the car. She imagined returning at high speed and running him down. She imagined finding a cliff and taking the car over it by herself. She imagined driving back to town and never looking back. When she reminded herself that it was his car, she imagined parking in front of his majestic home and handing Isabella Martin the keys.

When she returned, there was no sign of him. Suddenly she could not bear the thought of him out there alone, drenched, lost. She felt a wild panic and understood that you don't let go of someone in a single moment.

She found him wandering along a part of the old road protected by trees and where the rain was not so heavy. He looked like an invalid, a vagabond, someone who had lost a good portion of his memory. He glanced up at her with an expression that said he was beyond caring.

"You had the keys?" he asked.

For a brief moment she thought he was being funny.

"You lied to me?"

She nodded.

This was it. Time was chugging on, and Heather wasn't ready. Everything was moving away from this moment, into the awful future, and Heather wanted to grab onto it and dig her heels into the ground and pull it back. Stop!

"Benny — "

"Let's not talk anymore. It's all a bit much, don't you think?"

So this was goodbye.

Heather left her desk and came around to sit in the third, empty chair, knowing that sometimes her best tool was sympathy. She offered the tissues, and Donna took a clump. Tracey shook her head; she didn't need them. Not yet, Heather thought. She rested the box on her knees, inches from Tracey's thigh but within easy reach of either woman. For some reason, perhaps due to her sudden closeness to the women and the heat they were emitting, her milk let down. She usually made it to noon, when she rushed home to nurse her daughter. She folded her arms over her front and pressed down on her breasts, which were now tight and aching. Tracey seemed to sense the distraction in Heather, though she couldn't know its cause.

"If we could change the past," Heather said to Donna. "Most of us would."

Heather had realized there were more ways than one to fall in love, to come to love a face. With Benny, it had happened in a moment: a face with an opening that she went straight through. Not a moment of resistance. She suspected this had been Tracey's, and likely Donna's, response to Derm. Perhaps this was love at first sight.

But there was another way. Meeting a face that grows on you. You have one or two glimpses. A sneak preview. A promise. At first standing in the woods with your feet numb and birds like chatterboxes overhead, you think: never. But then you begin wondering, until one day there is an opening and it takes your breath away.

*

Isabella was unable to sleep because of the heat. In the evenings, just at that point when she would have acquiesced to the idea of sleeplessness and lain in the dark and listened to sounds of Cooper, Inky, cars on the street, she got up and took a walk.

She was growing accustomed to her new neighbourhood, particularly at night. Suddenly it was an extraordinary world of crescents, cul-de-sacs and connecting footpaths cluttered with hockey nets, skateboard ramps, candy wrappers, knobs of sidewalk chalk, escaped hair clips. At the beginning she had been a newcomer, a single mother, a stranger, but during these warm nights both she and the world were transformed.

She felt alert. She felt she was climbing back into her life.

She circled the same route over and over — one crescent that linked to another crescent and up a cul-de-sac with a paved footpath connecting to the first crescent — as though she could not get enough of it. Midnight, and the laburnum still smelled like grape jelly, their drooping branches discharging papery blossoms that fluttered past her like popcorn. The clicking watering of lawns, now restricted to night-time hours under a new water conservation order, resulted in forgotten sprinklers saturating lawns until the water flooded sidewalks and ran down the sides of streets. Isabella watched a man cross his lawn beneath his weeping trees, moving his sprinkler in the tepid dark: a pale figure in white shorts and polo shirt, long returned from tennis but not yet in bed either. A lot of people were still awake.

She heard a flute being practised in an unlit upstairs room, the zany buzz of an electric guitar from a basement, a child squealing — or was it a teenaged girl? A pair of cats emerged from an open garage and approached her, mewing their complaint. One sprawled in the middle of the street, its tail swishing saucily. There was the padded crunch of a car door as it slammed shut, repeated three times.

She paused before an old bungalow set back from the street

and looked through its open door down a hallway to a kitchen where a woman in a dress and apron was standing at the counter, sorting through a pile of papers.

Another woman, in another house, cried out, "Wow, honey," and Isabella knew the woman really didn't care at all.

Near her home she stopped before a storm drain. It was quiet here, as she had hoped. She took the Super Soaker canister she'd been carrying in one arm and unscrewed its top. She bent and emptied the contents through the grated opening. The smell of gasoline rose up, but it was done. She thought of it making its way to Rennie's Mill River and mentally apologized to the ducks and fish that lived there.

She crossed her lawn and heard rustling in the hedge separating her yard from the neighbouring yard, then a single bell-like chirp: a bird, also fitful. Inky was sprawled on the doorstep, too hot and arthritic to move when she tried to open the screen door. She gave up and went around to the back of the house.

He was still there on the doorstep the next morning when she tried to get out. It was a Saturday, but she found a number and telephoned, a part of her hoping no one would pick up. But someone did, the vet, in fact, a woman who told her it would cost an additional ninety dollars to dispose of the body.

She called for Cooper, but couldn't find him.

She held open the car door and whistled to Inky. Twice he rose and ambled towards her and twice he thought better of it and turned back to the house. Isabella stood and watched, as though she had all the time in the world, thinking it was a peculiar thing to have a creature's life in your hands like that.

When she got to the animal hospital she opened the back door of the car and Inky stumbled getting out. He had been panting and Isabella saw he'd covered the backseat with that clear syrupy saliva seemingly unique to dogs. She felt chilly and dispassionate watching him straighten and stand. Wanting him to suffer seemed to be a secret only just surfacing. He hobbled with her into the building, always wanting to do the right thing, but as soon as he was indoors he began to tremble violently.

The vet had short blond hair and wore a number of earrings. Together, they lifted Inky onto the metal table, but he immediately began to slide off, his legs rigid as tent poles. The vet got him to lie down and told Isabella to cradle his head. His terror began to subside. The vet explained how the injection would travel through his bloodstream until it reached his heart, stopping it. This would take only a minute and the dog would feel nothing. While the vet readied the needle, she asked Isabella if there were any questions.

"Does it matter that he's not my dog?"

"Whose dog is he?"

"My husband's."

"Does he know you're here?"

"He's dead."

The vet nodded. She was impossible to read.

Isabella looked back down at Inky. Heather Welbourne had recognized this dog right away. How many other women knew him by name?

When Heather had first entered Isabella's kitchen, Isabella felt the floor slip sideways. She had never felt such hostility towards anyone before.

The vet was back at the table with the needle. Already Inky's head was heavy as a log in Isabella's arms.

"Wait," Isabella said.

The vet stepped back. Isabella could see that she took everything in stride.

"This dog is basically a hundred years old," the vet pointed out.

Inky had relaxed and seemed to be sleeping. His bones prodded his hide from within, his grey-black fur was greasy and unclean, his muscles were astonishingly atrophied. He smelled wretched. Ashamed, Isabella realized she was going to cry. She was going to cry and needed to get home quickly. Home. She thought of Cooper, balancing a spoon on his nose instead of eating his cereal and asking her last week, "What month did Dad die?"

She had been halfway across the kitchen. She stopped and noticed red stains on the floor. His tone was serious, but matter-of-fact. He had grown several inches over the summer and she sensed his voice was about to change any day.

"It was in December," she said. "You went to see him in the hospital just before. Do you remember?"

"No, I never. You told me I had to, but I hid under my bed." He laughed, pleased with himself. "You tried to bribe me."

Was he right about that?

"Christmas is in December, right?"

"Yes."

"Did we still have Christmas?"

"Yes, but it was — strange."

"I don't remember it."

"I don't really either."

"Did we already live here?"

"Yes."

"I kind of remember. But Dad wasn't here, was he?"

"In this house? No."

"So Dad doesn't know about this house."

"No."

Benny had loved Cooper. Though they had never discussed it, Isabella knew he never had any intention, before or after becoming sick, of leaving them.

But he had left them, in a sense. And he did leave them, in the end.

She hadn't told Cooper she was taking Inky to the vet. That wasn't fair. He deserved the opportunity to say goodbye.

"I've changed my mind," Isabella said.

The vet nodded.

They roused Inky and got him off the table and carried him to the car. The vet withheld her opinion, which Isabella appreciated. Isabella thought perhaps that man Byron might know how to prolong Inky's life more comfortably. He seemed clever that way.

But once Isabella got into the car, she realized she was breathing rapidly and her hands were shaking. She sensed she had narrowly escaped something dreadful, like a car accident or electrocution. Behind her, Inky groaned once, perhaps urging her to get the car started and them home again, out of this heat.

She did not entirely know the man Benny had been. Apparently, he had been a philanderer, but in a monogamous way. One mistress at a time. Isabella realized this came as no great surprise to her. When he met Heather Welbourne, he gave up Bridget Neal. Gave her up so completely he forgot to mail her photos of their last tryst — even forgot he had them. He had been as loyal to Heather as Heather imagined him to have been. No more, but no less.

Isabella opened her purse and removed the photos of Bridget Neal and tore them up.

The warm weather started early on the morning of July 18. Darren woke up to it. He couldn't get over how people complained. He wanted to shake them and say, it won't last, you'll wake up one morning and it will be winter again and you'll be cursing and complaining about that.

The bird flew onto the deck of a cargo ship forty-five nautical miles east of St. John's. The crew put it in a box and tossed in a slice of bread. Darren got the call at nine thirty in the morning but was too busy to get down to the harbour until late afternoon. From the crew's description he guessed American bittern. He took the box from the crew, put it in the back of the truck and headed over to Long Pond. He knew the bird was still alive because he heard it moving around inside the box.

Approaching the pond, he noticed several boys coming up the street towards him and he slowed the truck. They were carrying skateboards. One of the boys was dark-haired and Darren thought it might be Cooper, but the sun, already lower on the horizon at this time of year, was bright and blinding. Darren watched the boy lower the rear wheels of his skateboard to the pavement, then begin running beside it, leaning forward as he held the nose of the board with one hand. Then he stepped onto the board with one foot, using the other to push himself along, gaining greater and greater speed. Just where there was a dip in the road, he bent his knees and both boy and board rose several feet into the air.

Darren was not quite sure how it happened — what it was that had given the boy the power to leave the ground. During those few seconds of being airborne, the skateboard remained attached to the soles of the boy's huge sneakers as though glued. Then both skateboard and boy had landed and were moving in Darren's direction.

Darren could not remember when he had last seen Cooper. He visited Goodridge Place only once or twice a week now, to check on Jeanette. If this was Cooper, he had grown considerably over the summer. He looked too old for a wading pool and certainly would no longer be easy to lift. Darren recalled the boy's lightness, dripping wet with fake blood. He had picked him up and carried him out of the kitchen without thinking.

He waved at the boys as they passed him, but the gesture was neither acknowledged nor returned.

He pulled up to Long Pond and parked. He glanced at his rear-view mirror, imagining, as he still frequently did, a red Echo pulling in behind him.

He paused, the window down, drinking in the warm end-of-day air. Along a strip of grass beside him a pair of adult crows strutted, jabbing at the ground for grubs. Another two were perched side by side on the arm of a streetlight. One held a wine cork in its bill and the other was trying to steal it. Young crows were everywhere now. They were black like their parents, but Darren could distinguish them by their nasally call and the fact adults had better things to do than squabble over wine corks.

The moment he got out of the truck, the crows on the streetlight flew off, cawing maniacally, to a nearby stand of fir. The adults on the grass lifted and cocked their heads, getting a better look at Darren, then went back to foraging.

He put on his leather gloves and dropped the tailgate. The

box had fallen over onto its side and the untouched slice of bread had slid out. Both box and bread were covered in guano. The bittern was silently opening and closing its long bill. The slender legs were of an unearthly green colour that reminded Darren of Martians, and he felt briefly boyish.

Slowly the bird stretched its bill up towards the roof of the truck, revealing black streaks on a pale throat and belly. Two bulging eyes peered around the base of the bill and regarded Darren coolly. There was a drop of blood on one of the wings. Darren reached for the bird, knowing it would be as light as a leaf.

He carried the bittern out onto the marsh grass where it collapsed around itself like a small broken umbrella, then he backed away from it several metres and waited. Eventually the bird picked itself up and began taking slow, stealthy steps away from Darren until it stopped and pointed its neck skywards, its reed-like body now parallel with the grasses surrounding it.

When Darren was back at the truck he turned and searched for the bittern. The camouflage was a success. He brought the binoculars to his eyes, but knew he would never find the bird again. He looked down at his feet, up at the sky, then searched one last time with his naked eye. No luck. While he was re-assured that tens of thousands of years of natural selection had an unequivocal purpose, he also felt a peculiar loss. He almost took a step back out onto the marsh, but that would have been counterproductive.

That night Darren was working at the kitchen table on his laptop, reviewing data from several years of oiled bird surveys. Predictable patterns were emerging. When he heard the crying, he panicked slightly, assuming it was the baby. She was sleeping in her own room now and in a crib — a huge rig for such a creature — and if she were feeling lost and abandoned, it would be no surprise to him.

But when Darren opened the door to the baby's room he was met by silence. She was asleep, little pockets of air passing rhythmically in and out of her body in the manner of any living creature at rest. His concern took a new course.

He found Heather sitting upright in the bed, looking bewildered, self-conscious, just-awoken.

"Is she okay?" she whispered.

He nodded. "Asleep." His voice felt gravelly.

"Are you all right, Darren? You look tired." She raised herself to a kneeling position and gave him a look that was a little sheepish, a little sly. She opened her arms to him.

She was such a small thing, he thought, holding her, so much smaller than you would expect.

They stayed like that for a while, and he thought some embarrassing thoughts about being together forever and being perfect for each other. The more he thought them, the more he wanted to voice them. He closed his eyes, loving every place on his body that came in contact with hers. He felt like he was flying.

Many thanks to my editor, Bethany Gibson, for her invaluable insight and advice; to my agent, Anne McDermid, for her kindness and enthusiasm; to members of the Burning Rock Collective for their affirmation and encouragement — particularly Claire Wilkshire, who read earlier versions of this novel and was instrumental in its progress; and to Patty Wells for her astute comments and suggestions. I am also grateful to Paul Linegar, Bruce Mactavish and Pierre Ryan for generously sharing with me their knowledge of avian life, and to the Newfoundland and Labrador Arts Council and The Canada Council for the Arts for their support.

The story of Suse Hayes told here was inspired by events described by Gerald L. Pocius in his book *A Place to Belong*.

The production of the title **The Darren Effect** on the Rolland Enviro 100 Print paper instead of virgin fibres paper reduces your ecological footprint by :

Tree(s) : 15
Solid waste : 424 kg
Water : 40 094 L
Suspended particles in the water : 2,7 kg
Air emissions : 931 kg
Natural gas : 61 m^3

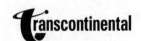

Printed on Rolland Enviro 100, containing 100% postconsommation recycled fibers, Eco-Logo certified, Proceded without chlorinate, FSC Recycled and manufactured using biogaz energy.